Bone Pit

Books in the Gina Mazzio, RN Series

Bone Dry
Sin & Bone
Bone of Contention
Bone Dust
Bone Crack
Bone Slice

Other novels by Bette Golden Lamb & J. J. Lamb

Sisters in Silence
Heir Today...
The Killing Vote

By Bette Golden Lamb

The Organ Harvesters
The Organ Harvesters-Book II

By J. J. Lamb – Zach Rolfe, PI Series

A Nickel Jackpot
The Chinese Straight
Losers Take All
No Pat Hands

Bone Pit

by

Bette Golden Lamb
&
J. J. Lamb

TWO BLACK SHEEP PRODUCTIONS
NOVATO, CALIFORNIA

Bone Pit
Copyright © 2013 by Bette Golden Lamb & James J. Lamb

www.twoblacksheep.us

ISBN-13: 978-0-9851986-2-6
ISBN-10: 0-9851986-2-1

Cover Designer: Rita Wood
www.ritawoodcreative.com

Dedication

To Peggy and Charlie Lucke,
our long-time and valued dear friends,
who may or may not be related to
one of our protagonists.

Acknowledgements

To all the sincere and dedicated
critique groups, especially ours –
Peggy Lucke, Shelley Singer,
Nicola Trwst & Judith Yamamoto.
Thank you.

Bette Golden Lamb & J. J. Lamb

Prologue

"Stay down, bitch!"

Need to get up. Get up or pee the bed. Oooh, shoulders hurt. Glass crunching inside. Fire in my knees. Hot. Hot like Hawaii! Ocean hanging upside down, hanging from the sky. Oh, God! Rocky, stop it! Stop stabbing me! Stabbing my arm! Ouch! Ouch! Ouch!

"Hold her!" Rocky yelled. "Crissake, I can't do this alone."

Pete snickered. "She's only a bag of bones. You could crush her with one hand."

Move ... inch ... inch ... inch. Careful. Careful.

"Damn it! Hold onto her or I'm gonna pop you in the mouth!"

Light bouncing. Dark ... light ... dark ... light. Supposed to remember. Promised if I took the medicine I'd remember.

"Man, I hate going into that friggin' lab with Ethan lookin' like some freaky scientist straight outta the comics. And those floatin' brains. Gives me the creeps."

* * *

Ocean falling. Snake dangling, falling into my hair. Can't scream. Hit me when I scream. Oh, my God! It's sliding across my neck. Curling around my head, moving through my hair. Squeezing tighter and tighter.

"Rocky, get the snake!"

"Shut the fuck up, lady!"

"Did you give her the meds?"

"Course I did, Doc."

That sound? Buzzing?

"No! Don't!"

Hammering in my brain. Boom! Boom! Boom!

1

"The two of you are idiots. I told you to sedate her. How am I supposed to work on someone who's flopping around like this?"

"Hey, Doc, I gave her the juice. Right in the vein. She shoulda been long gone."

Burning, throbbing. Eating me inside.

"Get away! Get away!"

"All right, you fools, get her out of here! This was a total waste of my time. Why can't you ever do anything right?"

"Don't know what happened, boss."

"Wheel her out! Now!"

* * *

"Jesus, can't you give her more dope? She's creepin' me out with those crazy eyes."

"Used up all the shit."

Deep breaths. Swim away in the cool ocean. Waves crashing down. Ocean coming. Breath hurts. No air. Swimming. Swimming harder. God, God, dear God! Father in heaven, please help me. Save me! Air. Need air. Someone help me! Save me!

"Throw her in the pit."

"Sounds like a goddam dying animal. You really fucked up. Should have been dead by now."

"Give her a few more minutes and she will be, asshole."

Help! Oooh, oooh, hurts.

"Rocky! Pete! Don't leave me! Don't go!"

"Shut up, bitch!"

"Come back! Stop the water! Please stop the water!"

2

Chapter 1

Gina and Harry inched along in a deserted silver mine north of Carson City. She refused to think about the ancient, rotting timbers that were supposed to hold back the tons of rock over their heads. Instead, she concentrated on the dancing beam of light coming from the flashlight Harry was holding to guide them through the inky blackness.

From their first step inside, she'd grabbed the back of his jacket, bunched it up until she was grasping a sweaty clump with one hand, while the other hand trailed along the exposed jumble of rock in the vertical wall. For some reason, touching the inanimate rocks was reassuring even if they were scary companions.

"What is this cockamamie fascination you have with mines, anyway?" Gina said. "You know how claustrophobic I am. I can barely breathe in here."

"Hey!" He wrapped an arm around her. "You could have waited outside."

"No way! I'm not letting you out of my sight, Harry Lucke. Besides, waiting alone in that creepy canyon would have been just as weird. I swear there are ghosts hiding behind every single rock—some old miner with an axe or a frustrated gambler with a six-shooter."

"A city girl from the Bronx; what would you know about Nevada ghosts?"

"I have news for you, mister. The alleys in the neighborhood where I come from could make even you wig out."

"Well, Ms. Mazzio, if you were raised in my neck of the woods, you'd know not to keep poking your fingers in between those rocky crevices. It's a great spot for black widows to hide."

She jerked her hand away from the wall and stuck it in her pocket. "Very funny."

"So who's laughing?" Harry said, laughing.

Without warning, the flashlight blinked out, leaving them both gasping in surprise.

Gina's voice was shaky. "Oh, God, this is like being blind." She grabbed for his arm and squeezed him with all her might. "Harry, please, please, please put the light back on. If this is supposed to be some kind of joke, it's not funny."

"It's okay, babe. Give me a moment and I'll have it working."

She squirmed. An invisible hand was crushing down on her chest. "Harry, I can't breathe!"

She heard him going through his pockets, clothes swishing with his movements. "What are you doing?" Her voice sounded hysterical even to her; it bounced around them—not really an echo, but something like it. No matter how hard she squinted, all she saw was a flat black wall.

"Batteries, doll. Always carry an extra pair if you're exploring a mine. Big daddy taught me that."

The light was back.

Gina threw her arms around his neck, thought she was going to cry with relief, but a smile won the contest. "I love you, do you know that, Mr. Lucke?"

Then his mouth was on hers and they were lost in each other in the middle of the deserted mine.

Gina yanked away. "Did you hear that?"

"Just some rocks. They drop all the time."

"You know what? I've had it. If this is panic therapy, it's not working." She tugged his sleeve, taking backward steps. "First the light disappears. Then the mine is collapsing. I get the message— time to run, live to fight another day."

"The mine's not collapsing. Land moves, rocks shift all the time. A few are going to drop here and there."

"You might be right; it's a perfectly logical explanation. But get me out of here." She tugged at his arm again and again until he gave in. They walked back out of the mine.

* * *

Gina and Harry agreed that all the electricity required to power the blinking outside lights of The Silver Dollar casino could have powered a small town.

It was like stepping back in time when they pushed through the wooden swinging doors. The sawdust-covered plank floors creaked with every step; old guns and mining relics clung to the walls and ceiling, filling every inch of available space.

Gina thought this must be one of those old leftover gambling joints she'd heard about that had gone through the gold and silver rushes of the 1800s. But it had somehow managed to slide through later eras of transformation without losing its original mining-era vision of hard times.

She couldn't imagine how this historic casino could compete with the ultra-modern places in the center of Reno and Carson City. There, electronic slots, convenient credit tickets, glitz, glitter and showgirls gave the illusion of no tomorrow. Riches all round were there for the taking.

That's what the suckers came for.

The place was jam-packed, the customers surrounded by the clatter of slots being well-fed with coins and the wild shouts of the three-deep crowds around the blackjack and craps tables. Gina felt a rush of adrenaline.

The restaurant area was also mobbed. Gina and Harry had to cool their heels for thirty minutes before they were seated.

And it was a Sunday night!

"You know, when I was going through nursing school," Gina said. "I never quite pictured myself working in Nevada. And tell me, how the hell can anyone breathe in here with all the cigarette smoke? You could scratch your name in the fumes."

Harry smiled at her. "But look at how happy everyone is, even while losing their money." He reached across the table to take her hand. "How about I move my bod over and crowd the hell out of you?"

Gina laughed as his bottom bumped her against the wall of the small booth. She made a point of ignoring his hand creeping up her thigh as she fingered her way through the menu. She stopped at the double-page, 24-hour breakfast section.

"You may be the sexiest man alive, Harry, but I don't think I'm ever going to get over being in that creepy mine today."

"If you'd only go with the flow, you might even find it exciting."

"Yeah, sure."

When the waitress asked for Gina's order, she pointed at a breakfast combination plate of eggs, pancakes, and bacon. Harry nodded for the same.

"This last week exploring the area has been fun. I could even use another seven days," she said. "But reality says this is our last night before we start work." She handed her menu to the waitress. "I'm a little nervous. I've never been in charge of a prenatal clinic. I wish I were going with you."

"Yeah. That would have been the best-case scenario. But we're still within shooting distance of each other." Harry's hand advanced farther up her thigh. "And there's always the nights in our own little condo in the sky."

"Sex." Gina laughed. "You're always thinking of sex."

"Not all the time. That whopping sign-on fee also got my attention."

"Twenty grand between the two of us!" Gina let out long whistle. "*Now* we can really plan for that trip to Italy."

"And you needed to get away from Ridgewood Hospital and all that, what is it you call it, *cacca?*"

"I know," she said. "But I love living in San Francisco."

"It's only a three-month contract," Harry said. "It's not forever. And if we don't like it … we're out of here."

The waitress set their orders in front of them, pulled a bottle of syrup from her pocket and set it on the table. The tempting aroma of bacon and coffee was almost lost in a battle with the casino's heavy smell of tobacco smoke. Still, they grabbed their silverware and started eating. An overhead announcement shouted a $50,000 progressive slot winner along with *dah-dum* music. A chorus of wild cheers blasted the place.

It didn't slow either of them.

When the volume dropped, Gina said, "That Comstock auxiliary unit where you're assigned sounds … I don't know, strange. Why isn't it part of the hospital campus here in town?"

"I asked the same question and never got a real answer. All they said was it's basically an internal medicine facility and they wanted someone with extensive experience." Harry buffed his nails on his shirt. "You know, someone like me."

Gina's cell rang out Madame Butterfly's *Un bel di*. She pulled the phone from her purse and gave Harry a puzzled look.

The inquiring voice was pleasant. "Hello. Is this Gina Mazzio?"

"Yes, this is Gina." She nodded.

"Welcome to Carson City. This is Katie Velick, the staffing supervisor for Comstock Medical. There has been an unexpected change in your assignment. Of course, you're under contract, so there's no question about using your services. But we won't need you for the prenatal clinic after all. I hope this doesn't disappoint you too much."

"Well … what happened?"

"Nothing we need go into. It was an administrative glitch. But I think you might be pleased to know we have a sudden vacancy at our auxiliary unit. I believe your fiancé is starting there tomorrow. Is that something you might be interested in?"

Gina's face broke out into a wide smile. "Yes, of course. It sounds perfect."

"Fine. I'm glad this is working out. They'll expect you on site tomorrow at seven."

"Yahoo!" Gina tossed the phone into her purse, reached out, and threw her arms around Harry.

Chapter 2

The moment Harry turned the Jeep Wrangler onto the narrow mountain road, he was forced into quick steering maneuvers to avoid huge potholes that could have sent them into free-fall. Gina gripped both sides of her seat to keep from being flung into the metal door with each swerve. She rubbed hard at what was sure to turn into a colorful bruised shoulder.

So much for seatbelts.

She saw the look of concentration on Harry's face, but knew he was happy. He was a car freak, a truck freak, a vehicle freak. If it had wheels, he loved it. She held her tongue, caught up in his excitement as he manhandled the wheel through the many switchbacks that climbed toward the tiny town of Nugget—barely a spot on the map.

With the top down, Harry's long hair was defenseless against the wind; the top strands stood straight up as though someone was yanking him into a sitting position. Her short curly hair barely riffled in the breeze.

She glanced at her watch. "Maybe we should have left more time for the trip. Not too cool to be late on our first day."

"Nugget is probably only another mile or two," he said with a smile. "The Comstock facility's supposed to be right outside of the town. We'll be fine."

Fine. The universal lie. Now she knew they were in trouble.

To distract herself, she surrendered to the gods, let go of her seat, and held a hand out. With her fingers spread, she imagined riding the wind stream as it turned warmer and warmer with the rising sun. The air was so dry she could feel the moisture being sucked from her body with every breath, but the land was beyond parched; it looked lifeless. Even the gray-green sagebrush, had all but disappeared.

"Oh my God, look!" Gina pointed ahead of them—the road was covered with a spread of black crawling creatures. "Harry! Stop!"

He came out of his road warrior trance and hit the brake. "Tarantulas," he said, chuckling. "I've heard about their migrations in the fall. Don't worry about them. They're not going to hurt us."

"Yuck! They're big and creepy and look like they could eat us in one bite. What are we going to do, just sit here and wait for them to get out of the way? They're everywhere. It'll take forever for them to cross the road."

"Close your eyes, doll." He hit the accelerator and the Jeep sprang into action, leaving behind them a heavy spray of rocks.

"You're not going to run over them, are you?" She screamed. "Oh, this is too gross. I want to go back to San Francisco."

"No you don't. Remember, this is supposed to be an adventure. Chin up." He gave her another brilliant smile. "Especially since they're out there and we're in here."

"I don't care. They're hairy and they're jumping around. What if one gets in the Jeep?"

Loud crunching sounds sent chills down her spine as a whole slew of spiders gave up their lives so the two of them could get to Nugget and their new job.

"First you drag me into the bowels of the earth, now we're riding over creepy-crawlies … even New York cockroaches aren't this scary."

"We're almost there … check the map."

Before she could unfold it, they made a sweeping turn that brought them onto a cluster of weathered wood buildings that looked like they could have been lifted from a movie studio's back lot. A battered, tilted sign said, "Nugget. Pop. 83".

"Do you think they have a Walmart?" Gina said.

"Hell, I'd settle for finding someone who's alive."

10

"I'm glad you don't want to stop—the town looks ghoulish to me."

"And we really don't have the time," Harry said.

"Thank God!" She'd no sooner spoken and they were back into the emptiness of the high desert.

"Okay, I think the turn-off we're looking for should be coming."

Gina pointed. "There's the sign: Comstock Medical Auxiliary Campus. That's what I call minimalism. It's tiny and covered with dirt, to boot." She pointed to a turn-off that looked more like an overgrown bike path.

"Good thing you spotted it. We could have easily driven right past it."

Harry made the sharp turn onto a dusty trail between two huge boulders. It was so narrow that ribbons of paint would have scraped off the fenders if they'd been driving something wider, like a Hummer. Gina smiled at the imagine of one of those ugly heaps of metal wedged permanently between the rocks.

Harry checked his watch. "Okay, we're now officially late. You're right. This is not a good way to start a new assignment."

The lame excuse for a road started out straight, but suddenly there was a tight curve, almost 180 degrees, and then they were into a small clearing. Gina cried out, "Look! We made it! There's the building."

A tall man dressed in pressed jeans, white short-sleeve shirt, and a bolo tie, was standing in front of the three-story building. His smile was welcoming, but Gina's eyes were drawn to the second level, where a line of windows were recessed behind iron bars.

The ground floor was a wall of adobe brick that appeared to have no windows at all, at least on the side they were facing. To top it off, the entire place was surrounded by the same kind of huge boulders lining the road they'd just traveled.

They couldn't possibly have been placed there deliberately, could they?

"This building is pretty strange looking for a hospital," Gina said under her breath as the Jeep rolled to a stop. "Why are there bars on the windows?"

The man walked over to the driver's side and held out a hand, which Harry shook. "I'm Ethan Dayton. You must be Harry Lucke."

"That's me."

"And you're Gina Mazzio," Dayton said, looking over at her.

"Sorry we're late," she said. "Didn't expect it to take so long to get here."

"No one ever does." He looked at his watch. "You're closer to the appointed hour than most people. Come on in, I'll show you around." When Harry didn't move, Dayton said, "Leave the Jeep here. No one will bother it."

Harry still didn't budge. "There'll be no room for anybody else to park."

The moment became awkward—Harry and Gina staring at the administrator, who was becoming perturbed, but shrugged it off and smiled widely. "Really, not to worry. We don't get many visitors here."

Gina shifted in her seat.

Mmmm. This is pretty weird.

Harry opened the car door and Gina watched Dayton's gaze shift to her. She could feel his eyes crawling all over her body as she lifted her purse from the rear seat and hiked it onto her shoulder.

* * *

Seated in Ethan Dayton's office, Gina studied the administrator's steely gray eyes and his skin that was as white as the day he was born. His smile seemed forced, pasted on his face. But with her employee history, she wasn't known for her love of people in administration.

12

The only picture on the office walls was one of the facility, and, whenever it was taken, there were no bars on the second-story windows. His desk was neat and clean, except for his name plate: Ethan Dayton, Administrator. There wasn't a single family picture on his desk, not even one of a dog. It was as though he'd rented all the office furnishings, like props. The man was a blank slate with no real information to flesh out Gina's initial impressions. She shifted her attention to the window behind him; it looked out onto another huge boulder.

Imagine that. A view without a view.

Dayton followed her eyes. "Our plants out here are beautiful rocks. They *are* beautiful, don't you think?"

Gina smiled, didn't say anything.

"We get tremendous wind storms," Dayton continued. "Those boulders are a protective barrier ... they keep us from blowing away."

"Makes sense to me," Harry said. "So, can you give us a run-down on our assignment? The agency really didn't give us much more than a bare-bones job description."

The administrator stood. "First, why don't I take you on a tour, then we'll go to the lounge and talk about what you'll be doing at Comstock."

* * *

"There are three floors to the facility," Dayton said, as they rode up in an oversize elevator.

Gina wondered about the warehouse-size lift, but at least she wasn't forced to stand too close to Dayton. He continued to make her feel restless. He looked like an average person, maybe a little stern, but that wasn't it. There was something not quite right about his white buzz cut and his flinty gray eyes that strangely matched the rocks outside his office window. He was friendly enough, but humorless, and about as parched as the landscape they'd driven through. Yet, Harry seemed all right with him, obviously relaxed with his lets-just-move-on-with-the-job attitude.

The elevator stopped at the second floor; two guys in scrubs, guys that Gina wouldn't have wanted to come across in a dark alley, stepped aboard. Their almost expressionless faces morphed into leers when they saw Gina. She cringed inside.

"Ah," Ethan said. "These are our two orderlies, Rocky and Peter." He introduced Gina and Harry to them.

"Which wing *you* gonna be on, Ms. Mazzio?" the one named Rocky asked.

"That hasn't been decided," Ethan said. Rocky gave him a noncommittal shrug.

When they arrived at the third floor, everyone got off. A bright, modern lounge lay straight ahead, with a long corridor on either side of it. Ethan pointed to the right. "That's where my apartment is." Then he pointed to the left. "That's where your living accommodations are."

Rocky and Pete walked away down the corridor on the left.

It took a moment for it to sink in; Gina and Harry looked at each other and said in unison, "What living accommodations?"

"That's where our staff stays. Let me show you your place."

Gina and Harry again spoke at the same time. "No!"

Ethan's pasty face turned a bright red. He looked first at Harry then at Gina. "You mean they didn't tell you about living on the premises?"

"Not a word," Harry said. "They only told us about the company digs, and we've rented a condo in Carson. That's where we're planning on staying for the next three months."

Gina was floored. She sure as hell wasn't going to spend twenty-four hours a day on site. She'd rather go back to San Francisco's Ridgewood Hospital, or someplace else, and maybe fight with an administrator who didn't keep looking at her chest like he needed breast feeding—and not the maternal kind.

"I don't know," Harry said, taking Gina's hand.

"Well, let's sit down and have some breakfast, a cup of coffee, and talk about it. I don't think you'd appreciate driving that road twice in one day."

As they followed Ethan, Gina squeezed Harry's hand until he winced.

Bette Golden Lamb & J. J. Lamb

Chapter 3

Ethan Dayton served them a full breakfast of scrambled eggs, French toast, and bacon, all of which arrived via dumbwaiter from a kitchen somewhere in the bowels of the building. Although they'd had juice and toast before leaving Carson City, Gina and Harry ate as though they hadn't been fed in days.

While the administrator refilled their espresso cups from a thermos, Gina took in a deep breath of the aromatic Italian coffee and looked around the eating area. They sat at one of two small Formica-topped tables near a mini-kitchen that was equipped with a small fridge, microwave, hotplate, and sink. At the other end of the room was a lounge, with a large flat-screen TV, a sofa, and a couple of leather arm chairs.

It was a fairly pleasant room, with a window that offered more of a view than just monstrous boulders. In the distance, she could see mound after mound of dirt, probably tailings from some kind of long-abandoned mining operation.

Bright sunlight filled almost every corner, but she wondered how long she would feel this sense of relaxation if this was where she had to eat three times a day, almost every day of the week for the next three months. Thinking about it made her antsy—she just wanted to leave even though Harry had one of his let's-wait-and-see looks on his face.

"Look, Mr. Dayton," Harry said.

"It's *Dr.* Dayton, but please call me Ethan. We have a small staff and we're very informal here."

"All right, Ethan. I've been involved with travel nursing for several years, but I've never once been *required* to live in company-supplied housing. And if I had, I would have refused the job, for obvious reasons—I need time away from my work, and anything connected with it."

"This may be my first travel assignment," Gina said, "but I certainly agree with Harry."

"We've tried it your way ... where the staff lives off campus. Our experience is that because of the region and the roads, people were either late or didn't make it to work at all—cars broke down, roads were blocked by landslides, casino nightlife was too addictive. It was always something."

"Still, this is not what we expected when we took the job," Gina said.

Ethan tapped his gold Cross pen on the table. "Our work is very specialized here. We can't run a facility under the conditions I've mentioned, no matter how small or efficiently planned it is ... we've had to establish strict protocols."

"Did you say *specialized?*"

"This is a research facility, Gina."

"A *research* facility?" Harry's face turned bright red. "I can't believe it. This is like being hijacked. You lied to us to get us out here?"

"And you never wondered why the sign-up bonus was especially generous?"

Gina and Harry shifted in their seats, looked at each other, and remained silent.

"It's been extremely difficult to get nurses out to northern Nevada, and twice as hard to tempt them to live on site. I'm sorry if we weren't completely straight forward with you."

It was a long moment before Harry said, "Suppose you tell us about the job before we settle the living arrangements thing, or even decide to stay?"

Harry Lucke, what the hell are you getting us into?

"I can't do that unless I know you will abide by our rules, and agree to sign a non-disclosure agreement. We are a cutting edge research center and everything we do is highly confidential." He paused, looked at Harry for several seconds, then turned and did the same with Gina. "Our greatest concern is industrial espionage. It's a crucial factor we can't afford to ignore."

He tapped the pen again and said, "I cannot stress enough the critical nature of our work or what it would mean if details were leaked to the competition. You need to understand that right from the git-go. The bonus we offered to get you to come here to this isolated and extremely environmentally unfriendly part of Nevada would probably be a pittance compared to what a competitor would offer you to deliver the details of our research. Even the most ethical person would be tempted to cooperate."

"Are you questioning our ethics?" Gina said. Ethan was exploring her chest again, or was he looking straight through her?

"Not at all, Ms. Mazzio." He paused for a moment. "Perhaps it would help you understand if I told you that we are involved in a vital national research project for Zelint Pharmaceuticals. That much I *will* tell you."

"Dr. Dayton—"

"Ethan." He said softly to her. "As I said before … we are quite informal at this facility."

The switch in demeanor caught Gina off guard. In her experience, there were very few people in administration who didn't treasure that *Mr.* or *Ms*, or *Dr.* before their name. "All right … Ethan … I think we can sign those papers for you. But, if we don't like what we see, we're out of here. We've made it plain, neither one of us wants to live in your hospital. So, persuading us is going to be a major task."

She could feel herself revving up, knew she was starting to get confrontational, but that resident evil twin inside of her refused to shut up. "And you also need to know that if we do decide to leave, we might or might not give back the bonus money." She smiled sweetly at Harry. "And if this place and what it does is such a big secret, you're not about to take us to court."

Harry glared at her, cleared his throat. "We've come here in good faith, Ethan. And I agree with Gina that our time is worth something." He softened the moment with a wide smile.

* * *

Where is everyone?

Gina noticed that they'd been alone with the administrator for more than an hour. No one had even walked by the lounge, let alone come in. It didn't *feel* like a hospital. It was way too quiet.

She didn't know if she could live with this total sense of isolation day after day. She'd felt this way from the very moment they'd reached Nugget and turned onto that almost nonexistent road. It was like they had been scripted into a sci-fi movie and plunged into another world.

And what about those iron rods on the windows?

"As you can see, this is a very small facility" The administrator chuckled at the obvious, interrupting her thoughts. She watched him emphasize his words by gently tapping the table with his pen over and over again. "Aside from housekeeping and the kitchen staff, there are only two other full-time RNs and two relief RNs for our 30-bed hospital. Of course, we fill in with temps whenever necessary."

"That's all?" Harry sputtered his full mouth of food while his eyes morphed into two large blue saucers. "You've got to be kidding! You really expect us to work twelve hour shifts, with a patient load of fifteen each, five days a week?" He shoved his plate away. "No wonder the agency was so closed mouth about this assignment. When I get back to San Francisco, they're going to get an earful."

"You won't be alone," Ethan said. "You will be assisted by aides, and Zelint will make it well worth your while."

"And how do you plan on doing that?" Gina was ready to stand up and go.

Ethan Dayton didn't blink. "An additional ten thousand per month, over and above your salary, if you go the full three months."

Harry had a weird look in is eyes, but Gina started thinking about what the combined $60,000 would buy. She could put some money into her Fiat, and living on-site, they could save most of it. Then she stopped.

There's gotta be another catch here.

Ethan pushed forward a set of non-disclosure forms for each of them. "I need you to read through these and sign off on them. I can't discuss, or move ahead without your signatures."

Harry pulled the papers to him, glanced at them, and signed. Gina speed-read through the words and scribbled out her signature.

"And *now*... maybe you can tell me, Ethan, why you have bars on the second floor windows?"

Harry gave her a *look* and the administrator was speechless for a moment. "I was about to explain all of that, Gina." He was pleasant enough but there was an aggressive undertow of anger that surrounded him like a fiery aura.

I always bring out the worst in these guys—or is it that they bring out the worst in me?

"Comstock is part of Zelint's national clinical study of a new drug for the treatment of Alzheimer's."

"That's incredible!" Harry's jaw hung open. "And you're actually into human trials? That's what this is all about?"

The administrator beamed at them. "Yes, it really is phenomenal. Zelint is very excited. We're all very excited. If this works out, in a year or two we'll have a real treatment for a disease that's plagued humanity generation after generation."

"Wouldn't *that* be wonderful," Gina said. "Oh, my God, now maybe I won't freak out every time I forget where I put my keys." The three of them laughed.

"So you can see why it's essential that all of this has to be kept under wraps."

"How have you kept the media at arm's length?" Harry asked excitement in his voice. "I can't believe they haven't somehow gotten wind of it? I mean, this is really huge."

"Zelint Pharmaceuticals," Dayton said, "has advised the media in a limited way. But there have been so many hits and misses in Alzheimer's R&D, it's become a wait and see attitude with *any* potential drug. No one jumps at rumors anymore."

"Well, I admit you've really gotten my attention," Harry said. "What do you think, Gina?"

Staring at the boulders, she still thought about those barred windows on the second floor, but she gave him a tentative thumb's up and began to relax.

Chapter 4

On the trip down to Carson City to their in-again, out-again condo, they had to drive over the migrating tarantulas again. Gina closed her eyes and tried not to imagine what was going on under the car as the tires crunched the black, furry creatures.

She hoped that if there was really such a thing as reincarnation, she would never come back as a tarantula, or as any number of other things she could think of—a yapping Pekinese, a fat gray rat, a slithy tove.

Ethan Dayton kept his word. As promised, he'd settled up with the condo manager, who was really nice about their leaving; even helped them load up the Jeep. Not that they had that much to tackle—just a couple of over sized suitcases, a cosmetic case, and a laptop.

Before heading for the hills around Nugget, they stopped and bought some groceries, even though they'd yet to see their new living quarters. All in all, everything took under two hours before they were headed back.

When they arrived, Ethan was waiting at the entrance. Just like the first time.

"*Cacca!*" Gina said. "Does that man do anything but stand guard at the front of the building?"

"Don't be so hard on him. He's just trying to be nice." Harry reached for her hand "What's the matter, babe?"

She tried to silence her inner warning system—it was making her heart race. She took a deep breath and thought about it. "I don't know, Harry," she said, squeezing his hand. "I'm jittery about this whole assignment."

"Hey, you're used to working in a big hospital with a large staff … travel nursing, all of this stuff, it's new to you." He looked into her eyes, ran his fingers across her cheek. "You're a great nurse. You can work anywhere and your patients will love you … so, it's going to be okay. Trust me."

Gina looked back at his soulful eyes and started to relax. "You're probably right. It's only me being my insecure self." She smiled. "You know, Harry, you're the best."

"Isn't that what you deserve, my little buttercup?"

"Ick! That's the worst one you've come up with yet." But she was laughing again. He leaned over and kissed her on the cheek.

She peeked out at Ethan Dayton waiting patiently in front of the building. "Well, here goes nothing."

The administrator took them directly to their apartment and pointed out the details of their new living quarters. A large flat-screen TV, microwave, coffee-maker. His parting shot, "I hope you'll be happy here with us at Comstock Medical."

As soon as the door closed behind Ethan, Harry spun Gina around in a full circle. "Well, what do you think of our new digs, Ms. Mazzio?"

"Not bad. I think we can make it work." She pointed at the living room window. "And, guess what? Another hunk of granite."

"Admit it. Isn't it nice to have something you can depend on? Sort of solid, like … a rock."

"Yeah, yeah!" She moved closer to the window. "Take a look at that … if we get desperate we could probably jump right out the window and onto this one." She pointed for him to see a weathered-sculpted ledge on the side of the huge boulder.

"You are an absolute nut," he said, standing beside her. "Besides, who cares about these monsters anyway?"

"I do," she said, kissing his nose. "Tell me, you can't possibly think that's a natural formation?"

"Why not?"

"Because all these boulders are uniform in size and shape. That's not the way Mother Nature works, not even in the wild, wild West."

"A nature freak from the Bronx?"

"Go ahead, make fun of me. But I'll bet they were placed there to either keep something out, or something in."

"You are the most suspicious broad I've ever met."

"And I don't know how you've managed to live this long calling women broads. So dated; right out of a noir movie." She flicked her fingers at him.

"Right about that. A male nurse surrounded by all those women … I should be dead, my balls hammered to the wall."

Gina giggled.

"But you're my solo target and it's worth it to watch you go into hyper-drive." He pulled aside an accordion-pleated partition to reveal the small kitchenette. "Come on, admit it. This is a great apartment."

"Go ahead, change the subject."

Harry laughed. "Survival instinct to the rescue."

They both began to unpack their suitcases and claim drawers and a share of the closet. "Sort of like a large studio," Harry said. "And our bed is stashed up and out of the way into the wall. Hmm. Never had a Murphy bed before. With the screened-off kitchen, it becomes a really nice living room with plenty of space to chase you around and then nail you on the sofa." He bounced down onto it and leered at her.

Gina gave him a wicked smile and leaped at him. "I only let you think you're nailing me."

"Uh, huh." His hands slid to her bra strap.

"Harry Lucke, I'm much too excited to mess around with you right now. I want to see what's on that second floor…besides bars on the windows." She stood and tried to pull him up.

"Hey, I was just beginning to warm up." He checked his watch. "Look, we have an hour to ourselves before we meet the boss for an official tour … and we're getting paid for it." He patted the cushion next to him.

"I want to check it out now. Why would a place like this have bars on the windows of the second floor? It's a drug study, not something illegal that needs a cell."

"We'll see everything later." He patted the cushion next to him again.

Gina, hands on hips, said, "Why does everything have to be about schedules with you?"

"I get into less trouble that way."

"Yeah, and what does that do for you?"

"Three squares and a fistful of dough."

Gina turned her nose up, gave him an I-don't-believe-you frown, and walked up to the window again. "Did you get an eyeful of those two orderlies who rode the elevator with us on the way up earlier? Kind of rough and tumble for a hospital facility, don't you think?"

"I gotta admit they didn't look much like orderlies to me, more the mop and pail type, but this is Nevada, remember?"

"Yeah, so?"

Harry shrugged. "I'm more concerned about the fact it takes a card key to get the elevator to stop on the second floor."

"How do you know that?"

"I'll bet if those muscle-bound guys hadn't been headed for the third floor, you would have seen what I saw—the button for the second floor was slotted for a card key. My take? No key, no visit to the second floor."

Gina grabbed an apple from their newly filled fruit bowl and started munching. "And that's where our patients are."

* * *

Gina went into their new bathroom and washed her face with cold water. It was the kind of ritual she often used to slow herself down so she could think about whatever was bothering her. When her ex-husband, Dominick, bullied her—tried to make her give into some scheme or idea he thought would bring him "millions," or when he'd been drinking and getting mean and physical—she

26

would head for the bathroom. It not only got her away from him, it gave her time to think, to find some kind of inner grit to outsmart him.

She looked at the bathroom mirror as she patted her face dry with a flowery hand towel.

Whatever makeup she'd had on when she started the day was now gone. Her eyes looked darker than usual, large and frightened; her short black hair barely stood up as she ran her fingers through its thickness.

Why did she feel so scared, like a trapped animal wanting to scoot into a corner, scrunch up, make itself smaller and smaller, so no one could find it, hurt it?

No!

She might be afraid, but she wouldn't allow herself to be like that. She would not, could not live in the shadows.

Gina reached for her makeup kit and did a pencil job around her eyes and left her dark eyebrows *au natural.* She finished the job with a touch of lipstick.

"There," she said to the mirror and left the bathroom.

* * *

"Stop looking so guilty, Harry. We're employees. We have a right to walk around the place, with or without Ethan."

"The last time, your curiosity almost got you killed."

"Don't be such a wuss." She pulled him toward the staircase. "I just want to see if we can get onto the second floor. What's wrong with that?"

"In another thirty minutes we can do everything on the up and up. This seems invasive."

"Bulltaki!" she said as they headed down.

They'd only taken a few steps when Harry held back. "Do we really have to do this now?"

"Yes, we do."

27

"Why? Can't you at least wait for Ethan, do the very same thing, and avoid getting into some kind of mess?" He sighed. "Gina, it's our first day."

"Number one, I don't like those disclosure papers we had to sign. That was a red flag. If it had been about patient confidentiality, that would've been one thing. But all that legal mumbo-jumbo about industrial espionage had a steel edge to it. More like a warning ... and I don't mean a slap on the hand."

"It's a drug study, Gina. Caution seems logical with all the cut-throat competition in the pharmaceutical industry."

"So, you think it's all about money?"

"Yeah. What isn't?"

She ignored him. "Number two, those rocks lined up on the road and all around the building. I swear, it's like being in a prison."

"The rocks again? Do you know how weird that sounds?"

She shook her head. "Number three, the census ... thirty patients. How do they get by on the kind of staff they have? Or should I say haven't? All I've seen are two muscle men and Ethan Dayton. Weird, huh?"

"It *is* weird," Harry said, "but I'm willing to wait and see how it all shakes out. Maybe the tour will explain it."

"I don't like it."

"Okay, babe. I do agree this is the craziest assignment I've ever had ... and you know I've put many years into this type of nursing. But sometimes off the wall can turn out to be interesting and challenging ... and the money is damn good. At least let's give it a chance. If you don't like it after a few days, I promise we'll leave."

"I wasn't finished." Gina gave him a big smile. "Number four, and don't you dare laugh at me," Gina said. "The place doesn't have the right smell to it."

Harry laughed out loud. "That's the nuttiest thing I've ever heard."

When they got to the landing, Gina looked into one of the security cameras over the door. "Something tells me, we're being watched right now."

He caught her around the waist, and hugged her to him. "Stop it, Gina. Please stop it, right now! Let's go back up." He looked into her eyes with his I-love-you softness and all the fight went out of her.

Why did he always have that effect on her? She went limp as his lips found hers.

The door to the 2nd floor opened, startling them.

"A little early for our tour, aren't you?" Ethan Dayton said from the doorway of the second floor.

Bette Golden Lamb & J. J. Lamb

Chapter 5

"Oh, hi, Ethan," Gina said in her friendliest voice, though her wobbly knees had their own agenda ... they shook so much she had to shift from one foot to another, or look like a total freak.

Can't I ever get away with anything?

She said, "Thought it would be fun to explore the building before our meeting."

Ethan's flinty eyes said he wasn't fooled for a minute.

And Harry didn't help. "Yeah, we hit the stairs early for some exercise." His forced laugh made everything even worse.

A smile that never touched the administrator's eyes cracked the lower half of his face. He made a point of looking up at an observation camera over their heads, which made Gina feel really stupid—they'd been watched the whole time. Had Ethan also heard every word they'd spoken since they arrived? She wracked her brain, jumping from one thought to another like a crazed grasshopper, trying to remember any specific negative things they'd said. Her mind drew a complete blank.

And I thought we were being so smart.

They should have realized that the bars on the second floor windows, along with all that talk about industrial espionage, meant that Comstock would have an air-tight security system.

"Now that you're here, we'll bring you in the *back* way." He stepped aside so the two of them could walk into the second-floor patient unit.

Gina wanted to grab Harry's hand and run, but she was a professional and would stand on her own two feet and do what had to be done. Still, she crushed her thumb and forefinger together—her secret fear neutralizer—and entered the second floor, with Harry close on her heels.

Her mind had conjured dark and dingy rooms and corridors, with patients wandering and crashing into each other like zombies. Or maybe there would even be loud screams of terror.

She'd been wrong about everything.

At first glance, it was no different than most other hospital floors she'd worked on—long corridors lined with rooms that could be closed off with wooden doors for privacy. Soft, classical music floated through the air, making her feel totally foolish for thinking there was something sinister about the place.

Not exactly a snake pit.

Ethan pointed ahead to the nurses' station. The three of them ambled over to where one of the two husky mop and pail orderlies sat. Close up, she studied this one's large, flat nose and black-button eyes that stared back at her. He was big, his huge shoulders made her shiver.

Steroid freak!

He nodded and gave them what could be considered either a smile or a leer, depending on your point of view. He was sitting next to the floor nurse—middle-aged, dressed in burgundy scrubs, and wearing a very, very tired face.

"Hi. You must be Gina Mazzio and Harry Lucke." She stood and walked over to them, hand extended. "I'm Delores Scott. Great to meet you. And this is Rocky." She pointed to the gorilla next to her. He nodded.

"Delores, why don't you show our new nurses around. I'll see them when you're finished." Ethan walked back down the corridor toward the elevator and turned around. "I'll catch up with the two of you later in my office." Before Gina or Harry could respond, he was out of sight.

"So how do you like this gig?" Harry said to Delores the minute Ethan was gone.

Gina noticed Delores' whole body language had changed to not only wary, but antagonistic now that Ethan wasn't around.

"I'd like it a hell of a lot better if I had more staff, or if those we have weren't so damned lazy."

Rocky watched the exchange with an empty look on his face, as though he couldn't have cared less. But his eyes bounced back and forth between Delores and them. Gina could tell he was listening very carefully.

Mmmmm. Looks like a dork but there's something more going on that head.

"You can make a lot of money," Delores continued. "And other than the killer hours, how bad can it be?" She paused. "Well, there is the fact that the patients are ... let's just say ... a little loopy."

"Ah, loopy? A brand new medical term." Gina forced a laugh.

"Come on, I'll show you around." Delores walked down the hall; they followed close behind. The first stop was a glassed-in spa that held a small hot tub and massage table.

Harry and Gina opened the door; steam drifted up, filling the room; the air was heavy with the moisture. Gina smiled at Harry. Being on the unit, in the actual work place made her feel more assured about the whole assignment. After a twelve-hour shift, this could be just what they'd need to become human again.

"Hey, does the staff get to use this?" Gina said laughing.

Harry smiled. "Pretty classy. Don't see these very often in hospitals."

Delores ignored Gina's question. Instead, she turned to Harry. "Well, we're not officially a hospital," she said, "more on the order of a rehab facility."

"Rehab? That's seems weird," Gina said, raising an eyebrow at Harry.

Delores again ignored the comment.

They visited some of the rooms; each held a single patient. It was pleasant enough: high ceilings, brightly colored drapes on the windows, matching spreads on the beds, fairly spacious, and generally the kind of upscale environment Gina wasn't used to seeing in medical facilities.

Delores introduced them to some of the residents, most of the people they met had dazed, drugged looks, and weren't very responsive.

"These people look absolutely stoned," Harry said.

Delores laughed. "Not stoned, but definitely heavily medicated."

"Doesn't it make it difficult to deal with them when they're medicated like that? I mean, most of them can't even talk. Can they answer your protocol questions?"

Delores looked at Gina in a puzzled way. "Didn't you know?"

"Know what?"

Delores's face turned a bright red. "I just assumed you knew. It's not my place to give you the particulars. I'm sure the doctor will explain everything."

Gina and Harry looked at each other.

"Looks like Ethan continues to have a lot to explain," Harry said, taking Gina's hand. "I wonder what other secrets he's sitting on."

* * *

They sat across from Ethan in his austere office. After giving them the necessary card keys and setting up their identification information, he ran through the care protocols. Gina was starting to feel very antsy again; she kept tugging at the magnetic ID that they were required to wear at all times. It felt like an anchor chain around her neck.

She could see now why the second floor needed so few licensed personnel. Every patient on the unit was so tranquilized they were more like the walking dead. Well, at least none of them had blood dripping from their teeth. But the barred windows made more sense now—couldn't have stoned patients climbing out the windows.

"So this facility is participating in a clinical drug study for the treatment of Alzheimer's?" Gina said. "That's really fantastic. What health professional wouldn't want to be a part of something as exciting as finding a real treatment for such a devastating disease?"

"Of course," Ethan said, nodding like a bobble-head doll planted on a dashboard. "As health professionals, I understand your dedication. It's plain to me that the two of you are humanitarian types, so the extra thirty thousand for your three-month commitment would have nothing to do with your willingness to stay."

The words were spoken in a reasonable voice—the kind administrators use when they don't want to tell you everything. But there was also an undercurrent of cynicism that jumped out and slapped her in the face.

Out comes the viper.

"Don't hold a carrot out in front of us if you don't want us to eat it," Harry said in a crisp voice that Gina recognized as part of his on-going battle with *his* demons.

"And you think we need to sit here and swallow your cynicism," Gina said. "We really don't need your money as much as you seem to think we do."

Ethan held out his hands, palms up. "I wasn't trying to put the two of you down. I'm sorry if you took it that way."

Gina looked at Harry; he stared back at her. She was ready to walk, had been from the moment the Jeep edged down that creepy driveway. But travel nursing was Harry's career choice. Any final decision would have to rest with him.

"So far, this has been a pretty hostile environment," Harry said, obviously still pissed with the administrator's jab at their motives for taking the job.

Gina couldn't stop herself. "Why are the patients we saw so …" Gina waved her hands around trying to find the right word "so … neutralized? How can you evaluate the efficacy of any new drug, especially one for Alzheimer's dementia, with people who can barely talk?"

"These patients are no longer receiving Zelint Pharmaceutical's new drug."

"What!" Gina knew her eyes must be bugging out as she gaped at the man. "So they were on the drug but they aren't any more?"

"That's correct," Ethan said.

Gina could barely breathe; she might as well have been back in the mine Harry had taken her into. "Why?"

Ethan stood and walked to the window. He stared outside while the room dipped further into silence. When he returned to his chair, he steepled his fingers under his chin and spoke slowly, as though they were children.

"Every patient who's accepted into our clinical trials has definitive biomarkers for Alzheimer's. All have undergone costly testing—spinal taps, positron emission tomography, and on and on. This intense kind of testing costs thousands of dollars for every single individual before they can even become a part of Zelint's study. And you have to realize, many applicants never become eligible. It's a costly and highly selective procedure designed to answer specific questions about the safety and effectiveness of the drug designated AZ-1166."

"All very interesting, Ethan," Harry said. "But—"

"But some of this doesn't make sense, Ethan," Gina said.

Ethan sat back into his desk chair, leveled his gaze at her and said, "Why would you say that?"

"We all know Zelint is not being altruistic," Gina said. "There are unbelievable barrels of money to be made if the trials are successful, right?"

"That's true," Ethan said. "And even more to be lost if it's not successful."

"Then why *aren't* these patients receiving AZ-1166 anymore?" she asked.

Ethan shifted in his chair; he couldn't hide his uneasiness with the question. "There are always some subjects whose response to a test drug … falls outside the protocols of the clinical study. They are considered failures. Simply put, the participants on the second floor are those kinds of failures."

"Well, what are they doing *here?*" Gina and Harry said in unison. They gave each other a knowing look.

"They're being treated for the negative side effects of AZ-1166. Part of Zelint's contract with the participants is to provide all medical care. We are fulfilling our part of the contract."

"What kind of side effects?" Gina asked.

"I think all of that will become clear when you read the computerized charts on the floor." With that, Ethan stood, ending the discussion. "So we'll see you at seven at the nurses' station tomorrow morning. And welcome aboard."

Gina wanted to grab the administrator by the shoulders and shake him until his brain rattled. She and Harry stood and started toward the door.

"Oh, by the way … don't forget to turn in your personal computers. We'll hold them for the remainder of your employment at Comstock."

"What?" Harry said loudly.

"Hey, that's *our* property," Gina added. She felt the bile rising in her throat.

"That's a helluva lot to ask," Harry said. "We need to be able to stay in touch with family, friends, and our professional agency."

Ethan looked from one to the other. There was a hint of a smile.

"Sorry, those *are* the rules," he said. "Paragraph three, subsection B of the disclosure statement you signed today."

Checkmate.

Chapter 6

They practically flew out of Ethan's office, caught the elevator to their apartment. Gina's face was so hot it felt like it was on fire. She headed for the sofa, then changed her mind and paced around the room.

Might as well be back in San Francisco, back at Ridgewood ... during the bad times.

The hospital administrator there had done his best to try to get her fired before the two of them finally made peace. If it hadn't been for the nurses' union, Gina would have been out the door.

Gina had a reputation for not being silent when bad things were happening to patients, particularly patients under her care. Most recently, she'd risked her life when she discovered her Oncology patients' treated and stored bone marrow had been stolen and was being held for ransom. Those cancer patients would have died without their treated cells, and the hospital had proved to be more worried about its reputation than in finding the perpetrators.

Did it even matter where she worked? Hospital? Clinic? Freelance? Administrators seemed determined to put her down for trying to do what was best for her patients.

I'll bet Ethan will be no exception.

Weren't hospital administrators supposed to be patient advocates, too? Wasn't that their priority? Maybe not their only concern, but it had to at least be somewhere high up on the list.

Well, sorry. I'll do what I have to do to protect my patients, even if it means hanging out like a big, fat pimple ready to pop.

"My head is spinning ... I've got to get out of here," she said to Harry. "Let's go for a walk before it gets dark."

"Slow down, babe," Harry said. "You know we'll work it out."

They stepped into the elevator. She looked up at one of the security cameras—its probing eye looked right back at her. She bit down on her lip and decided she would keep her thoughts to herself until they were outside the building.

The elevator stopped at the second floor. Rocky was waiting with an elderly lady in a wheelchair. He hesitated for only a moment before he wheeled her into the elevator.

"How's it going?" Harry said.

The man barely nodded. He was definitely uneasy about being in this confined space with them even though it was roomy enough to carry two full-size hospital beds.

The old woman was worrying a locket at the end of a long chain around her neck. She kept turning it with her gnarled fingers and seemed to have no interest in her surroundings. She was in pain—that was pretty obvious. With every movement the lines in her face deepened. Gina reached out and tucked a stray lock of hair behind the woman's ear.

The patient looked up with dark, troubled eyes and suddenly grabbed Gina's hand. The movement made her thin shoulders shiver. "Help me, nurse. Please help me."

Gina crouched down to eye level. "What's your name?"

"Emma. Emma Goldmich."

Rocky wrenched their hands apart and stepped between them. The patient screamed; globs of drool ran down her chin.

"Hey, man. There's no need for that," Harry said, his voice low and menacing. But the orderly ignored him.

Gina was stunned into silence. She glared at Rocky; thrust her balled fists into her pockets. At the ground floor, they waited for Rocky to push the patient out first. Maybe he was taking her to the laboratory or one of the other diagnostic areas on the first floor. Instead, he waved a hand, waited for Gina and Harry to step out.

The patient looked at them. "Help me! Help me call Tuva!"

Before they could respond, the door slammed shut.

* * *

40

Rocky was rattled. He smashed a knuckle into the second floor elevator button again, and then again, stared down the two nurses, who looked at him with puzzled expressions until the sliding door slammed shut in their faces.

"Rocky," Emma Goldmich said, her pleading eyes looking up into his. She clutched the arms of her wheel chair. "You promised to give me medicine." She started bawling, blubbered out the words. "Help me. My bones hurt! I can't stand it! I can't stand it! I can't stand it!"

The orderly hated the old woman. Her trembling hands were like claws as they reached up to him, and her eyes were crazed like a wild, trapped animal.

It's her fault that he was in trouble now.

He couldn't stop himself. He slapped her cheek and said in a low guttural voice, "Shut up! You hear me? Shut the fuck up!"

She whimpered and bent over, rocked back and forth, back and forth, a low hum coming from somewhere down deep in her throat. When the door flung open, he shoved the chair out and down the hallway to the nurses' station.

Delores Scott was studying her watch, probably counting the hours until she could escape. She looked up at Rocky. "I thought Emma was being discharged? I've already packed up her things. What's going on?"

"Delayed."

"I'm glad we didn't redo her room."

"Yeah."

Emma continued to rock and moan, which was creeping him out. He squeezed his hands together to keep from smacking her again. "I'll take her back to her room, but she needs meds for the pain, or she's gonna be screaming."

Delores shrugged, reached into her pocket, and retrieved the keys for the narcotics cabinet.

* * *

41

Rocky stood outside Ethan Dayton's office, planning what he was going to say. He couldn't let Ethan think Petey and him were pushovers, that he could shove them out the door. Their prison records weren't going to be the man's ace-in-the-hole.

If the dude thinks he can get rid of us that easy, he don't know dog shit.

But Emma Goldmich—she'd been a real screw-up.

Oh, yeah!

One thing for sure, he and Petey were never going back to that pen in Carson City. They'd done their time, hard time for a botched up B&E. It may have given him a body of steel but it also left him with a reamed out ass. He'd rather die than be tossed into that hell-hole again.

But that's not gonna happen. Me and Petey know too much about what goes on here for ole Dr. Ethan to just toss us out.

Besides, he liked this job, and there were not too many good slots around for ex-cons.

He finally knocked on the door and waited.

"Come in!" Ethan was seated at his desk. He smiled, but his gaze was cold and suspicious.

Rocky closed the door behind him. "There's been a problem."

"Oh?"

"Emma Goldmich is back in her room."

"What?"

"The new RNs were in the elevator when I was taking her down. Emma told them her name."

Ethan jumped up and leaned over his desk. He was practically in Rocky's face. "Even an idiot would have known not to get on the elevator with those new nurses."

"Hey! It couldn't be helped. It all happened so fast. I couldn't think—"

"Of course you couldn't think. Does an ex-con even have a brain?"

Good thing it's me dealing with this asshole instead of Pete. He would have freaked.

"They won't know anything. I took Emma back to her room."

"Well halleluiah for small favors. Now get the hell out of here."

Rocky stood his ground and stared at Ethan for a moment before turning away.

Don't push me too far, old man.

* * *

Gina laced her arm into Harry's, dragged him through the lobby and out through the front door.

"Maybe it would be faster if you carried me," Harry said. "What's this about?"

"Sorry. I was afraid you'd say something and they would hear us."

"Dammit, Gina, we have no proof that our conversations are being bugged. Three months of this kind of tension is going to tear us apart."

"Wait a minute, Harry. That's not true. How did they know we'd be at the second floor exit door earlier today if they hadn't overheard our conversation?"

"It could have been a coincidence. Or maybe they saw us in the security cameras."

Gina looked at the diminishing light—the sun was low in the sky, making it eerie to walk down the road in the shadows of the rocks.

"Okay, why didn't Rocky get off the elevator?" she said. "Where was he going with that woman, Emma Goldmich? There's nothing for a patient on the third floor. So what was that about?"

Harry looked away.

"That patient in the elevator, how did she know I was a nurse? I'm not in scrubs."

"Hell, Gina, you look like a nurse in or out of scrubs. It's who you are."

"But she was in so much pain ... and she was scared to death."

Sudden weariness washed over her. She'd had it. The whole day had been overwhelming. She walked over to the side of the road and onto the sandy terrain. When she was smack up against the nearest boulder, she leaned back and tugged at the sparse needles of a stray juniper that had fought its way through a large crack in the granite. She would not move any farther until they straightened this out.

He stood still and stared at her.

"Harry, don't just stand there. Say something, for God's sake. We need to talk this out."

His voice was soft and calm, but his body looked tense and wired. "Hey, Gina!" He gave her a weird smile. "Listen to me very carefully, and no matter what I say, don't jump. Okay?"

"This is ridiculous, Harry. What are you talking about?"

"Do not move! There's a rattlesnake near your foot."

Her heart sped up double-time, pounded so hard it felt like her whole body was throbbing. It took all of her self-control to stand stock-still while she allowed her eyes to wander downward. Her feet seemed to have a life of their own and were straining to run.

A foot or so away, a gray diamondback was coiled and staring right where her leg was quavering under her pants.

"It's all right. Just stay put; it won't bite you if you don't scare it."

"Scare *it*? *It's* scaring the hell out of me!" She wanted to be funny and laugh this off, but her mouth was so dry it felt like it was stuffed with cotton balls.

First tarantulas, now rattlesnakes. What's next, Komodo dragons?

"Harry, I don't think I can stand here much longer."

"Hang on, babe. I promise he'll move on soon."

44

But he didn't. She watched his vibrating tongue and beady eyes. They seemed to be watching both her leg and Harry edging in closer and closer.

"Try to relax, doll. Think of our trip to Italy three months from now."

She closed her eyes but all she could visualize was that evil-looking snake with its long teeth loaded like syringes. She started counting, forced herself to say each numeral very slowly. When she got to twenty, she opened her eyes.

Harry held a long stick. With quick movements he jabbed it under the snake and tossed it into the air. It landed about ten feet away, stretched itself out, slithered off, and disappeared between the black shadows of the boulders.

"Oh, my God!" Her stomach was resting somewhere near her knees.

Harry ran and pulled her into his arms. "You were fantastic! I'm so proud of you."

Her heart wouldn't stop pounding in her ears. Her legs gave way.

She grabbed Harry around the waist, squeezed hard, and held on until she could stand on her own two legs.

* * *

The elevator ride back to their apartment was smothered in silence. The minute they were inside, Gina stepped out of her clothes and raced to the bathroom. Her face was covered in tears and she couldn't stop trembling. She flung open the shower door and spun the faucets until the water was gushing freely and the steam was thick enough to make her stabbing headache start to ease.

Why am I here? What am I doing in this strange place? Everything feels disconnected and lonely. I don't want to be here—especially not for three months.

The hot water was like soft, electric needles jabbing at her body. Her chest was so heavy she could barely breathe. Wild, disconnected thoughts fired in her brain.

Love defeats me, make me do things I don't want to do. Why couldn't I let Harry go off by himself? I could have stayed in San Francisco, allowed myself time to think; worked out the misery of the past few months. Did I really need him so desperately that I had to follow him to a place so alien everything inside of me is screaming: Turn around, run?

And I'm still here. I need to let this man go.

Why can't I let go?

She poured a puddle of shampoo into her hand, rubbed it through matted strands, and scrubbed hard to wash away her negative thoughts and the scary happenings of the day.

Music filtered through the pounding water. Harry had turned on their iPod; through the heavy splatter she recognized the mellow jazz of Clifford Alden. The plaintive sounds of *Eleanor Rigby* grounded her, made her feel calmer. She closed her eyes and leaned against the stall, hummed along with the music until her hands stopped shaking.

She opened her eyes when she felt Harry slip in beside her. His strong arms drew her to him and he murmured soft, disconnected words of comfort. Bathed in silky soap, their naked flesh rode, slid against each other while tiny water fingers caressed them. His hands were everywhere, drifting down her back, onto her hips, around her thighs, between her legs. Puffs of steam rolled into her lungs. Words were lost when his tongue slid down her neck, onto her breasts, causing fiery tentacles of heat to curl through her groin. When his lips smothered hers, the steel vice that had squeezed her chest finally relaxed, and she knew she was safe again.

"I'm sorry for being such a wuss today."

"Shh! That was some weird shit out there. And this is new for you. It's okay to be scared. I was scared, too."

His voice was filled with passion, but at the same time soft and kind. She knew he loved her, and she loved him, but could she totally surrender, really share all her fears and allow him inside, allow him to settle in her heart?

* * *

Gina wouldn't let Harry touch the pasta sauce. She said, in her best fake Italian accent, "Keepa da hands away froma my pasta." She held a wooden spoon like a sword and waved it through the air, aiming for his midsection.

Each time he tried to mix or taste the sauce, she ground a hip into him until he finally said, "You do that one more time and that robe is coming off."

She leered at him wickedly. "You and what army?"

He grabbed her and held her up in the air. "Just because you're tall doesn't mean you can't be tamed."

"Mmmmm. Maybe we'd better eat now, Mr. Lucke, before we forget about dinner and everything gets cold." When he set her down, she tousled his long, curly hair and gazed into his soft blue eyes.

The small kitchen area was efficiently designed and well equipped. It had pretty much everything they needed, making it fun to cook in a new place. She poured the pasta into the colander and divided it onto their plates before spooning out the thick marinara sauce while he set out the basket of bread and lit the candles on the tiny dining room table.

"I already miss the sourdough we get in San Francisco," she said.

"I'll bet this brown-and-serve will be almost as good."

They both tasted the bread and said in unison, "No way."

"Harry?"

"Yes, beautiful?"

"I'll really try harder tomorrow. Really, really try to make the next three months work for us."

He reached across the table for her hand. "I know you will, babe. We'll breeze through this together. And after that, we'll be off to Italy for a whole month. Maybe we'll turn it into a honeymoon."

Gina smiled, then took in a large mouthful of pasta.

Why did he have to go and ruin a perfect evening by talking about marriage?

Chapter 7

Tuva Goldmich thought about her mother and brushed away her tears. She'd slept fitfully for the past few weeks and she'd been useless at work; she'd even fallen asleep at her desk in the middle of reformatting a brochure whose deadline had a red-flag countdown.

Her art director had found her with her head down on the desk, out like a light. She was awakened with a not too gentle shove.

"You can snooze on your own time, Tuva. Here, you're a graphic designer and you do the job." The woman tapped her Versace watch and said, "You've got two hours to finish that layout or you're out the door." She pointed a burgundy tipped finger at Tuva. "And you know I mean it!"

"Hey, I'm sorry but—"

"No *buts,* Tuva. Everyone always has some excuse, although I've got to admit, sleeping at the desk is a first. Bottom line: you've got two hours. Either the brochure is done or you are." The woman stomped away in her custom-made red power suit and four-inch Sami clogs without looking back.

Tuva was rattled but instead of diving in to make the final touches for the brochure, she studied the picture of her parents on the shelf above her desk—the one right next to the photo of her ex-boyfriend whom she couldn't seem to emotionally separate from ... even though he'd "moved on."

She really liked the shot of her parents, probably because it also showed one of her own paintings, a purple-red flower hanging in the background.

Right now it was her mother's penetrating eyes that reached out to her. Even in an inert photograph, she seemed to climb into Tuva's soul.

Did I do the right thing for you, Mom?

When her dad died, her mom had not only gone downhill physically, her mind had vanished. Every doctor Tuva took her to diagnosed Alzheimer's, but Tuva wouldn't accept that. Her own diagnosis: her mother was in a crushing depression with a broken heart—lost in a world of grief. Not very medical sounding, but it was real enough.

As her mother's condition continued to worsen, and the doctors held onto their diagnosis of Alzheimer's, Tuva had no choice but to accept what was happening. But where was her mother to live; who would take care of her? There was her mother's Social Security and a small IRA, but those wouldn't cover the cost of nursing home care. And Tuva had little to contribute from her meager salary as a graphic designer—rent, food, clothing, and an occasional movie consumed almost every penny. There seemed little choice but for her to move into her mother's condominium and be her caretaker. Just after she'd given notice to her landlord, she read an ad from a pharmaceutical company seeking Alzheimer's victims to take part in a long-term, in-patient drug testing program ... at no cost.

The call was made, papers were signed, and Tuva's mother was transferred to a Zelint Pharmaceuticals facility on Long Island. Not only was she relatively close by, but within a short time all the Alzheimer's symptoms had disappeared and there was talk of sending her home with continued treatment as an outpatient. But before that could happen, there was an unexplained setback.

Now her mother was far off in some way-out hospital in Nevada.

And I'm stuck here in New York ... can't even see her.

She shoved her unfinished work aside and pulled out her cell phone, hit the button for the connection to her family physician.

* * *

It was two hours to the minute when the art director returned. Tuva was calmly packing up her personal items into a box on her desk.

"What the hell are you doing, Tuva?" The director's voice slid through a climbing crescendo.

"I'm leaving." Tuva hated confrontations; she tried to ignore the woman instead of screaming back at her. She took a deep breath and silently placed her parents' photo in the box with exaggerated care before picking up her ex-boyfriend's picture. Even with the bitch standing on top of her, breath blowing hard on her neck, she slipped into a time-warp recollection—like falling from a twenty-story building with everything flashing through her head. She looked into her ex's eyes, remembered his body wrapped around her, and she sighed heavily before tossing him into the trash. That was behind her.

So was her art director, standing with hands on hips, fire in her eyes.

"Where's the layout?" Her voice was shrill and mean.

Tuva retained an air of dignity and remained silent. She lifted the box filled with her personal items and retrieved a blue folder tucked underneath. She hefted the file as though knowing what it weighed could have some special meaning. But like so many things in life, it was light and useless. In an envelope clipped to the folder was her letter of resignation.

"I think you'll find everything you need here," Tuva said in a calm voice. "And I e-mailed the file to the client, too."

The woman looked at the envelope as though she already knew what it was and instead, opened the blue folder. She quickly fingered through the graphic work with her long painted claws. When she finished, she pointed a finger at Tuva.

"Don't even think about coming back here again, Tuva Goldmich. And if I were you, I sure as hell wouldn't use this company for a reference, even if you have worked here for two years." She pressed her lips together, turned away, and carefully flicked a speck of nonexistent lint off her sleeve.

Tuva, who always controlled demanding, high-maintenance personalities by remaining calm, later splattering them on canvas in wild, throbbing colors, felt her composure sink.

"Fuck you, you self-centered bitch."

The art director kept moving without missing a step.

Tuva covered her mouth and looked around at the surprised office staff staring back at her.

* * *

It was 8:00 PM before Dr. Markas finally responded to Tuva's message. By then her imagination had gone into overdrive.

"There's something wrong! I know it!" She paced back and forth in her small living room, clutching the phone to her ear.

"I'm sure Emma's fine."

"Don't patronize me, Dr. Markas. She's not a child and she's not fine or I wouldn't have had to sign a proxy so she could be in that clinical trial."

"Tuva, you know it was only a technicality. Her decline—"

"Her *decline* grew worse when you talked me into placing her into that damn neurological evaluation and treatment center."

"Let's be realistic. You couldn't afford to take care of her anymore. It was a wonderful opportunity to help her, and everything is paid for."

"I would have been a great caretaker." Tuva's face was covered in tears as she collapsed into her leather sofa and tried to compose herself.

He's right. In a few months I would have been flat broke.

If only her mother would stop showing up in her dreams, screaming for help. Two to three hours sleep each night for the last few weeks had thrown Tuva into a state of exhaustion.

"This is an important opportunity," Dr. Markas said. "Your mom is 70 years old. There's still time for her to have some kind of life. Being part of this Phase III national trial may give her a real chance to be cured."

Tuva could hear the exasperation in his voice, but she didn't care. It was her mother—she couldn't let it go.

"*Real* chance? You don't even know if she's getting *the* drug. She could be on a placebo for all we know."

"Even so, the drug could be available very soon if the study shows that it works. You've got to realize, the entire scientific and medical community from around the world is sitting on the edge of its seat, holding its collective breath in anticipation. Tuva, this is big. Really big! And your mother's a part of it."

"But they took her out of the treatment center and sent her to Nevada." Tuva started crying again and could barely get the words out. "I can't even see her … she's so far away."

"I want you to think carefully about this, Tuva. You're thirty-five years old and you sound exhausted. You need to take care of your own life."

She leaned back into the sofa; put her feet up on the coffee table.

He doesn't know the half of it.

Chapter 8

At 5:45 AM, Gina awoke with a start. The radio alarm blasted their apartment with down-and-dirty Rock—no going back to sleep with *that* roaring in her ears. She slammed a hand down on the off button.

The sudden silence was a relief; it allowed her to take a few deep breaths and get her thoughts around the fact that today was the beginning of a new chapter in her nursing career. She'd been in the profession since she was twenty-two and she'd always given bedside care, except for her last job as an advice nurse at Ridgewood General. But she'd never had any travel nurse assignments, like Harry. And she'd never thought she would.

Her mind continued to drift. It was hard to believe she'd almost been murdered only a month ago. Who would ever think sitting at a telephone dishing out medical advice could be life-threatening? Somehow her violent upbringing had hitched a ride on her back to San Francisco. That thought gave her the shivers.

Get thee to a nunnery—or at the very least, move into a cave.

As usual, Harry didn't budge when the alarm went off; he continued to snore softly. She stretched out her arms, reached for the ceiling, then rolled over and gently blew into his ear until he opened one eye.

"How do you ever manage without me when you're on the road?"

"I never have anyone interesting to snuggle, so I might as well get to work." He opened his arms; she slid up against him. "Did you sleep well?" he asked.

"Totally." He was so warm and cuddly she wanted to throw the covers over her head and cancel the day; just relax and fall back to sleep with her head buried in his chest. But she forced herself to roll away and sit on the edge of the bed. And as she had so many times in the last few days, she ignored that inner voice that told her to pack her bags and go back to California. Instead, she set one foot on the floor, then the other, and pushed off.

She started singing, *Oh, What a Beautiful Morning,* in a high, broken falsetto, while she danced around the room, her voice getting louder and louder.

"Okay, I give up." Harry leaped out of the covers and raced to the coffee machine, getting everything together for breakfast. His movements were so fast it made her head swim. In a flash he took off for the bathroom.

"You rat, how do you always manage to beat me to the BR when I'm the first one out of bed?"

He poked his head out the door. "Talent, my dear Watson."

Gina rummaged through her drawer of scrubs and picked out a burgundy set that had seen enough washing to be soft and comfortable. She quickly got dressed.

Harry finally ambled out of the bathroom stark naked. He wasn't tall, but years of working out gave him the hint of a six-pack and nonstop muscular shoulders. When you threw in his baby blue eyes and curly mop of hair, Gina thought he was really something hot to look at.

"Too late to tempt me now, Mr. Lucke. I only have enough time to use the potty, eat, and get to work on time. And that's because we're only a floor away from the action."

He laughed, reached out, wrapped himself around her and pressed everything he had against her. "There's always later, beautiful."

* * *

They stepped out onto the second floor and the elevator slammed shut behind them, Harry immediately tuned in to a distinct clatter coming from what had to be a climbing dumbwaiter. The sound emanated from the opposite wall. It took him a moment to zero in on it—the access door was well camouflaged, with only a small, protruding aluminum knob to indicate it existed at all.

He pointed. "See that? That's what I call a logical food delivery system for this small facility. I barely noticed it before."

Gina nodded.

The second floor landing's walls were painted a soft gray-blue. Opposite the elevator was a tall artificial palm whose fronds spread up and across the ceiling as though it was searching for a way out. The phony plant was housed inside a huge Asian celadon-glazed pot; it sat on a thick gray carpet that effectively muffled most sounds on the floor—footsteps, voices, and even the noise of the dumbwaiter.

Harry's imagination turned the corridor, where he would tread onto a narrow bridge between two exciting worlds. That was why he'd become a travel nurse—he'd wanted to see the world, see strange and exotic places. Almost instantly reality kicked in and he knew he was merely poised between the two patient wings of a Nevada medical facility in the good old U.S. of A.

Gina looked nervous; she was running a hand through her black curly hair, and her dark eyes were wide open, blinking rapidly.

He squeezed her hand. "You'll be great."

She gave him a quick peck on the cheek and walked toward Wing A, while he turned and went into Wing B.

He caught sight of the nurses' station and the orderly he would work with.

Looks like I'm about to meet the other muscleman from the elevator ride yesterday.

"Hi, I'm Harry, Harry Lucke, one of the new nurses." He extended a hand; the man gave him a lopsided grin.

"Are you really lucky, Harry?"

"Lucky enough," Harry said, refusing to let his hand drop.

"I'm Peter," the orderly said, barely returning the handshake. "You'll never guess why they call me Peter the Great."

If you're anything like Rocky, it's because you're a great big pain in the ass.

"No, I can't imagine why."

"It's because I'm a great cocksman ... *big* with the women ... if you know what I mean." Peter gave him another one of his half-assed grins. You couldn't ignore the idiot, because like Rocky, the man had muscles popping out of his eyebrows.

Enough of this bullshit.

"Where's the charge nurse, Pete?"

"Allison had to leave early. I'm with you on this shift." He tossed Harry a ring of keys.

An orderly passing me narcotics keys? Hmmm. Pretty loose operation.

Harry moved behind the desk, pulled out a tattered Procedure Manual and did a quick thumb-through. He looked around—nothing unusual about the area. Well, nothing except that it was an undersized nurses' station with a narcotic cabinet twice the size found in a standard hospital unit.

"And the census?"

"Fifteen patients, as usual." Pete's eyes bored into his. "Fifteen on A and fifteen on B. Although I hear we're gonna be cuttin' back real soon."

"You have a constant turnover?"

"You could say that. They just keep movin' them in and movin' them out."

Harry was losing patience. The guy not only had attitude, he had a huge black mole in the middle of his chin—it kept yanking at Harry's attention.

"As I mentioned to Ethan, the facility seems understaffed. This wing holds a lot of patients for just the two of us to handle safely."

Yes. I do see why they're paying us so much money.

"We used to have another pair of hands until a month ago," Pete said, "but they just keep droppin' off like flies." He gave Harry a knowing smile, which made the mole on his face look like it was a fly about to jump off. "One day they're here, the next day, they … ain't."

A sudden scream pierced their conversation. Harry's inner alarm went off., making his scalp tingle.

"What the hell is that?"

Pete was unperturbed. He stood. "They'll all be doin' that if you don't move your ass and get them their dope."

* * *

Delores Scott was waiting at the Nurses' station for Gina; she had that blood-drained face people have after they leave a roller-coaster ride that was supposed to be fun.

"Rough night?" Gina said.

"No more than usual."

They both turned to look at Rocky as he arrived at the desk whistling. His movements were a study of contradictions—heavily muscled, yet light on his feet, like a dancer. He looked at Gina with testosterone-filled eyes. The man was really creepy.

"This is Rocky Salvo." Delores's voice climbed enough for Gina to know something was out of kilter. "He'll be assisting you with the patients."

Gina looked at the orderly. "We met right here yesterday, remember?"

Gina couldn't believe it. Rocky had not only ignored her question; he'd already turned his back on both of them.

Delores kept right on with her orientation. "You'll find a complete computer profile on every patient on the floor. An oral report won't be necessary," she said in a snippy voice. "So there won't be one."

"Maybe you could tell me *something* about the patients," Gina said. "I'd like to know—"

Rocky interrupted, whistling again as he walked away from the station toward the patient rooms.

"Is he always this rude?"

Delores's pale complexion turned a shade whiter. "I think you'll find that both Rocky and Pete, the other orderly on the Wing B, pretty much do their own thing."

"Their own thing?"

Delores started gathering her stuff together. She rummaged around in her purse. "When I first started here I was feisty and curious like you. My advice to you, Gina: mind your own business and just do the job, which is mostly checking custodial needs and handing out pain meds."

"What about the study? What's the lowdown on these patients?"

Delores hefted her purse onto her shoulder and was definitely ready to take off. "What lowdown?"

"Okay. What do you think—?"

"What's there to think about?" Delores started down the corridor, looked back at Gina and said, "Didn't Ethan tell you … the patients in this facility are finished with the study."

"Yes, but—"

Delores just kept walking and was gone in an instant.

Chapter 9

Gina was at a loss for words; she was actually dumbstruck as she watched Delores leave the unit, move toward the elevator, and vanish from the floor.

How unprofessional.

The departing nurse had not given a report or breakdown for expected patient care. No guidance, no direction of any kind for the new girl in town. Boom! Gina Mazzio, RN, would be giving nursing care to fifteen people she knew nothing about; their lives had been entrusted, no, thrust into her hands.

This wasn't the way it was supposed to be. In fact, nothing like this had ever happened to her before, except during an emergency. She needed some insight—the ins-and-outs of the facility, hard facts about the patients on the Wing A unit. That's what nurses did for each other, part of what made them professionals.

And this whole set up feels out of whack.

She mentally back-stepped and went over the introduction to the facility step by step—Ethan had specifically told her and Harry that although these patients had been part of a Phase III national clinical drug trial, they were the failures. They were only here for medical care.

What kind of medical care?

"You better get a move on," Rocky said, "or we'll both be in trouble." He'd come back to the nurses' station without her seeing or hearing him.

"What do you mean by trouble?" Gina snapped. She could feel the muscles in her neck bunching up. She didn't like or trust this goon. Now he was telling her—the charge nurse—how to do her job. That was no small matter. There was a lot at stake here for her. She had a license on the line; she didn't even want to begin to think about what would happen to her if she lost that.

"Where are the patient profiles, Rocky?"

He sneered, yes, sneered at her, putting her flat-out into attack mode. "I don't see you moving," she said, looking around the desk; pretending to be lost in a search. She shifted papers, deliberately looked under the desk, shrugged her shoulders. "I still see no charts here."

"This is the twenty-first century, lady. They're in the computer."

And there it was, just like when she grew up. Another bully trying to push her buttons, shove her around, stake out a territory at her expense.

She paced out a long stride, putting her into his personal space. "Let's get one thing damn straight here, Rocky. When I say jump ... you jump! Don't give me a lot of smartass back talk. Pull those profiles up on the screen ... and do it now!"

She could see he didn't exactly know how to change gears, but he planted his butt in the chair at the computer and scrolled his way into the nurse's notes for every in-house patient.

Gina sat down in a rolling desk chair, waved her hand for him to scoot over so she could move in front of the monitor. She scanned through the entries, and without exception, they all only dealt with a variety of drugs for pain management for each individual. Not only that, all of the patients were due for their first morning dose *now*.

"Where are the medicine cards?" She had to slow down, calm down; she heard the panic in her own voice. These patients were pretty much getting narcotics like clockwork, four times a day, and right now they were probably climbing the walls.

"Go check up on everybody, Rocky. Tell them I'll have their meds PDQ." But he didn't move; he just sat there. "Look, man. We've gotten off on the wrong foot with each other this morning, but we'll settle that later. Right now we've got to take care of these people." She waved toward the patient rooms. He held out a packet of medicine cards and she took them. The orders on them would allow her to move at top speed. She held out the other hand for a high five. "Truce?"

Rocky's eyes narrowed but he smacked her open palm—a little too hard.

* * *

A piercing scream echoed throughout the unit. Harry bolted down the hall; it was coming from the far end of the corridor.

He checked the posted name outside the room: Rhonda Jenkins.

He stepped inside and saw the woman hunched over, standing at the barred window crying. She was leaning with all her weight on the sill, trying to hold herself up.

Harry moved to her side and slipped an arm around her fragile waist. She jerked as though he'd punched her.

"It's okay, Ms. Jenkins. I'm one of the new nurses and I'm here to help you."

She looked at him with the opaque eyes of a trapped animal. "The pain. I can't stand it anymore." She held out a pleading hand; her fingers were disfigured by tight contortions that made Harry wince.

"Here, Ms. Jenkins, let me get you to a chair, then I'll be right back with your medicine." He tried to support her arm but the pressure made her cry out. "Let me bring the chair to you. He stretched out and grabbed onto an armrest and dragged it over.

She was still sobbing, but she'd calmed down and had stopped screaming. "What's your name?" she asked. "Are you a nurse?"

"Yes, I'm a nurse. My name is Harry Lucke. But you can call me Harry."

A fleeting glimmer of humor reflected in her eyes. "And you can call me Rhonda." He placed a hand on her head and gently smoothed her hair. "I'll be back with your medicine very soon."

Harry returned to the nurses' station to find a display of red lights. Everyone on the unit was buzzing for help. He quickly read Rhonda's medicine card, then opened the narcotics box

Demerol 100 milligrams, IM.

Considering her age and condition, it was a lot of juice to take on a regular basis. He quickly brought up her profile on the computer. It confirmed what he already guessed: Rhonda had an advanced case of osteoporosis. Along with being almost blind, her whole body was not only crumbling, she was in a deep depression, complicated by total exhaustion.

He drew up the med for Rhonda, rushed down the hall, and found her in her chair, head almost bent to her knees. Intermittent sobs wracked her body. Pete was in the room straightening her bed. He seemed oblivious to either one of them. For the moment, Harry ignored him and gently moved the patient's underclothes aside and gave her the injection in her hip. She gave a soft whimper.

Pete and Harry left the room at the same time.

"I noticed Rhonda was dressed already. Did the night shift dress her?"

"Yeah." The orderly moved into the next room while Harry continued down the corridor.

Once again in the nurses' station, Harry quickly arranged medicine cups and syringes on a large tray; every medication was an opiate of some kind. The dose level in each and every case was in the stratosphere. He worked quickly and it didn't take him long to get everything ready.

He went from room to room at top speed, introducing himself and administering the pain killers.

Every patient looked at him as though he had in some way betrayed them.

Chapter 10

It was 4 pm when Gina buzzed Harry. "It's quiet enough now ... I can get away. How about we coordinate and have our dinner break together?"

"Wish I could, babe, but I think my evening meal is going to consist of catching up on nurses' notes."

"Rough day?"

"You don't know the half of it. See you back at our apartment around 7:30."

Gina was disappointed; she'd looked forward to seeing Harry before the end of the shift, but his response didn't surprise her—this was the first time she'd had a free moment the entire day. She'd spent most of her time with agitated patients and a sulky, aggressive Rocky. She wanted to talk to the orderly about their edgy start, but he continued to make her jumpy. Each time she was on the verge of apologizing for not playing nice, she was back to snapping at him for some new insult he'd tossed her way. When he called her a "California short-timer," that ended any kind of truce between them. She got the message, in a not too subtle way: He was telling her that she would be gone in three months, and so who cared what she thought? Sort of a king-of-the-mountain mentality. It was so childish she didn't really get mad, but she was still irritated—the guy kept pushing her buttons. Besides, it seemed strange for anyone to call her a Californian. She still thought of herself as a New Yorker.

When the two of them had delivered all the patient dinner trays, she took the elevator to the third floor and wandered into the cafeteria. She wasn't terribly hungry, but not eating wasn't an option—she faded quickly without having food every couple of hours. She usually carried some kind of snack she could pop into her mouth when her energy dipped. Today it had been raisins. But they were long gone.

The place was empty. The heavy silence made her lonely for the normal hospital cafeteria environment, a place where people from all the different units and specialties had a chance to exchange information and gossip. There was always something going on and it was rare that she ate alone.

She looked at the vending machine, with its limited assortment of sandwiches. She chose turkey on a roll, then went to the soda machine and bought a diet Coke.

It was hard to get comfortable in the room's molded fiberglass chairs. When she took the first bite of the sandwich, she knew it was the last time she would be buying anything from that machine—the bread was dried out and the poultry was more like mystery meat. She drowned the small bite with the Coke and wondered if all her dinner breaks were going to be this bad. At least if Harry had been here they would have found something to laugh at.

Man, it's way too quiet here.

Her watch told her she still had enough time to hurry to their apartment and make a bowl of soup, or at least find something else. She tossed the sandwich into a trash basket across the room, gave herself two points for the shot, and left the lounge. At the hallway leading to their apartment, she hesitated, then walked back to the elevator.

She decided to go see Harry, see if she could help him. When she started to press "2", she noticed a black square under "1." Just a plain square with no writing. Underneath it was a narrow three-inch slot. It had to be an unadvertised destination to a lower floor.

Probably the kitchen. Maybe I can grab a free meal, or at least nose around.

She tapped it.

The car moved down and then clunked to a halt. The door remained closed.

Wadda you want, "Open Sesame?"

She laughed at herself and quickly checked her watch. At this rate she knew there'd be no food until after work. The slot and the closed elevator door kept staring at her. She pulled her ID card from around her neck and shoved it into the slot.

Whoosh, the door jerked open.

Mmmmm. Funny, Ethan didn't say anything about this.

At first her feet refused to drag her into the dimly lit area, but then she forced herself to step out into the corridor. She'd been holding her breath and was startled when the elevator snapped close and started its climb again.

It was a weird, shadowy area, and hard to see much of anything. But like the second floor patient units, there seemed to be only two wings. She could either go left or right. No, wait a minute: straight ahead was a narrow tunnel-like pathway that disappeared into darkness. Her eye did that twitch thing, like it always did when she was scared or cornered.

Well, I'm not going there. No way!

The tunnel made her think about being a kid again, about the deserted old studio in her rundown neighborhood. Most kids said it was haunted—they all stayed away from it, including Gina. But one day the place became the only way to get past a gang of boys without taking a beating—or something worse.

That was when the twitch started.

* * *

Five boys, ranging from 10 to 12, were standing in a don't-cross-me line on the sidewalk. And they were only a short half-block away. They tried staring her down, stood tall with their thumbs hooked into their jeans, sure that she was going down, was going to have to take whatever they tossed her way. And they were in no hurry—they wanted her to think about it, wanted her to be *really* scared.

Her eye started twitching. Gina had almost been caught by these same boys before and she'd seen them beat on some hapless jerk ... like her. It would be serious.

She stood near the ten-foot, iron-bar-fence that surrounded the creepy deserted movie studio; she wouldn't be climbing up and over it, that was for sure—each bar had a spiked top. Her only way in would be to squeeze through. The bars were pretty close together and she wasn't sure she could suck in her gut enough to get through to the courtyard.

She walked past the old studio most days. The place was falling down, and she was sure it was haunted. That's what everyone said. Her apartment house was right next to it but at the other end of the two-block-long building. She would stand on the fire-escape outside her bedroom window and try to see inside one of the dirty windows of the old studio. But she never saw anything.

The boys must have figured she had enough time to freak out and would really be scared; besides, they were probably tired of standing around and doing nothing. They began to walk slow and easy in her direction. She checked behind her again, but thugs from the same gang were standing at the other end, blocking her escape.

They suddenly let out a war whoop and ran full out. She held her breath, sucked everything in and tried to squeeze through the bars. She didn't think she was going to make it, but she pulled her gut in so hard she couldn't breathe ... And finally slipped through.

The five of them now stood right outside the spiked fence, looking in at her. One of them yelled, "You stupid bitch, you better come out of there before the vampires suck you dry." Then they laughed.

Someone else screamed out, "Leave that to us, you little pussy."

"Here, kitty, kitty. Here kitty, kitty."

She knew they couldn't get in this way—they'd never fit through the bars. Besides, all their tough talk didn't hide their fear of the old studio. She was safe here.

Or was she?

One thing she knew: she wasn't going out where they were. No way. She'd just have to run through the two-block length to the other end of the studio. It was the only way home.

I gotta, gotta.

Gina started running in large circles to work up speed. With her eyelids half closed, she took off.

Dear God, please, please, help me. I promise I'll never be bad again. I promise ... I promise ... promise ... help me ... help me."

She ran flat out, her heart hammering in her chest, her shoes crunching down hard on scattered glass, which made her slip and slide, over and over again. Creepy moans were all around her. She ran harder, faster, until she was panting so rapidly she couldn't catch another breath. She stopped, bent over, hands on her thighs, and looked around.

When she calmed down, not only an eerie sense of courage, but a feeling of inner peace made her really look at her surroundings. She studied the spooky building.

One wall of the three-story structure was crumbling. Dirty old stucco was peeling off the other walls. She'd never seen the inside before.

She walked up a cobblestone pathway to a loading platform. Rotted, splintered crates were tossed everywhere. A thick rope hung from an open second-floor window over the platform; it swayed in the breeze, frayed strands spread out like pleading fingers. And the moaning? It was coming from the wind blowing through broken doors and smashed windows. One long moan that never stopped.

There was nothing here to be afraid of ... at least if she stayed on the outside.

She whooped, tossed out a wild laugh, and did an Indian dance of joy, round and round in a circle before she walked the rest of the way home.

* * *

Gina looked at the dark underground tunnel-like area and smiled. But she still wasn't going in there. Instead, she turned toward a buzz of voices far down the dimly lit corridor. She walked carefully, trying to keep her sneakers from squeaking.

The male voices got louder and louder the farther in she went. There was light ahead, coming from a pair of swinging doors. Each door had a glass panel high up and there was a two-inch or so crack where the door's rubber flaps didn't quite match up.

Gina tried standing on tiptoe but the glass was too high to see inside. She bent close in to the flap and could make out a long kitchen counter against a wall and a wooden cutting block in the middle. She leaned into the door and slipped—knocked her shoulder hard against it.

The conversation behind the closed doors stopped. Gina jolted up, turned and ran down the long hallway back to the elevator.

She heard the men far down the corridor as she hammered the button with her fist. "Come on, come on!"

The elevator door sprang open, but a large hand grabbed her arm.

"Where do you think you're going, sister?"

Gina's heart froze in her chest. She tried to pull away as she looked into the man's intense eyes—they seemed to burn a hole through her.

"Hey, Bernie, can't you see you're scaring—" the other man leaned over and read her name tag, "—Gina." He lifted the hand away from her arm like it was something slimy or diseased. The man smiled and said, "I'm Jeff. Don't let this animal scare you. We're just not used to seeing any pretty ladies down here." He reached over to a switch on the wall next to the elevator door and gave the area more light. The place was still pretty creepy, but Jeff seemed friendly enough. He was tall and slender, and he seemed to be going out of his way to make her feel at ease.

"What's going on? What are you doing here?" Jeff's voice was probing, but polite.

"Actually, I just started this job … it's my very first day and I came looking for the kitchen. The food in the vending machine in the cafeteria was a disaster." She smiled at the two of them. "I mean, it's not like I can run into the Golden Arches down the street. I was hoping you had something decent to eat down here."

She could tell neither of them was buying any of it, but Jeff said, "We only put together enough food for the patients." His voice changed almost imperceptively harder. "So we don't expect to see you here again. Right, Gina?"

"Right!" She stepped into the elevator. As the door closed, Bernie glared at her, but Jeff only nodded.

Chapter 11

Ethan Dayton sat at his desk, fingers tapping a nervous beat on the two new employee folders that were side by side in front of him.

Unfinished business. That's what papers on his desk usually meant.

Is that what these two new nurses are ... unfinished business?

Gina Mazzio, RN, and Harry Lucke, RN.

He didn't bother opening the files. There wasn't much in them other than their employment histories, and he knew those by heart. Usually, his computer held all the vital and trivial information he needed, but these two files hadn't been scanned and tucked away in the cyber world, yet.

For a moment he allowed himself to visualize the virtual world that held all of his letters and secrets, big and small, floating in outer space ... scattered like pearls of wisdom across a vast and glorious cosmos. He knew it was romantic drivel to view the cyber world that way. Pure logic told him that the information was really in some kind of contained electronic storage that he couldn't even begin to see in his head.

He tapped the computer keyboard lightly, patted his pants pocket to assure himself that his backup flash drive was where it was supposed to be—safe, next to his body, in his control. He'd been doing that a lot lately. And why not? Every single detail of Zelint's drug trial AZ-1166 was stored in there. His future depended on presenting all of the necessary evidence of the clinical study—and he needed to get his part done flawlessly. If he didn't ... well, his life would turn to shit again.

He'd sworn he'd never go back to working in a hospital environment.

Never.

No more carving his way through an endless assembly line of dead bodies that flowed through an autopsy lab. No more pressure from the police, hospital administrators, state investigators.

Constant pressure. Constant dead bodies to cut up.

He stared hard at the telephone and thought about his conversation with Jeff a few minutes ago. If there were any kitchen problems he was the one Ethan talked to. Bernie, the other one, was dumb as a fence post. But he did do what he was told. And that's all Ethan required of kitchen help.

Jeff had called about the new nurse, Gina. It seems she was wandering around the underground floor of the building. Jeff said she was looking for something to eat—something other than the junk in the vending machine. That really irked Ethan. He'd been trying to get the vending machine people to change the food on a daily basis, but they'd refused. Too much trouble, not cost effective to service them more than twice a week.

Heck, maybe she was really only looking for something to eat.

He leaned back into his chair and remembered the couple carrying bags of groceries from the car yesterday after coming back from Carson City.

Am I being paranoid?

No, she *was* nosing around. Just the edge of panic made him restless.

Ethan tapped out a staccato beat on the two nurses' files, alternating from one to the other. He was having serious second thoughts about having brought Lucke and Mazzio on board. And he'd even had to really sweet talk Comstock General Hospital's OB supervisor into changing Mazzio's travel assignment so he could steal her from the main campus, with its out-patient prenatal clinic. That had been her original assignment—temp nurse-in-charge of the busy, low-income clinic.

Maybe instead of him doing the manipulating, maybe somehow he was being manipulated.

Maybe there was another layer to this whole set-up with Zelint.

Maybe there was an underbelly of hidden currents he was missing?

Hadn't the OB supervisor given in to Ethan's request much too easily?

Be careful what you wish for.

His ex- wife used to say that all the time, but Ethan found that wishes never did much of anything for him, one way or the other—and neither did his wife. That realization came to him much too soon after they were married.

What worked for him was being in the right place at the right time, willing to do anything and everything, bad or good. That's what brought him here to Nevada from a thriving metropolitan hospital in LA. That and a huge pile of money and Zelint stock options. Growing up poor had taught him a thing or two about not taking things for granted; about how not to be a loser, how to turn something into a profitable deal.

He looked back again at the files on his desk: The male nurse seemed more solid and less inquisitive. More compliant. He flipped through Lucke's file and scanned his employment history. The man had done everything from ICU to rehab.

Soup to nuts—tons of experience.

And he has glowing references.

The woman was the outspoken one, which usually didn't bother him. Most of the nurses he'd been around in hospitals were always more independent and mouthy. And he needed that kind of person here; someone with self-confidence who could make the right decisions in an isolated environment like this. Besides, it didn't take much to squelch questions after working a twelve-hour day. They were usually too tired and more than willing to put ethics aside when they were that bushed. All they wanted to do was sleep and try to fit in some kind of life of their own.

Yet, right off the bat, this nurse seemed to be sticking her nose into things.

He opened Mazzio's file. This was her first independent travel nurse assignment. Did she need a little more time to settle in? After all, it was only day one on the job. But her references were guarded; there was an undertow of something unexplainable. They indicated she was a good nurse, but the language didn't add up to outstanding. He remembered noticing and ignoring that before.

Maybe I was too hasty bringing her here.

A worse thought:

Could these two possibly be undercover agents from the FDA's Office of Criminal Investigations?

Undercover agents!

That would be a disaster. We can't have the FDA's criminal unit sticking its ugly nose into our AZ-1166 trial.

He picked up the phone and punched in 06, the autodial to David Zelint.

* * *

The founder and co-owner of Zelint Pharmaceuticals had just come from a board meeting, and was ecstatic. Not how he usually felt after those long, bitter meetings that mostly dealt with the heavy costs of a recent trial failure—a cancer drug that turned out to have only a positive side effect of slowing down an extremely rare disease that he couldn't even remember the name of. It certainly hadn't produced the promised remission for Stage IV breast cancer.

The board hammered the Zelint twins about the money that was never going to be recovered from the R & D expenditures. His brother Saul didn't see it that way; the failed cancer drug could help some people, even though it would become one of those orphan drugs that brought in low returns on their investment; it certainly wasn't going to rake in the multi-millions they'd anticipated.

Saul wanted to continue manufacturing small production runs of the drug to help the people who would benefit from it. David agreed with the board that they should just drop the medication all together.

His brother was a do-gooder and he couldn't be taken for granted. He was someone who really cared about people.

Maybe someday I'll be that way... probably not.

Still, David loved his twin brother and AZ-1166 had finally made not only Saul happy, but the board was wild with anticipation about the Alzheimer's study results. It was going to be a winner—rake in money beyond their wildest dreams, while doing something monumental for the human race.

David Zelint reached for the ringing telephone. He ignored a lot of calls, but never his private line.

"David, it's me, Ethan. Sorry to bother you, but it's about AZ-1166."

He felt the slight stirrings of discomfort. Ethan never used to call unless there was a critical problem. His whole rural Comstock operation had been created with the sole purpose of taking care of AZ-1166 problems. But lately, Ethan had been calling much too often.

"Hi, Ethan. I hope you're not going to ruin my good mood. Not often I can say that after a board meeting."

"When are you presenting the lab data to the FDA?"

It was none of Ethan's business when David did that, or for that matter anything in the step-by-step process he was going through to get AZ-1166 approved.

"Soon, but, of course, it can't be soon enough."

"I need to run a few things by you. See what you think."

"Shoot!"

David listened as Ethan reviewed his suspicions about the two nurses he'd just hired.

"I don't know," David said. "We've absolutely no indication that the OCI is nosing around in our affairs."

"I think the male nurse is okay, and they are a couple. But she has very little experience in temp or travel nursing, and she's straight out of the hospital/clinic labor force. Why would she choose to work here? I'm worried that they might be working undercover."

David thought about all the complications heading their way if Ethan's suspicion was correct. The company needed a big win with AZ-1166 and they needed it soon, or money was going to become a real issue for Zelint Pharmaceutical's survival.

David let the silence grow as he thought about losing their company.

Ethan piped in, "Do you think I'm imagining things? I mean I've asked myself that question a dozen times. What's your take, David?"

"Maybe it's only because the nurse is a new hire. Maybe what you're seeing is an imaginary monster in the closet." David listened to Ethan's breathing. Short, tight breaths. "Listen, man, we need this trial to be a winner. You asked for this job ... asked us what we needed ... that's what we need. A winner!"

"I already know that, David."

"Do you really think you've got two undercover agents? *Really?*"

"At this point, all I can say is, it's possible. But too early to be sure."

"Well, find out for sure!"

"David, you know I've been holding up my end of our deal."

There was a long moment of silence as David thought about the criminal unit of the FDA. About OCI, sticking its nose into Zelint's operations.

"Remember how you said you were never going to work in a hospital again, Ethan?"

"Of course I do."

"Well, do your job … get rich. Don't come to me whining about problems you're expected to handle. I have enough of my own. You hear me?"

David didn't wait for an answer. He slammed the phone down—his good mood already evaporated.

Bette Golden Lamb & J. J. Lamb

Chapter 12

The overnight orderly had been right on time for the 7 pm shift turnover. After a brief hello to Gina and a high five to Rocky, he wandered down the corridor, popping into patient rooms to take vital readings. Rocky gathered his things, and without a word, left the unit.

Gina sat at the desk waiting, jiggling the narcotics keys and rereading her nurses' notes. Delores finally arrived thirty minutes into the night shift.

"Sorry," was all she said. No real or phony excuses—for which Gina gave her points—but she turned her back on Gina and began putting together a tray full of narcotics as though Gina didn't exist. The woman never said another word and never asked for a report or any patient status. A repeat of how the day began.

"Hey, don't you want to hear about the patients?"

Delores turned and gave her a strange look. "Not necessary. I'll read your nurse's notes later."

Well, now it's official—that's the way they run this operation. No reports. No nothing.

And when Gina started down the hall to leave, Delores didn't even return Gina's goodbye.

What a bunch of dorks.

Gina continued to feel let down, unsettled, and annoyed at the gods … no, the whole flipping universe.

Her skin was crawling with exhaustion when she shoved the key card into her apartment door and found the place silent and dark. Where was Harry? Why wasn't he here?

She hit the light switch, walked to the sofa, dropped like a stone, and began to sob.

* * *

She barely heard Harry come in, but he folded her into his arms and rocked her.

"Hey, what's the matter?" he whispered.

She felt small, like a little girl again. When things went wrong, her father would hold her close and smooth her hair the same way.

"I hate it here."

Whine, whine, whine.

"Everyone is so unfriendly. I feel like I landed on the moon. There's no one to talk to when I'm not with you, and it was terrible when I got back and you weren't here." She looked up at him. "I feel so lonely."

"I'm here, babe."

"I know, but it hit me really hard when I walked into a silent apartment and realized I'd spent the whole day only listening to irritated patients in terrible pain." She took the tissue he offered and blew her nose. "Is that the way it's going to be for the whole three months?"

"It's only the first day. Give it a chance."

"I know it sounds stupid, but I miss our apartment and my little Fiat." She blew her nose again and the tears finally stopped gushing. "The thought of it sitting all by itself in a garage back in San Francisco … it's horrible."

Harry laughed. "Well, I have to admit *I* don't miss that temperamental Italian *prima dona* for one second. It never runs smoothly for me. I swear it has double pneumonia the way it coughs and snorts." He looked at her with laughing eyes. "Well, at least you're smiling again."

"Why were you so late?"

"The overnight nurse was swamped. I stayed and helped out for a while."

"How are they running this place on such a minimal staff? It's crazy."

"You've got to admit, except for their narcotics," Harry said, "most of the patients are pretty self-reliant—especially after they have their fix." He laughed again. "Nothing but a bunch of junkies."

"I still don't get it," Gina said. "I thought these patients had failed the study because of side effects. Yet, I haven't found anything in their charts about individual treatments for those side effects. Isn't that why they're here? These people are in a lot of pain. Someone needs to help them, not mask their problems with narcotics."

"Guess I was too busy jousting with Pete, getting all the meds straight, and juicing up the patients to spend a lot of time thinking about that. It didn't even cross my mind. Not too bright."

"Well, that's all I've been thinking about," Gina said.

"What puzzles me," Harry said, "is that the people I've seen show no sign that they ever had dementia. That AZ-1166 must be one helleva drug … they're all as clear thinking as you and I … well, at least me."

"Aren't you the funny one?" She fake-punched him in the arm. "Anyway, remember Emma Goldmich? The one who was in the elevator with us yesterday?"

"Of course."

"She's on my unit."

"Well, I didn't have a lot of time to hang out with any one person," Harry said, "but I did spend some time with an interesting woman: Rhonda Jenkins. She was a marketing CEO; worked for a New York firm for most of her career, but in later years she became a medical assistant. She's almost blind now. But the worst part is her arthritis. I've never seen anything that severe."

"It's the same for Emma Goldmich."

Harry gave her a wicked smile. "Rhonda almost sounds like you with your New Yawk accent. Only very refined … if that's even possible."

"Okay, I've whined enough. I don't have to sit here and listen to an air-head Californian. I'm going to make dinner." She went in to the kitchen area and took a couple of cans of soup from the cabinet. "Soup all right?"

"I sort of had my heart set on a thick sandwich of some kind … and a pile of French fries on the side."

"Spoiled rotten," she said, pulling out a package of frozen fries and popping them into the oven.

"You're supposed to wait until the oven heats up," Harry said.

"Listen, my little butternut," she said, throwing him a kiss," *you* cooka da dinna, you waita for the heata. *Capish?*" Then she gave him a wicked smile and repeated herself in pure Bronxese, hands flying in every direction, "When I cook, we do it my way." She pulled out a wrapped package of hamburger and began to make thick patties. Peeling an onion, she cut a thick slice for herself, a thin one for him. "Tell me more about Rhonda Jenkins."

"Sure you don't need some help?" he said, lying down on the sofa, smiling.

"Nah. I got it tonight. But tomorrow … it's your turn, and I'll be on that sofa, you can bet your cute little butt on that."

Harry finger-gunned her. "Rhonda is really a sweet woman … after the pain meds kicked in. We briefly talked about the stock market. She gave me some great investment tips."

"You can invest. I like to handle my own money," Gina said, pulling the catsup out of the cabinet and setting it on the table.

"You mean stuff it under the mattress, don't you?"

"Eh! Whatever!"

"Anyway, Rhonda said she did really well, more than just put bread and butter on the table to support herself and a small child, after her husband died."

"Ugh … finances and numbers." Gina pulled the fries out of the oven, slid the broiled hamburgers onto the rolls while he stood up and grabbed a brand new Dijon jar from the cabinet. He set it down next to the catsup.

"Mmmmm, a veritable feast. I couldn't do better at MacDonald's," Harry said, sitting down.

"Sometimes," Gina said, "I don't think you care about staying alive."

"l don't, unless I can spend it with you." He reached across the table and squeezed her hand, his eyes all soft and dreamy.

Gina's face felt hot. "Don't say that, Harry. It makes me feel weird."

"You are weird. But let's eat anyway."

After a few bites, Gina dabbed her mouth with her napkin. "I guess I ought to tell you about something that happened today."

"Uh huh," Harry said, stuffing his face with three French fries all at once, dripping gobs of catsup into his napkin. He wiped at his mouth before Gina could warn him and smeared the red sauce all over his cheeks.

Gina started laughing. She jumped up and brought him another napkin. "Try this." She held out her hand and waited until he placed the red paper mess into it. "As I was saying, I think I got into a little bit of trouble today."

Harry was suddenly all ears. "Trouble? What kind of trouble?"

Gina leaned back in her chair. "Well, I tried eating a snack in the cafeteria."

"Don't stall, Gina. Tell me about *the getting in trouble* part."

"I was only giving you some background, telling you the whole story—"

"—skip the build-up."

"Okay, so I decided to see if maybe they had some extra food in the kitchen."

"How on earth did you find the kitchen?"

"Well, you see," she said, "if you use your ID card, there's a slot on the elevator panel … I'll show you tomorrow."

"Go on," he said, ignoring the rest of his dinner.

"It's really pretty creepy down in the basement, but I wandered down one corridor and found the kitchen. I was just peeking inside at these two guys in the kitchen, and I guess they heard me."

"So what happened?"

"I kind of freaked out ... so I ran ... you know ... to get out of there. But they caught me before I could get back into the elevator." The silence in the room was closing in on her, she could barely breathe. Her voice sounded small and timid to her. "I only wanted a sandwich. What's wrong with that?"

"I don't understand why you can't try to stick with the program ... do your job and stop looking for trouble."

"I wasn't! I only wanted something decent to eat."

"You could have come here to grab a bite. You didn't have to wander around, dig into places you have no reason to be." He paced around the room before coming back to her. "This is exactly how you almost froze to death in that butcher's freezer in San Francisco." He grabbed her elbows, then pulled her into his arms. "I almost lost you then. I can't go through that again ... do you hear me?"

Tears rolled down her cheeks. "I do, Harry. I really do."

"Promise me you won't do anything like that again? Please, Gina. Please!"

She wanted to say something comforting ... something to reassure him. But her voice was lost and the room remained smothered in silence.

Chapter 13

Carl Kreuger was grumpy, or, as his wife would say, he'd gotten up on the wrong side of the bed. Man, he hated that trite, stupid, hackneyed, ridiculous expression. But he loved his wife—she was the best thing that ever happened to him—so it was a good thing he was usually more of an "up" kind of guy and didn't often have to hear those inane words.

No matter what his wife said, getting up on the wrong side of the bed had nothing to do with the black cloud hanging over his head today. No, it was the third friggin' time in six months that his transfer request to move from the FDA's New York Office of Criminal Investigation to its Los Angeles division had been turned down.

Shit, I hate New York City and every last one of those pushy, funny-sounding people who live piled on top of each other and think nothing of it.

His attitude was stupid, he knew that. But when he left the FBI in Albuquerque to hitch up with the FDA's special investigative unit, he'd thought moving to New York was a dream come true. So did his wife. The difference between them: she loved the big city.

Oh, if I didn't adore that woman life would be so much less complicated.

He scooted down into his chair, would have crawled under the desk if he thought he could get away with it and still have a job. He didn't want to see or talk to anyone.

He scanned his schedule for the day. Right at the top of the list was a 10 o'clock appointment with a Tuva Goldmich. His secretary's note said something about a drug study problem.

Drug study, drug addiction, drug control, drug trial. And on and on. Sometimes I think if I hear that "D" word one more time,

I'll yell my head off. Bad attitude for an FDA criminal investigator, that's for sure.

Well, he'd better get his rotten attitude under control if he wanted to bring home the bacon.

Ugh! Hate that one, too.

He stood, lifted his jacket from the back of the chair, poked his arms through the sleeves, crossed the office to his small closet, and checked himself in the door mirror. He immediately cinched up his rep tie and ran a hand through his short blond hair. He looked all right, except for that volcano welling up on his cheek threatening to erupt like Vesuvius. It never failed. Any emotional problem and zits blossomed like daffodils in springtime. Not so pretty, though.

To squeeze or not to squeeze? That's the question.

Before he could give it any more thought, he was out the office door to the reception area. There were three people waiting; only one was a woman.

"Ms. Goldmich?" he called out to the woman and smiled.

The petite, brown-eyed brunette stood and walked up to him with a nervous gait, but she held out a hand and shook his firmly. "Call me Tuva, please."

"I'm Carl Kreuger." He chuckled. "But you can call me Carl. Why don't we go on back to my office, Tuva?"

She followed him down the narrow corridor. Once they were in his office and seated, he waited a moment. What she said in the next few minutes would either really motivate him or put her request on the bottom of his work pile. Didn't know why it was that way, but that's the way it was.

"Tell me about the problem."

Tuva Goldmich crossed her ankles, tucked them under the chair. She looked off into the distance before meeting his eyes. "I'm not sure how to start."

"Tell me why you're here."

"My mother—"

"Her name?" he interrupted.

"Emma Goldmich."

He wrote the name on a memo pad.

"She's been a participant in a national drug study for Alzheimer's ... has been for the past year."

"A national study? Are you certain?"

"That's what they told me."

He held up a finger for her to wait while he searched through the "A" file in his computer for ongoing drug studies for that specific disease.

There was a long list of different Phase I investigations, where fewer than one-hundred volunteers were being tested with a new drug "Which pharmaceutical company are we talking about?"

"Zelint."

He scanned the pharmaceutical companies until he found it—a small company with very few active studies in the works.

Looks like they'd completed Phase I ... used fewer than one hundred healthy subjects for their new drug, AZ-1166.

"Sorry, "he said to Tuva. "Just give me another minute."

And they also completed Phase II—with a few hundred volunteers

Before he could stop himself, he let out a long whistle. "Zelint is the only Phase III study in that disease category at this time."

"What does that mean?" Tuva said.

"It means that Zelint Pharmaceutical's study will provide evidence for the safety and effectiveness for the Alzheimer's drug your mother has been taking. Then the drug will be considered for FDA approval. If they approve it, it will be released to the public. That's when they move into Phase IV for post-market monitoring."

"How many people are in the Phase Three study, the one my mother's in?"

Carl looked at the numbers. "Over a thousand across the US."

How did the company managed to keep this away from the news hounds?

Tuva sat up taller in her seat.

"This could be a real break-through for the treatment of Alzheimer's." He hesitated for a moment before adding, "I think your mother's lucky to be in this study."

"I had to be talked into it by our primary care doctor. I was resistant to signing her into the study because she had to be moved into a special facility for constant observation. But it was worth it. After a few months, it was actually amazing. She became my mom again."

"I hear a *but* in there," he said.

"Well, her mind definitely improved but the rest of her has gone downhill. I mean, she's always had arthritis. Some days were better than others, but she managed to take care of herself once she got moving." Tuva pulled a tissue from her purse and blew her nose.

"Did your mother have a job"

"She was a professor of fine art … she retired three years ago." Tuva looked away. "Within six months after taking the test drug, her Alzheimer's was in remission, but her arthritis exploded. It got so bad she could barely stand. She was in horrible shape."

"Did the investigators think it was from the test drug?"

"No. They insisted it was part of the same symptoms she'd always had. But that's not true. She was so much worse. I told them that, told them there must be something wrong with the drug they gave her." She gave Carl a forlorn look. "I mean, isn't that possible?"

"Anything's possible," Carl said.

"The investigators were very nice about it. They said they were going to help her, move her to a special facility in Nevada where they would treat her arthritis and give her advanced medical care."

Advanced medical care for arthritis? I guess they planned on replacing every joint in her body.

"Have you gone out to Nevada to see your mom?"

"Everything is so expensive and I just lost my job. I hope to visit her …soon."

"What exactly is troubling you? I mean, the fact she's not close and you can't see her doesn't mean there's something wrong."

"That's true. But I've written to my Mom every day since she left. She hasn't answered one letter." Tears rolled down Tuva's cheeks again. "That's just not like her. I've even tried calling her, but they tell me she's never available." Tuva reached for a tissue from her purse. "Something's wrong. She's in some kind of trouble. I just know it."

Carl tapped his pencil on the desk top. "Tuva, let me do some digging around and see what I can come up with."

She studied him very closely. "You're not going to bury this in some slush pile, are you?"

Carl Kreuger shook his head, stood, walked around the desk and escorted her to the door and down the narrow hallway. "As I said, let me give it some thought. I'll get back to you. I promise."

She gave him a forlorn look before opening the outer door to the OCI offices and heading for the elevator.

Carl returned to his desk and stared at the computer screen. For a while he was caught up in the stats for the random, double blind study Zelint Pharmaceutical was involved in.

He thought about Tuva Goldmich's observations about her mother. But still, AZ-1166 could be an exciting drug.

Yeah, how many of those have I seen go down the tubes in the last year? So many failures. So many duds.

In a few minutes his mind was wandering and he was caught up in planning the next steps he would have to take to transfer the hell out of friggin' New York City.

Chapter 14

Gina tossed and turned, stared into the dark night, while Harry slept like he didn't have a care in the world. She couldn't settle down. No matter how hard she tried not to think of her ex-husband, her mind drifted back to him and how he had almost killed her in a drunken rage. He'd beaten her, jammed a bottle up inside, tearing her insides until she'd almost bled out ... died.

She looked at Harry's shadowy outline—peaceful, calm, sleeping on his side of the bed. When she lived with Dominick, he would spread out, shove her to the side until she could barely find a spot to hang on. Every time she would talk about getting a king-sized bed, he would laugh at her. That's all. Just laugh.

Gina forced herself to inhale through her nose and exhale through her mouth. Concentrate only on her breathing. She finally drifted into a light sleep. When the alarm went off, Harry kept trying to wake her, get her going. It wasn't easy.

"Bad night?" he asked.

Gina nodded.

"Dominick?"

"Uh huh."

"You know I won't let him hurt you," Harry said. "I promised before, and that promise is forever."

"But he's out of prison now..." Shivers raced up and down her spine; it took a long moment for her to finish the sentence. "...it's scary, Harry; he swore he'd kill me."

"He's not getting anywhere near you, doll." Harry reached out, pulled her into his arms. "He's in New York, three thousand miles away. And we're here."

"I hope that's where he stays."

Harry held her at arm's length. "Aren't you the one who's always saying: Take it one day at a time? I promise we'll get through this."

She could barely smile.

* * *

Gina was caffeine-wired, sleep-deprived, and jumpy all morning. She kept her eyes on Rocky, but the creep seemed to do a great job getting patients ready for breakfast while she worked at top speed to get the pain meds out. He acted as if she didn't exist and she returned the favor.

When she had one med left to administer—*not* a narcotic for a change—she began to relax. She walked into Derek Kopek's room and immediately detected a hint of nicotine polluting the air. But there wasn't a sign of tobacco anywhere—no ashtray, no cigarette pack.

Nothing.

Kopek was standing at the window, his breathing labored; he was fighting for every breath just to remain upright.

"Okay, Mr. Kopek. Where did you hide those cigarettes?" She wanted to call them coffin nails, but she thought it might be a rough way to begin a relationship.

He completed a slow arc and looked at her. "You mean where are the *coffin nails*, don't you? That's what you really wanted to say. Right?"

"Maybe. But I don't have to tell you how uncool it is for someone with a ticker problem to smoke." Her eyes swept over the swollen ankles sticking out of his carefully pressed pant legs.

"Uncool? Stupid is probably what you want to say."

"Mr. Kopek—"

"Oh, for heaven' sake, call me Derek, will you" There were long pauses between every sentence to give him time to catch his breath. "And I'll call you by your first name. That's the way the world is today. We're all 'friends.'"

94

"You seem to think you know exactly what's on my mind, Derek." She lifted a small paper cup off the identifying med card on her tray and handed it to him. Then she walked over to a dresser where there was a pitcher of water and an empty glass. The room was spacious, and it looked professionally decorated, with matching rust-colored curtains and bedspread. Pictures decorated the walls, along with a large framed map of South America.

She filled the glass and brought it back to him. "So why don't you take your pills and I'll leave you alone, since there's no real need to verbally communicate. You already seem to know what I'm thinking or what I'm going to say." She gave him a big smile and waited for him to swallow his meds.

A pink flush spread across his face as he tossed the wadded medicine cup into a waste basket next to him. That minimal effort increased his breathing rate dramatically.

"I suppose I am acting like an idiot." He looked into Gina's eyes for the first time since she stepped into the room.

"Well, I might have chosen different words." She laughed. "But it would have been something like that." She pointed: "Nice map."

"I spent most of my life there in the jungles, mostly the Amazon, searching for plants that could contain healing compounds." He moved slowly, collapsing into a chair.

"And where are *you* from?"

"You have to ask? That's a first."

He smiled. "Okay, so how long has it been since you left New York?"

"About three years." She walked up to the window, sat on the sill. "Other than the Amazon, where are you from, Derek?"

"Not too far from here. I was brought up in Reno." His eyes drifted as though he was seeing something other than his room in the Comstock Medical Facility. "But I'm a stranger here. As I said, I've spent most of my life wandering through the Amazon rainforest."

A sudden coughing spasm shook his body. His breathing became even more rapid, shallower. He bent over, caught between coughing and trying to breathe. A small oxygen tank was close to him, but Gina could see he had no intention of using it. It was hard for her to sit there and not rush to place the oxygen jets into his nose.

"How about using some oxygen to help you breathe?" she finally said.

He shook his head.

"Give the meds a chance to kick in. It'll help soon," Gina said. She took his hand and squeezed it.

He finally sat up taller, but he rubbed hard at his chest. "Don't bullshit … a bullshitter … Gina. This is never … getting better." He ended the sentence with another bout of coughs that didn't seem to want to stop.

She thought about his chart, his diagnosis, his prognosis, and most of all, her observations. She could see what Derek Kopek had to cope with every single day and night. He was in the final stages of congestive heart failure.

He's right. He's never getting better.

She reached for a blood pressure cuff on the side table next to his bed and wrapped it around his thin arm.

"Rocky took my BP earlier," he said.

She lifted the stethoscope from around her neck. "I know. But now it's my turn." She pumped and pumped the cuff for a reading.

"It's high isn't it?"

"Yes." She put a hand on his shoulder. "Maybe it would help to ditch the cigarettes, Derek."

"Maybe it would, but it's not going to happen." He looked back toward the window again. "There's not much that I live for now. A couple of those coffin nails a day is not going to matter much one way or another."

* * *

Derek watched the tall, attractive nurse leave his room. There was vibrancy and strength in her body movements, a "full-of-life" drive that he couldn't help but admire. He'd always been drawn to people like her. He'd thought of himself as strong and energetic until his mind started slipping away.

No other way to describe it. Slipping away.

The loss of memory happened bit by bit, until he couldn't classify even the simplest organic molecular structure, or remember his closest friend's name. The changes left him feeling helpless and estranged.

He looked at the map on the wall and was grateful for the extra time of clarity Zelint's AZ-1166 had given him. He knew this particular drug that was being tested had been discovered, synthesized, compounded from a tiny rare plant that *he* had found deep in the jungle. It brought a sense of ownership, of pride.

He'd lived a life of adventure, of never allowing himself to fall in love or establish a home. A life where he traveled deeper and deeper into Amazonia, always searching for natural plant curatives.

There were months spent in semi-darkness, under the umbrella of trees, months when he rarely saw the sun, where his aloneness brought him face-to-face with his own primal drive for survival— times of horrible hallucinations, that in the end, brought insight into his own tortured soul.

Those were the times spent with the people who lived in the forests, who spoke little or no English. But it was the kind of life that had taught him to finally surrender his trust to strangers, to people who blended with their environment, left few or no footprints on the fragile surface of the earth. His life depended not only on their kindness, but their knowledge. Their humanity kept him alive. He never thought of it then, as he moved deeper into the interior, but if they'd left him, had not healed him the times he'd been bitten by poisonous creatures, he would have died while wandering alone through the massive forests. And that death would have been a lot more painful than the crotch rot that plagued him every day.

He'd planned on a life where he would always be a seeker. Then one day everything went wrong.

Zelint made sure he was placed in the double-blind study, made sure he got the real medication and not the placebo. He was grateful for every moment of clarity the test drug had given him.

* * *

Gina was at the nurses' station, typing updates in the patients' computer charts, when Rocky entered and pulled up a chair next to her. "I don't see the vitals for the patients from this morning," she said to the orderly.

"I haven't put them in the computer, that's why."

"What do you have for Derek Kopek's BP?"

He flipped out a pad, opened it. "One-fifty over one hundred."

The tension in Gina's neck was like a rubber band about to snap. "Did you pull those numbers out of the air? "I got two hundred over one-thirty!"

"What's the difference," he said, "the man's gonna check out any minute. Why are you busting my balls?"

"Did you ever hear of medical management? The docs might change his meds; do something to make him more comfortable."

She watched him bite back a retort.

She tapped a few keys and opened Derek Kopek's chart.

Strange—Derek started out with his congestive heart failure barely symptomatic. In a ridiculously short time, he's gone from Stage One to Stage Four.

Scanning further through his history, Gina saw that the admitting MD, Ethan Dayton, had listed Derek's occupation as a Biologist, with a sub-specialty in herbal medicine.

He wasn't kidding. He did spend most of his life searching through the Amazon looking for plants that could be tested for potential therapies.

"Did you know Mr. Kopek is a scientist?" she said to Rocky. "That he worked for Zelint, the company running the drug study?"

"*Was* a scientist," Rocky said with a sneer. "Now he's only a dead man."

"Why are you working with sick people if you only have contempt for them?"

He stood, took a long body stretch. "Like you: M-O-N-E-Y!"

* * *

After dinner, Derek sat at his window smoking one of the two cigarettes he allowed himself each day. He knew the tobacco only made things worse—breathing became more difficult and his chest felt as if it was sinking into his spine. But he loved the feeling nicotine gave him. And what did it matter? His time was almost gone anyway. There simply was no other pleasure he was capable of now except inhaling the fumes of a cigarette.

He watched the sun go down behind the boulders. As dusk evolved through its darkening shades of blue, and the sky turned to jet black covered with a smattering of stars, he thought back to his nights in the Amazon.

Deep in the jungles, he never saw the heavens—the wide umbrella of trees in the dense forest gave a different night sky, a different world. It was a place of pungent smells, of a healthy, fertile earth filled with luxuriant growth. He'd been a lucky man to feel the planet breathe around him, engulf him with its splendor.

He could see it all, alive in his dreamy memories:

The copper-skinned woman returned, as she did so many nights, and crawled into his sleeping bag. Her smooth, hot skin trembled as his hand slid across her body and into her moistness. Her strong legs surrounded him then, and even now he could still feel her soft breasts burning through his chest, feel his groin fill with the heat of passion.

He jolted awake. Someone was in his room. After a moment or two, he recognized Rocky, and the other orderly, Pete, standing near the door, whispering to each other.

"What's the matter, Rocky?" Derek's voice was breathless, and a sharp pain clutched his chest.

"See you fell asleep smokin' again," Rocky said. Both orderlies laughed as they walked to his bedside. "The doc ordered some medication to make you feel better."

Derek was puzzled, couldn't make any sense of it. Pete reached down and took his arm, stretched it out straight for Rocky to jab in a needle.

* * *

The lights were bright when Derek opened his eyes. His chest was heavy and he felt sick to his stomach. Pete and Rocky were lifting him onto a table, an icy cold table.

"What am I ... doing ... here?"

"It's okay," said another voice. "Remember me, Derek? Dr. Dayton?"

Derek looked at the man's head floating above him.

"Yes. I remember ... you. What ... am I ... doing here?" Was there a vice clamped around his chest? He almost couldn't speak.

"There are a few last tests I have to do for the study you've been on." Ethan leaned close and spoke in his ear. "We're both scientists, so I know you'll understand how important it is to get all the data we possibly can."

Derek turned his head from side to side, examined the room.

There were large jars of human brains floating in preservatives. The containers were everywhere. He then realized he was on an autopsy table. A scale hung over him, and off to one side, near his head, was a tray of instruments, including a small saw.

I need to go. Get out of here.

He tried to move his arms but they were cuffed to the table. He wanted to fight but an overwhelming weakness left him helpless.

Rocky and Pete both snickered.

"Oh, for God's sake, get out of here, you two!" Ethan snapped. "You're disgusting. I'll call for you if I need you."

"Why am … I … here?"

"As I was saying, Derek, this is only to get final brain function data. I will be examining your cerebral signals for answers that can only come from living cells."

"Living … cells?"

"Yes. Serious questions remain—like why AZ-1166 has caused age-related diseases to go into hyper drive in so many subjects."

"Many … of whom?"

The doctor was obviously annoyed with him. His sunken eyes burned through Derek.

"Study subjects. People like you," Ethan said.

Derek tried to follow the doctor's thin lips, but he had trouble understanding the jumble of words.

"I'm going to give you more medication. It will lessen the discomfort."

"Let me go back to my room … let me go … please!"

"It'll all be over soon, Derek."

The doctor reached out, jabbed his arm with another needle and everything turned into a blur. He closed his eyes and when he opened them, he saw the doctor was holding—what? A scalpel?

Before he could process the information, excruciating pain tore across the top of his head and a searing burn spread out and raced down his neck.

"STOPSTOPSTOPSTOP."

The doctor's face peered down at him again. "It's all right, Derek. We're almost there."

"PLEEEASE!"

Before he could grab another breath, he heard the sound of the saw.

Chapter 15

Searching through the computer records, Harry found the files for all the participants in his unit … they had successfully completed the AZ-1166 study's requirement. Their status had been reclassified—*in remission*. In remission? Ethan said these patients were failures, here only for medical treatment associated with having taken the test drug

But why were they even here at Comstock? There were no special treatments that Harry could see. Most of the people here had crippling arthritis and were taking medication for their pain. Couldn't they do that in a home environment? A nursing facility?

He continued scanning through the unit's charts, then scrolled through all the records, searching for the final questionnaires and documentation for the study. They weren't in the computer.

Why?

During his and Gina's interview and orientation with Ethan, the administrator only talked about the patients as having been active participants in the Zelint Pharmaceutical Study of AZ-1166. And they were here now for medical treatment.

The hairs on Harry's neck did that weird bristling thing, and a sudden chill raised goose bumps on his arms. He could feel Pete watching him.

Again.

The orderly seemed to make it his business to check out whatever Harry was studying on the monitor.

The back of his Harry's head was burning. The guy was definitely spying on him.

Why?

"Something you need, Pete?" Harry did a fast swing around, stared into the orderly's eyes.

Pete shook his head and moved to the other end of the nurses' station.

Not far enough, jerk.

Harry scrolled through the patient census and again clicked on Rhonda Jenkins's chart.

He brought up the different screens of her medical record. There was nothing currently new charted about Phase III of the AZ-1166 study. But her complete history referred to having been on the test drug, with excellent results. Her dementia had gone into total remission within six months. He read further into her detailed history.

She'd been a marketing CEO for the majority of her working years. Late in life she changed careers and became a medical assistant who specialized in assisting vascular surgeons with office surgeries and treatments. Two years ago she started having acuity problems and retired. It was then she was diagnosed with Alzheimer's. A close friend told her about an ad she'd seen—a new clinical study that was seeking subjects with a dementia diagnosis. Rhonda could become a part of the new study, if she qualified.

Rhonda qualified.

The chart carefully documented her initial physical exam—a healthy seventy-five-year-old woman, with mild arthritis and the usual age-related problems. Nothing with severe pathology that would interfere with receiving the experimental drug.

He skipped to the final entry of that exam.

The patient was provided a packet of information that included informed consent and a list of expected positive results, along with a separate list of potential side effects. Rhonda Jenkins received a full explanation of the goals for the experimental drug designated AZ-1166. She and a first cousin signed the papers.

Harry skimmed through the listed potential side effects: nausea, vomiting, diarrhea, headaches, dizziness, insomnia, problems with balance, It went on and on, listing only relatively minor negative symptoms.

Nothing here about the bad shit.

This wasn't the usual multi-page document that covers everything from an ingrown toenail to spontaneous combustion.

It certainly doesn't cover the acceleration of age-related diseases. Did they deliberately hide that info from the patients?

Throughout the study, Rhonda had no significant side effects, at least none that were noted in her chart.

Mmmmm! The Rhonda Jenkins on this unit is almost totally blind and her arthritis is very severe. Why isn't that mentioned here?

He again went quickly through her most recent physical examination. Nothing! Absolutely nothing in the study chart noting that she had become virtually blind or that she had crippling arthritis.

Harry leaned back in his chair, tried to be measured and objective. Gina was usually the suspicious one. She always said she didn't go looking for trouble, it just landed in her lap. With her New York background, she usually mistrusted people right off the bat. She never took anyone at face value.

Hell, the truth is, Gina always sees the dark side of people. And too often she's right.

He was glad he'd grown up in California, but it hadn't been a bed of roses for him either. He'd done a short stint in juvie before he wised up. But he knew Gina's experiences were even worse. Being a female was definitely not a plus.

He thought about what it must have been like for her growing up on the Bronx streets—gang threats, beatings, constantly living in fear of being raped … or murdered.

She should have been treated like someone special; instead, she'd been forced to grow like a raggedy weed, fighting its way back to life every day.

* * *

Harry stepped into Rhonda Jenkins's room. She immediately snapped to attention.

"Who's there?"

"It's me, Rhonda."

"Oh, Harry. I haven't gotten used to your sounds yet."

"You will soon enough."

He moved to her side and took her hand. Her gray hair was long enough to be neatly pushed behind her ears, and she'd managed to put on lipstick without smudging it. He recognized the scent she was wearing. Gina had recently started wearing it, too—Chanel No. 5.

Rhonda was seated in a chair next to the window. He knew she could still see some light coming in, but he would appear only as a shadowy figure.

"Too bad I won't get to know you better, Harry. We've barely met, but I like what I see ... so to speak."

Harry chuckled.

"Dr. Dayton said they're going to release me in the next few days. I'm kind of excited. He suggested I call my friend to take me home, but not until he lets me know the exact date. I don't want her to come all the way from Texas and just hang around waiting for me to get out of here." She turned away. "I won't tell her about my eyes. She might not come ... might not want to play seeing-eye-dog. Pretty selfish of me, I suppose."

"She might surprise you. Besides, you seem to get around really well."

"You mean for a mole."

"Nothing wrong with being a mole." Harry hesitated, then said, "Have you always had impaired vision, Rhonda?"

Her smile drooped. "No, I developed thick cataracts in both eyes within six months of taking the test drug. Still, it was worth it to be able to think clearly again. But the loss of vision happened so quickly ... almost in the blink of an eye." Rhonda laughed weakly.

"Do you plan on having the cataracts removed?"

"When I'm back home, I'm hoping to have that done. Mind you, no one's saying it will be successful. I guess there's a lot of damage ... they think it's some kind of response from taking the drug. That's what Dr. Dayton said. At least the costs won't be a problem. The study and Medicare will take care of everything."

Harry pulled up a chair next to her. "Still, it's gotta be hard on you."

"It is." A single tear rolled down her cheek. Harry snagged a tissue from the box on the table next to the bed. He gently dabbed her cheek.

She pressed her hand against his. "You seem like a very kind man, Harry. I'm glad we met. I would have liked to have spent more time with you."

"You'll be happier going back to your own home."

"That's true. I'm really looking forward to it."

"I see from your chart that you worked not only in the business world, but in the medical field, too. I would have loved to hear about your experiences."

"It was hard work," Rhonda said, "but I loved working with the doctors ... the patients. You learn a lot about people when they're sick or suffering."

"That's true," Harry said. "It's a humbling experience to lose your health."

Rhonda looked toward the window again. Her face had turned very pale. "If you don't mind, Harry, I think I'm going to sit here and close my eyes for a while and try not to think about anything."

Harry stood. "I hope I haven't upset you, Rhonda ... you seemed happy until I dropped in to bug you."

She waved her hand at him. "No, no. It's not you. It's me. I tend to look at things on the dark side."

Harry laughed. "You sound like my fiancée."

"If she's your fiancée, I'm sure I would enjoy meeting her."

"I think you would. Maybe I'll bring her down to say hello to you before you leave."

"I would like that."

Rhonda reached into her pants pocket and pulled out a black Revlon tube and freshened her lipstick. He could tell she wanted to say something else. She slowly put the lipstick back in her pocket, pushed a stray lock of hair away from her face.

"You know, Harry," she said in a quavering voice, her eyes dull, unresponsive, staring at nothing in particular, "I can't help but think how quickly it all passes. One day your whole life is in front of you, just around the corner. The next, you're crossing a bridge to nowhere."

Chapter 16

David Zelint stared at the letter informing him that the FDA was postponing its hearing for the AZ-1166 study—for the third time. Fiery acid started working its way up into his throat. The news threw him into a deep depression.

What's the hold up, damn it?

Would the study now be lost in a bureaucratic eddy of paperwork and delays? Would all their investment monies disappear and leave them penniless?

The FDA, of all people, must know the importance of this study ... what it could mean to the world. For Christ's sake; we have a drug that can cure Alzheimer's. It's the start of a new era in medicine!

As if this FDA business wasn't enough, Ethan Dayton and his Nevada operation were turning into a real problem.

For two years Zelint had managed to stay clear of industrial espionage by simply toning down its publicity efforts. The study wasn't hidden, it wasn't a secret, but releases about it had been kept low-key to try to keep other pharmaceutical houses at bay— to keep them from trying to steal the formula for AZ-1166.

Zelint had been lucky so far.

Now Ethan had raised the ugly specter of OCI involvement. What if the investigative arm of the FDA started digging into their operation? What would happen to AZ-1166 if he were to actually be accused of health fraud? Was that the reason final FDA approval was being delayed? Were they getting ready to impound their records, nail the company?

A sudden chill shook him hard. He knew it had nothing to do with the weather in Reno—Northern Nevada was having a beautiful autumn.

I have only myself to blame.

If his twin brother Saul found out what was really going on, he would hate David. The man was an unrepentant idealist, and that made it hard to move ahead with any plan. David knew they *had* to make money.

Sink or swim.

Why did Saul always have to have that moralistic, good guy approach to everything? If he wasn't so noble, if he would get down in the dirt with everyone else, it wouldn't be necessary to keep him out of the loop.

And maybe I wouldn't feel so damn guilty.

David hadn't taken the chance that his brother would say no to what had to be done. And they'd had to move fast. The company was already too deep into the early studies to turn back.

I did what I had to do. Too much at stake to take a chance on Saul.

If Zelint was found guilty of criminal activity, Saul, as a partner would go down, too. He and his brother were not only born together in a single breath, they were pretty much joined at the hip. They would both go to jail.

He covered his eyes and rocked back and forth. When he could think again, he glanced at the pictures of his brother's family on the back wall. His niece and nephew adored David and the thought of not having them in his life was unbearable. They were all that he had ... other than his work.

And if anything goes wrong, Saul will never speak to me again.

His baby brother—a joke between the two of them because David entered the world first—would never smile at him in that special way again, and David would lose the one person who made life worth living.

He picked at a nail, looked at his brother's picture. Even after all these years, it was still strange to have another person with your face, staring back at you. But the two of them seemed to verify all the twin studies ever undertaken. It wasn't only the face; at fifty-five both of them still had a full head of hair.

Yeah, and a gut that I wish wasn't there.

He patted his middle and laughed for the first time that day.

Too much deli!

There was really nothing special about the looks of either one of them. You wouldn't give either a second glance. But Saul's wife adored the man, and when she looked at his brother, there was only love in her eyes. And both of their kids were wonderful.

David wasn't jealous; he'd been in the thick of things when he younger—had a great social life, spent his days with many women, some really fantastic. But he never clicked with any one woman. Not like Saul.

Why am I thinking about this now? No time for that. And damn Ethan for even mentioning OCI. Now I can't get it out of my head.

He tried to quiet himself, look at things logically. If OCI came barging in, what would they find? There would be nothing in the Zelint facility or the factory where AZ-1166 was made—nothing suspicious at all for investigators to find.

And what would the computers reveal?

Nothing.

He never fully trusted computers. It seemed like the whole planet was swimming in too much technology. Besides, it was very easy for *any* device to be hacked and its contents revealed to the wrong people.

No, he didn't worry about his computer; there was nothing in there to worry about. He looked across the room at his office safe. *There* was the weak point; the only place within Zelint where the step-by-step details of every action taken, every nuance of the AZ-1166 study, could be found. That weakness needed to be taken care of. Immediately, if not sooner.

Either a bonfire or a safe deposit box.

* * *

Ethan Dayton was still fuming.

He'd called David Zelint so the CEO would be up to date, know everything, know every single detail that Ethan knew.

That was the agreement.

That's the kind of relationship he was promised—the two of them would have each other's back, at all times. They would be full partners, working for the good of the study and its outcome. David would be the front man. Ethan would handle the dirty work.

The man sits in his secure office and has the nerve to brush me off. Leave me holding the bag.

Things were starting to feel out of control, something medical examiners didn't tolerate at all well. Cutting up a corpse, weighing, collecting, classifying organs was an emotionless, methodical, scientific procedure. The only thing that ever got in the way was the administrative process and Ethan had come to like doing things his way. He was beginning to see David in that administrative interference category, but with an important twist.

Remember, Mr. Zelint, I know everything. Everything! Before you talk to me like I'm a fool, or an underling, you'd better reexamine our partnership. That's right ... partnership!

Ethan's job in the Comstock Medical Facility was the dangerous one. David sat in his plush office building and deluded himself into thinking his hands were clean.

He'd better remember that he's the reason I'm here. You brought me here, David. Don't forget that.

He reached into the bottom drawer of his desk and pulled out an expensive, four-color brochure about Zelint Pharmaceutical. He toyed with each page, remembered how he'd applied for the position after seeing an ad in one of the medical journals. At the time, he'd looked at so many medical *Help Wanted* ads that he now couldn't remember exactly which publication he'd found the Zelint notice.

When he'd first met the head of the pharmaceutical company, the interview began with the usual dog and pony show. David Zelint started with the history of the fairly new company, provided all the details about its heavy investment in biologics from the rain forests in South America. Zelint's research into these substances had in the early stages produced a promising breast cancer drug, and now, their real winner: AZ-1166.

"This study, this new drug, will be an explosion in the field of cognitive neurology. Geriatric medical practices will be changed forever," David Zelint had said.

Ethan was excited. He saw it as a great fit for him.

But when he asked about the previous doctor who'd run the Nevada facility, David was not only evasive, he changed the subject all together.

Ethan couldn't turn down the opportunity, though. Not only would he get away from Southern California hospitals, he would be far away from his ex-wife, who didn't seem to understand that divorced meant *finished, over!*

Still, after slightly more than a year at Comstock, with the study in its closing phase and about to be up for review by the FDA, David Zelint was getting more and more difficult to deal with.

Even though Ethan knew the up-front numbers appeared outstanding and Zelint was more than ready to provide the chief paper evidence of its safety and effectiveness, they were now into the tricky part of the operation, the part that would determine whether the drug would move into the next phase. And although AZ-1166 would continue to be monitored for its long-term safety and effectiveness, Phase IV would put the drug into the market … and the money would begin to roll into the company. And into Ethan's pockets.

They could take care of anything when the money started rolling in. Ethan had tried, but he couldn't even imagine that much money. He had a huge number of shares in Zelint and as a principal holder in the company; he would never have to work again. He needed that so he could proceed with his own scientific investigations. Now it was Alzheimer's. Who could know what new projects he might become involved with in the future?

He had to drag his thoughts away from all of that and get back to the problem at hand.

Can I trust these new nurses?

Were they working undercover for the OCI? Was Ethan, or Zelint, being set up by those two?

He'd always hired travel nurses for three-month stints at Comstock. He liked them coming from out of the area—short-term employees didn't usually invest a lot of themselves into something that wasn't permanent. They were certainly more likely to overlook irregularities.

On top of that, he paid way over scale for their services. He might have spent his career dissecting dead bodies as an ME, but that didn't mean he knew nothing about human behavior.

Damn, I don't have time for this if I'm going to stick to the schedule.

Things were already screwed up. Emma Goldmich was supposed to have been out of his hair by now. If Mazzio and Lucke hadn't met her on the elevator, things would have proceeded as methodically as a metronome clicking out its beat. Now, everything was out of whack.

And all because of two California nurses. Damn!

Chapter 17

Rocky and Pete looked at Ethan, then at each other as they entered his office. It was strange the way they sat down like a pair of puppets, quick, but jerky.

"Tell me, what do you think of the two new nurses?"

"Lucke? Smartass Californian," Pete said, without hesitation.

Rocky chimed in, "Same for Mazzio only with a New York accent."

Ethan leaned back into his desk chair, looked across his desk at their snake-like eyes. "Okay, so the two of you don't like them, but neither one of you like much of anybody. Is there anything that stands out?"

"That Harry seems to always have his nose in the patients' friggin' charts." Pete said. "Every time I turn around, he's digging into their records for something."

"So?" Ethan said. "Nurses have to read the charts. No other way to document the care given, or to even know the history of a patient."

"Well, there's something unnatural 'bout it," Pete said, "his body's all tensed up like a cat with an eye on a mouse. He's lookin' for something."

"And I hate that skinny-assed bitch," Rocky said. "One of these days I'll show her a thing or two." He gave them a dirty laugh. "The bitch might even like it."

"Woman!" Ethan said. "How many times do I have to tell you not to call women *bitches*?"

Rocky ignored the comment; his eyes narrowed until the whites of his eyes were barely visible. "Yeah, well they're all bitches as far as I'm concerned, no matter what *you* call them." He seemed to blow out tension, relaxed, and elbowed Pete. They both snickered.

"Just keep your hands to yourselves! Otherwise, keep a close eye on them. Let me know if they do anything unusual."

With all the problems Ethan had encountered since becoming involved in the Zeilint drug study, hiring a professional staff for Comstock Facility hadn't been one of them. That is until Gina Mazzio and Harry Lucke walked into the Comstock satellite.

Nurses understood that a contract was a contract, were fully aware that they couldn't walk away from a legal agreement without consequences, serious consequences. They also knew the large payments they received were because the facility was part of an unusual experimental drug development program, and that staffing was set at a bare minimum. Except for Delores, every nurse had left after three months—with fat wallets. And that was the way Ethan deliberately planned it.

"I'm going to need the two of you tonight," he said.

The two orderlies sat across from him like a pair of cocky fools.

"What time?" Rocky asked in his smart-ass, alpha dog way.

Ethan ignored the attitude and looked at his watch. "In a couple of hours."

They both nodded, got up, and left.

* * *

Ethan thought back to how he hooked up with the two incorrigible orderlies.

He'd gone searching for staff at the Silver Mine Saloon in Virginia City one Saturday night. He wanted cheap, local help to train, not only as orderlies, but to do *whatever* else was necessary to carry out his plans.

He was sizing up the local talent when Peter and Rocky wandered in, slid onto the two stools next to Ethan, and ordered up a couple of boilermakers. When they'd tossed those down, Ethan offered to buy them another round.

The pair accepted without even asking who their new friend was, or why he was buying them a drink.

Ethan struggled to keep from laughing out loud at the two of them, but after scoping out the town, he realized he was out numbered by the many misfits and low-life characters that roamed the streets looking to start trouble just for the hell of it. He decided it was better to keep his mouth shut than end up on the floor with a broken nose, or perhaps hauled away and dumped in some ditch by the side of the road.

Hell, I'd rather spend hours cutting up a corpse than look at these two cretins for more than a few minutes.

On the plus side, he'd certainly come to the right place to snag the sort of people he needed to do what had to be done.

Each of the two was built like a brick shit-house—strong and square, and just as dumb.

They look like they were spawned from the same mold; they're even dressed alike, right down to their dirty jeans, plaid shirts, and scuffed Acme boots.

Rocky was by far the one with the most marbles. But he was also the one who would fight a house fly for violating his space.

Too damn aggressive for his own good.

Because of that, Ethan wanted to hire only Peter. But the more he talked to them he realized the two men came as a matched set. Having grown up in the same foster home in Winnemucca, they'd continued to live together after taking up residence in Virginia City. There would be no taking just one of them.

Ethan had been sorry ever since.

* * *

Gina and Harry sat at their mini kitchen table, looking at a beautiful mixture of fresh, raw vegetables, topped with vinaigrette dressing.

There was none of their usual back-and-forth chatter; they were both poking at their salads, not really eating much of anything.

The meal sat there glaring at Gina.

With a spark of annoyance, she realized that they were still in their work scrubs. After twelve-plus hours, she felt grubby and glued together; Harry's duds still looked fresh—not only that, they matched his baby blue eyes.

Can the guy do anything wrong?

After work, they almost always headed straight for the shower, not wanting to eat without *really* cleaning up after their shift. As a nurse, she never knew exactly what she might have gotten into, or what she'd been exposed to on the units. Even with the constant washing and disinfecting of her hands, she was still vulnerable to every microbe that existed. Gina and Harry never felt *right* until after they'd scrubbed themselves thoroughly in the shower.

Throughout her career, Gina tried not to spend too much of her time thinking about the God-awful pathogens she might be breathing, or the microbes swimming through the body fluids she had to deal with. But every now and then, she wondered why she was so willing to be in the defensive line of stopping disease and suffering.

She and Harry had talked about it many times and came to the conclusion that their choice of occupation had nothing to do with helping people. They were just plain crazy.

They both looked up at the same time and started talking, stepping on each other's words.

Gina laughed, "You go first."

He took a quick sip of his water before answering. She watched the ice cubes wash up against the lip of the glass, and then bump his nose.

"You were right, doll," he said after swallowing. "There's definitely something not right about this place."

Gina's surge of relief came with a rush of warmth. She was up and around the table, kissing his lips, his cheeks, then back to his lips again. "I can't tell you how much better I feel," she said with a wide smile. "I mean, I'm the one who's always so god-awful distrustful. Sometimes I feel like an idiot."

He drew her onto his lap. "Truth be told, you are a little strange … but damn, you're beautiful."

"What made you change your mind?" She nuzzled his neck waiting for him to go on.

"Several things. But what nailed it was a missing computer page, the one that covers questions and answers from the trial participants. No sign of that page … *anywhere!*"

Gina pulled her chair next to his. "Why would you expect it to be there? These people are the failures. They've been dropped from the study. I'm surprised you found anything. Besides, how do you know there was even a questionnaire like that?"

"Tomorrow, take a look for yourself. The clinical study packet *is* in the computer. Not only that, there's an index that describes each section of the packet. The final question-and-answer page is listed in there, but it doesn't exist. At least not for my patients."

That could be just a glitch of some kind," Gina said.

"Well, I'm not finished," Harry said. "Here's the biggy—all the patients are listed as *in remission.*"

"That can't be true. Ethan said these people had failed the protocol."

"I know. I can't get away from that either," he said. "And these people seem to come from all over the country. The paperwork establishes that they have been participants, but are now in remission because of AZ-1166. That doesn't sound like failure. That sounds like the drug was a success."

"Mmmmm. We certainly can't confront Ethan," Gina said. "He's the one who lied to us in the first place."

"I keep thinking there might be some plausible explanation … but what could it be?"

"Maybe we could ask to see the actual study protocol," Gina said "I mean, after all it's a logical request, considering what we've been told. We could have misunderstood Ethan … maybe these people are in a different phase of the study at this particular facility."

"Failed does not mean the same as in remission."

Gina pulled her salad across the table and took a few bites. She felt Harry staring at her. "I mean, it is possible we just don't have all the information."

Harry started laughing, and then he couldn't stop.

"What's so funny?"

"You," Harry said, "being the voice of reason."

"Ha, ha! That's not funny, Harry Lucke."

Chapter 18

"Here are some pills for you to take," Delores said, then up-ended a medicine cup to spill out two identical pills into Rhonda's palm.

Rhonda fingered the small tablets. "Have I taken these before?"

"No, they're a new medicine for your arthritis ... they'll also help you sleep. You've been very restless ever since you arrived. Anyway, Doctor wants to start you on these."

Rhonda carefully picked up each pill, held it close to her face, tried to set its identity in her mind, then swallowed it with a generous gulp of water.

* * *

How long ago did I take those pills?

Still can't sleep.

She couldn't stop her mind. She had questions, so many questions. But the worst part was having the same horrible words keep repeating, and repeating in her head: *I'm blind!*

No matter how many times she said or thought about those terrible words, there was no acceptance ... only cold sweat and a pounding heart.

During the daylight hours, she could see *something,* and though limited, it gave her a sense of time, a sense of space. In the black of night, everything changed—she turned into a cornered animal, trapped in a box with no way out.

What if the eye surgery fails?

What if they can't even do the surgery?

What if I can never *see again?*

Negative questions nagged at her, stole her peace.

When she'd had Alzheimer's she never thought about things like that.

Or did she?

What she *did* remember was the day she was driving her car and couldn't visualize where she was going, or even how to stop the vehicle. She'd thrown herself from the moving car into the street, heard her own screams as she hit the pavement. After a night in the hospital, she went back to her apartment and things became normal again.

But they really weren't. And they never were again. She'd finally accepted her reality. It was then that she talked her cousin into being her guardian and signing her in as a participant in a clinical study her doctor had recommended.

It was like magic. After being on the medicine for only five months, the Alzheimer's was gone! But so was her vision and her arthritis had increased to the point where her hands felt like clubs.

And then everything happened so quickly.

The pharmaceutical company said they were moving her to Nevada for special treatments for her problems. But if the cure was in the pills they gave her, she never saw any improvement in the time she'd been here. In fact, not only had her vision and arthritis gotten worse, so had her mind. It seemed to be slipping again ... gradually, but she noticed the difference.

It was so hard to be in this place. So many patients seemed to be in such terrible pain—arthritis, spasms, leg cramps, chest agony. She'd hear them coughing, crying in the daytime; the same throughout the long nights. They all begged and begged for something to alleviate their misery.

The doctors she'd worked for never allowed their patients to have this kind of constant pain. They wouldn't have allowed this to happen.

No one should have to suffer like this.

She started to drift off ... sounds were diminishing ... melting, melting away. Going home ... she would be going home soon ... soon.

* * *

122

"Did Delores give her the Ambien?" Pete asked, pushing an empty gurney.

"Gave her a double dose," Rocky said. "Told her it was a new medicine for her arthritis."

"That was pretty smart."

"Delores is smart all right … but I'm fucking smarter … and stronger!" He raised his right arm and flexed the bicep. "She knows better than to mess with me!"

"That's for sure," Pete said loudly, giving his buddy a look of admiration.

"Sh-h! We need to keep our voices down."

As they continued to move through the unit, Rocky glanced at his watch: 10 PM. They waved at the overnight duty nurse, standing in the station drawing up a medication, and at the orderly working at the computer. Neither responded with anything more than a slight nod.

Outside Rhonda Jenkins' room, Rocky touched a finger to his lips. He pulled a tourniquet and pre-loaded syringe from his pocket; the one that Ethan had given him.

"M-m-m-m! Good ole knock-out juice," he whispered to Pete as they pushed the gurney into Rhonda's room.

"Dark in here … can't see what I'm doing."

"Turn on the light, dummy," Rocky whispered. "Not gonna make any difference … she's fucking blind."

Rhonda was lying on her side, turned away from them. Her breaths were shallow and very slow.

The meds, as predicted, had totally knocked her out.

"Take her arm. Try not to jolt her!" Rocky said in a harsh whisper. "I don't want her screaming her head off and waking up all the other moaners and groaners."

Pete lifted the exposed arm; Rocky studied it, looked for a bulging vein. But there wasn't even a hint of one in her stick-thin limb.

"Shit, can't ever grab a break." He slipped the rubber strip around her arm and tightened it. She muttered something but was too out of it to make any sense. "Hold her arm good."

Pete held Rhonda in place while Rocky searched for a vein. "Damn it, there's nothing here!" He snapped the tourniquet open and retied it tighter. "Nothing! Shit! Where the hell are they?" He poked until he thought he felt something in the crook of her arm. "This better work."

The minute he jabbed the needle in, she began thrashing around, trying to break free from Pete's grip.

"She's fuckin' strong for an old buzzard," Pete grumped, trying to hold her down.

Rhonda suddenly sat up straight, started to scream; Rocky slugged her hard on the jaw and she fell back onto the bed, out cold.

"That's better," he said.

* * *

Gina checked the bedside clock: 2:30. The red-orange numbers seemed to hang free form in the inky darkness. She eased out of bed and dressed quietly. Harry was a heavy sleeper and she knew if she was careful, she could get out the door without waking him. It only took a few minutes before she was outside the apartment, a broom in hand.

She headed for the stairs and used the broom handle to gently redirect the two overhead stairwell security cameras so they were unable to record her presence. Although they might guess it was her, they wouldn't be able to prove it. She walked cautiously down the stairs; at each landing she repeated her silent attack on the security cameras.

Tightening her sweater around her, she tried not to think about what would happen if she *was* caught in the basement again. This time, there could be no cover up. She'd been told she wasn't supposed to be there; it had been made very clear. Besides, what

was she doing there in the middle of the night? No way to explain that away.

When she reached the basement, she rested the broom in a corner, took out her ID card and shoved it into the slot. The door opened with barely an audible click. As much as she wanted to leave it open, she closed it so the light from the staircase was blocked out.

Harry's going to kill me when he finds out about this.

The elevator was several feet down the corridor. She positioned herself, remembering what it was like when she was here last time—if she went to the left, it would take her down the long corridor to the kitchen. Once again she eyed the entrance to the tunnel straight ahead, almost hidden from this angle. She turned right. The corridor was about ten feet across, but she felt safer leaning, flattening her body against the wall as she edged forward.

The dimmed lights and the silence made everything seem strange; scenes from bloody slash movies popped unwanted into her head. She swallowed hard, forced herself to keep from jumping at every shadow, from expecting someone to rush out and try and kill her.

Cut it out! Stop imagining things!

She stood still, closed her eyes, and allowed her heart to slow down.

When she finally calmed down and started to move again, something soft brushed against one ankle, then the other. She jumped, let out a yelp, and slapped a hand across her mouth. She held her breath and looked down into the shining green eyes of a cat rubbing against her leg. It meowed, wanted to be petted; Gina waved it away.

She continued edging her way down the corridor, which began to curve. Judging from the distance and the location, she knew that she must be circling one of the huge boulders visible outside facility.

Ahead, she heard a buzz of voices. She needed to get much closer to hear what was being said. The cat continued to follow her, causing her to trip over it; she tried shooing it away, but it kept pace, moving between Gina's legs.

* * *

"What is the matter with the two of you?" Ethan said when Rocky and Pete arrived with the gurney. "You're more than twenty minutes late. Do you think I can stand here the whole friggin' night waiting for a couple of losers to get the job done?"

"It's not exactly a walk in the park," Rocky said.

"Did I say it would be easy when I picked the two of you out of the gutter for the job? No! I said it would be damn hard ... you signed on ... and now I expect you to get the job done." Ethan spoke to them like they were stupid delinquents. "Am I making myself perfectly clear?"

"Yes, Dr. Dayton," Pete said.

"Yeah," Rocky said. "I got you."

"Good! Now put her up on the table." He stepped back and watched. "I hope you didn't get her all riled up—I told you before, it screws up my analysis."

The two of them lifted Rhonda from the gurney, placed her on the stainless steel table, and shoved her head smack against the top edge.

"Don't stand there like two wooden posts. Wait outside until I call for you. For Christ's sake, do I have to tell you the same thing every single time?"

* * *

Gina identified the voices of Pete and Rocky; they were coming her way. She turned to backtrack down the corridor, almost went flying over the cat again. It screeched, clawed at her leg, hooked into her denim jeans. Gina whirled around, the feline still hanging from her pants. She grabbed it by the scruff of the neck and yanked it away from her. The cat stiffened in panic, the claws not only ripped the fabric, but it sank its teeth into her flesh. Gina swung her arm back and forth and finally tossed it far down the hallway.

The cat had not only gored her leg, it also had hooked a claw deep into her arm. She bit back the pain, but she still felt as though she'd been torn apart.

She started to head back to the stairwell, but saw she'd misjudged the distance—it was much farther than she remembered.

* * *

"There's somebody else down here," Pete yelled. "Did you hear that?"

"Don't get your bowels in an uproar. They keep a bunch of cats down here. They're probably wandering around fighting over some pussy." Rocky roared with laughter.

"Cats?"

"Cuts the rat population. Boy, are you stupid," Rocky said. "Don't you know nothin'?"

"I know enough to check out that noise."

"Yeah, yeah, okay, let's go. I'm bored standing around anyway, doing nothing but listening to you jabbering like a dork." Rocky stretched his neck from side to side, flexed his arm muscles. "This is the shits, man. I'd planned on a little visit to the Starlight Ranch tonight. Was gonna get my rocks off with some hot bitch. Then good ole Ethan fucked that up."

"Man, is that all the faster you can move?" Pete said.

"You keep yanking my chain and you'll see how fast I can move to beat the shit outta you."

* * *

Gina heard Rocky, Pete, their gruff voices getting louder, closer. She could almost hear them breathing. They were going to catch her. Fear shook her, screams jammed in her throat.

What would they do to her?

Sweat and blood soaked her clothes ... her leg was on fire ... shooting sparks burned holes in her flesh.

Need to move ... can't.

* * *

Ethan's voice echoed down the hallway. "Hey, where the hell are the two of you?" There was disgust in his voice. "Can't even do a simple thing like wait?"

"Be right there, boss," Pete yelled.

"Do you always have to lick his ass like that?" Rocky said, turning around. "It kinda makes me want to puke."

"He's the man with the bucks, bro," Pete said. "Ain't that why we're here ... why we came to Nevada?"

"Maybe you're not so dumb after all." A harsh laugh echoed down the corridor. "Except for making me chase after some cat in heat."

* * *

Gina let her breath out, heard their voices start to fade as they moved away from her and back down the corridor. She hugged herself as she bent over, fighting spasms of pain that made her want to retch.

When she was able to stop shaking and think again, she limped, slid along the wall until she was once again at the stairwell.

Chapter 19

Gina tiptoed into the apartment, closed the door with a careful click, and headed for the bathroom. Once inside, she turned on the light, stripped off her clothes, sat on the toilet lid, and examined the claw marks on her leg.

No wonder it burned like hell—they were raw and deep. The cat had really done a number on her. There was a stabbing pain all the way from her calf to her thigh. And her arm, though not as bad, still hurt and had bled profusely. She could barely lift it—it weighed a ton.

"Jesus, Gina! What happened?"

She jumped when Harry's voice cut into the silence. She was so focused she hadn't heard him come into the bathroom.

"Did you know they have watch cats in the basement?" She tried to treat it lightly, not turn it into a big deal, but she couldn't stop the tears from gushing down her cheeks.

Harry held her in his arms, just letting her sob until she quieted down.

"Tell me about it, doll?" He caressed the back of her neck, rubbed her back.

She'd done it again, done something stupid, done something that could have gotten her into *real* trouble. That she'd barely escaped discovery only made her realize how terrifying the whole experience had been.

"I know I promised, Harry." She pulled away and looked into his eyes. "But I had to know what the rest of the lower level was like."

"Sort of a case of curiosity killed the cat," he said with the hint of a smile.

"Obviously not the one that clawed me half to death."

"Let's get these wounds cleaned up." He reached into the medicine cabinet and pulled out a bottle of disinfectant, dressing supplies, and antibiotic ointment, set them on the edge of the washbasin. He went out and grabbed a kitchen chair, brought it back, and sat it down next to her. He washed her leg with warm water, then did the same for her arm.

"Man, this cat was definitely in attack mode," he said. "You must have the scared the heck out of that little kitty."

"The kitty? Scared *it*? You've got to be kidding. I'm the one who's all ripped up."

"When was your last tetanus shot?"

"About a year ago. I'm okay with that."

"Okay, so while I do the nurse thing on the nurse, tell me exactly what you've been up to. And don't leave out a single thing."

* * *

"You took a terrible risk," Harry said, putting the chamomile tea bags in their cups.

"I know."

"What do you think Ethan was doing down there?"

"I don't know. I never got close enough to see. Pete and Rocky were almost on top of me when they were called back. Thirty seconds more and it would've all been over." She ran both hands down the length of her face. "That's what I keep thinking about."

He lifted her chin to look into her eyes. "Why couldn't you just let it be?"

"I don't always have logical reasons for the things I do. I'm not like you. I guess I can't stand not knowing or understanding every part of an unknown equation. I hate feeling helpless and … and … used."

"What does that even mean?"

"Don't you understand? I want things to be right. I don't like to see people hurt and I really think the patients in this place are in danger."

"I know there's something wrong here, but, in danger? Are you sure you aren't overreacting?"

"I don't know. It's just that when something is wrong, or I feel people … patients … are at risk, I have to act, do *something*. But everything I've done here has been a waste, right from the start, especially sneaking down there, trying to find out what they're doing. It was all wasted. I didn't even get close enough to see or learn one damn thing. Nothing's changed, other than I've been clawed to shreds, and we still haven't found out what Ethan's doing down there, or even what he's up to. The only thing I know for sure is that this isn't what we signed on for."

"You know what?" Harry said, a worried look on his face.

Gina gave him her attention, but was silent.

"What I think is that we should pack our bags and get the hell out of here ... git while the gittin's good. This place, this job, was completely misrepresented by the nurses' agency, and Comstock Medical, as well. Shit, there's no drug study going on here. We've both discovered that."

"But what about the money?" Gina said.

"It's not worth it. We can't spend the next three months working under these conditions."

"And the patients? Do we just leave them? They're at the mercy of these people … so vulnerable. What's going to happen to them?" Gina turned away. "Don't you think we have to find out what's going on … for them?"

"There are only two of us. What do you think *we* can do? It's like jousting with windmills."

Gina smiled. "You and Don Quixote. You're both my heroes, you know?"

"Yeah, but I don't want to be a dead hero. And I have a hunch we're circling around a sink hole."

Harry poured hot water over their tea bags. They let the tea steep in the two large cups they'd been using for their first-thing-in-the-morning coffee. He reached into the cupboard and pulled out a jar of honey, poured a generous teaspoon into each mug.

"I did learn something down there: it was definitely Rocky and Pete bringing a patient to Ethan. That much I could figure out from what was said."

"But why?" Harry said. "What could Ethan possibly do for a patient in the basement? Don't you think it's a hell of a strange place for any kind of treatment … especially at that time of night?"

Gina took a sip of the tea, pulled away from the scalding liquid. "I wish I'd heard a name or knew which patient was there. That would be something to go on. We might have been able to question the patient later."

"I don't know, doll. I don't want to scare these people. They're going through enough as it is."

"Have you ever seen such severe cases of arthritis?" Gina asked. "Some are so crippled they can barely move. At least half of my patients are that way."

"Mine, too." Harry said. "Well, that along with congestive heart failure, visual impairment, and a host of other age-related diseases … it's damn sad."

"And why are the daytime orderlies bringing patients down for treatment at night, or whatever it is Ethan's doing? Shouldn't it be the night staff doing that?"

"That's how it usually goes down, but the entire facility is so understaffed, it doesn't surprise me that Ethan would overwork every employee he has. Wait and see. If we stay, we'll be called in for lots of extra jobs, too."

Gina looked at Harry as he concentrated on stirring the honey into his tea.

He finally looked up at her. "You're thinking of dragging us further into this, aren't you?"

"We have to, Harry. We can't just leave these people behind."
She took his arm and squeezed it. He was disheveled: hair flying in all directions, eyes at half-mast. But there was something so reassuring about him. She was excitable and quick to anger; he was calm and seldom, if ever, acted irrationally.

He'll make a great husband, a wonderful father, too.

That thought struck hard. Suddenly she could barely breathe.

A baby? That's never going to happen with me.

Her mind flashed back to that horrible night three years ago. The night when her drunken husband had not only beaten her, he'd made it so that she'd probably never have a child.

I'll never get pregnant—not after what Dominick did to me.

The medical team had saved her life, even her uterus, but no one was convinced she'd ever be able to have a baby. She'd spent a long time trying not to think about it. A lesson she'd learned a long time ago.

Don't wish for what you can't have.

She'd been telling herself that for three whole years. Harry was probably now part of that same "can't have" package.

She watched him sip his tea and finally understood one of the biggest reasons why she'd more than once backed out of marrying him—she would only be trapping him, holding him back, keeping him from finding someone who was not so damaged … emotionally and physically.

She knew getting him to leave or breaking up with him would have to be done in a logical, constrained manner. The last person in the world she wanted to hurt was Harry Lucke. But, once and for all, she should stop leading him on, allowing him to think they had a real future together.

But how can I live without him?

Her heart would be broken and everything inside of her would be empty again—lost and confused, like when she came out of the hospital after Dominick's attack.

Still, she had to do this for him. Somehow, when they finished this assignment, he would have to go on without her. And she would have to be the one to bring it to an end, make him walk away. Otherwise, it was never going to happen.

Chapter 20

Emma Goldmich lay awake, staring into darkness. She did this every night, waiting for something horrible to happen. From her bed, she could see stars pin-pointed in the sky. They brought none of the wonder she used to have when looking off into the heavens.

She didn't know why she was so jumpy or why fear had lodged itself in the pit of her stomach, but she knew it began the first day she'd come to this place so far away from her home and her daughter.

She shifted ever so slightly, trying to find a comfortable position in her bed. But the tiniest movement made her back feel as though it would snap. Her arms, legs, neck … everything … hurt with such acute intensity, it was difficult not to scream.

In the past week they'd placed a catheter inside her so she wouldn't have to get up to go to the bathroom so often.

"You're using up too much of our time with all your screaming and carrying on every time you have to get out of bed to pee," Rocky had told her. "You're not the only one I have to take care of, ya know?"

What made him say such cruel things?

Emma thought about the new nurse, Gina, the one she'd seen for the first time in the elevator when she was supposed to be on her way to have some kind of *special procedure.*

She'd been right—something terrible *was* about to happen … it just didn't happen then.

Somehow she sensed, she knew, the new nurse was someone she could rely on. When she'd reached out to touch Gina, the nurse's hand had been warm, reassuring. What was confusing was that after Gina stepped out of the elevator, Rocky turned around, took her back to her room. No procedure … no explanation. She'd tried to question him, but he wouldn't say anything ... just gave her a strange, disturbing smile.

Gina seemed kind ... not like Delores, who only raced into the room to give her a shot or meds, then disappeared without any conversation. Lately, the medicine barely deadened the aching, or the stabbing pain that smothered her body. When she first came here, they gave her pills, but it wasn't long before they shifted to injections. Now, those were as ineffective as the pills had become. All the shots did were deaden her mind.

Arthritis was not new to her, but it had been manageable up until a year ago when it flared with a vengeance, not long after she entered the study. Since then, the slightest movement was like holding her hand over a flame. She tried to meditate, to mentally reconfigure all her pain into wild sparks of color—orange, yellow, red, purple—that she would splash over a canvas floating behind her eyelids. She'd started doing that when her drifting, unfocused mind wanted to empty itself into dark passages. The swirling colors not only carried the spasms away, it kept her mind alive ... kept it from totally dying.

Tuva, Tuva! Could never understand why I refused to create the graphic art she loved so much. She thought abstract art was silly, ineffective.

My practical daughter. My beautiful child.

Would she ever see Tuva again? Emma wanted to hug her daughter at least once more before she died. That would be very, very soon. She'd overheard Rocky talking to the other orderly, Pete. It was as though she didn't even exist and couldn't hear what they saying. They talked about taking Emma away somewhere. Putting her somewhere else. They laughed a lot about it ... and not humorous laughter.

She couldn't remember much about her Alzheimer's days, except for her art ... and one other thing—the unrelenting sensation of life pulsating through every part of her. That force had a voice of its own; it wanted her to continue to fight, to live.

Tonight, she fought hard with that powerful inner being. Tonight, she wanted someone to kill her, take the pain away forever.

What is there to live for?

Without her daughter, her heart was breaking. No one could go on with this kind of crushing sadness pulling them down. No one could survive such terrible despair for very long.

If only she could hear Tuva's voice one more time. Not to complain. That's not the last thing she wanted Tuva to remember.

The nurse interrupted her thoughts by turning on the room's overhead lights without warning.

"Good evening, Ms. Goldmich."

"Hello, Delores."

"Time for your shot. Are you having a lot of pain?"

"It's terrible!"

"You don't have to move. I can get it into your hip just the way you are."

The nurse's words were kind, but her fingers were brusque and rough.

"This will help soon."

And with that, Delores left the room.

* * *

Emma's mind began to drift again. Thoughts jumped here, there.

Tuva ... Tuva ... beautiful baby ... beautiful child.

Grown ... independent ... accomplished.

Her father gone away with my best friend.

Gone ... everything gone ... beautiful home ... twelve-year-old child ... alone ... back to work ... teaching other peoples beautiful children.

Tuva ... sad little girl ... draws everything that moves.

Like her mom ... art buries her pain.

Emma reached out for her cell phone in the bedside table drawer. That slight movement made her whimper. Her mind became even fuzzier, but the pain remained.

Matter with me? ... no service out here.

"Regular phone?" she muttered, "what's to say?"

Tuva, get me out of here.

No!

This is all I have now ... I won't be a burden.

Waves of silent screams echoed across her brain.

* * *

Tuva Goldmich looked at her watch—9:45. She was stoked, yet at the same time she was beat. She'd just had another sleepless night, one that left her dull, slow thinking. And she really had to be sharp for that 10:30 interview. She needed that job, needed cash in the worst way.

I'm sitting here like an idiot, hanging onto a telephone for ten wasted minutes, listening to elevator music. How smart is that?

Tightness was growing in her neck. It reminded her of Babe, the German Shepherd that her mom brought home for her after her dad moved out. Babe's hackles would bunch up like a fist when she sensed a threat of any kind, especially if it involved Tuva. Someone at the door was enough to set her off. Right now, Tuva imagined her own neck probably looked as weird as Babe's did long ago.

Everything was off-balance since her mom had been taken away to Nevada. Tuva was run down, a mess. She was even starting to dream with her eyes open. And when she finally did doze off, her mom would be there, trying to tell her something.

Two weeks.

Not a word out of this Carl Kreuger dude.

If the OCI agent didn't pick up soon she would have to hang up. Have to get to that interview on time. She looked at her watch again. It was going to be close, very close.

She held the phone in the crook of her neck and paced to the mirror to check out her outfit. Her pin-striped, tan business suit, with a chocolate shell, was just back from the cleaners. The soft material nipped at her waist, exaggerated her petite figure, highlighted her brown eyes. She was pleased. It was the perfect outfit for her interview, even though she'd rather wear jeans and a tee.

That certainly wouldn't land her the job.

* * *

Carl had already taken ten calls since 9:15, and none of them had been worth his time.

Always a lot of damn questions, usually poking at him, blaming him for all the stifling bureaucracy in the world. It was all his fault … of course.

Blah, blah, blah.

Budget cuts had taken away most of the telephone screeners the department used to have. Now, when the calls were about numb-dumb questions, he usually palmed them off to one of the junior agents, or redirected them to the on-line informational outlets. His time was too important to handle the stupid questions most citizens tossed his way.

He took a sip of coffee and reached for the phone to take the next caller in line. Even though he was pissed off, he forced himself to speak in what he hoped was a pleasant, helpful voice.

"Good morning, Agent Kreuger here."

"This is Tuva Goldmich."

She said it like it was a name he should remember.

"Oh, can you hold one more minute, Ms. Goldmich?"

He hit the hold button before she could complain and tapped into his computer files.

Damn it! That name sounds really familiar.

"Oh, shit," he muttered, "that's the Alzheimer's study business."

How the hell did that get lost?

He thought back to the meeting he'd had with the woman, pulled out the notes from his bottom drawer:

Worried daughter re mom in Phase III Zelint (California company) study AZ-1166. Follow up with LA regional office.

There were no other notes … or any follow up.

Shit!

"Ms. Goldmich?"

"You didn't do anything, did you?"

"I've been checking with the LA Regional offices about your mother." He let the words spill out with no room for interjection. "Any action, of course, would have to be taken from our California offices since they're the ones who cover Nevada and the facility where your mother is in residence." He loosened his necktie and took a large gulp of coffee, which now was not only icy cold, but was making him choke.

"You're a liar—"

"—now wait a minute!"

"You did exactly what I thought you would do. My mother's case is buried in some pile on the corner of your desk. You don't give a damn about her, do you?"

Before he could answer, the line went dead.

Chapter 21

Ethan detached the flash drive from his car key chain and pushed it into the USB port on the side of his PC. Zelint's AZ-1166 study data was stored on it, as well as all of the completed altered results of the study. Not only that, copies of the submission papers for FDA approval were also stored on the memory stick.

The drive, a little piece of red plastic, also held the only copy of his personal testing, research, laboratory work, and clinical findings. Everything he'd done since joining Zelint had been compacted and exiled to a virtual reality that could fit inside a two-by-three-quarter-inch computer storage unit.

Thinking about how his huge accomplishments could fit into something so small agitated him. After all, he was studying and searching for answers to enormous questions. The only complete evidence of his work was staring back at him, housed in a tiny flash drive. He should have left the files safely in his computer. Deleting sections of them was stupid. Without documentation, everything he'd achieved could be dumped into that vast shit bucket called anecdotal evidence.

He drummed his fingers on the desk, but couldn't concentrate on anything.

What if I lose the drive?

The answer wasn't pretty.

David Zelint had a copy of the data, but that copy didn't include any of Ethan's private research or investigations.

Throughout his years as a pathologist, he'd pictured himself as an active research scientist. That's why he went into the field of medicine in the first place.

Researchers, pathologists, medical examiners didn't have to deal with the emotional outbursts of patients and their families. Working as a pathologist gave him the luxury of stepping back, standing off, treating people as an essential segment of a bigger, more important picture. They were subjects, building blocks to be assembled as a key to a solution.

He never had to put up with all the bad health news people were bound to get sooner or later. Specifically, he didn't have to inform people that some disease would kill them long before the thought of death had ever crossed their minds.

He wasn't cut out to deal with people—he just wasn't a touchy, feely kind of person.

And that had always been fine; after all, dead people didn't need hugs.

He hadn't gotten enough sleep last night. He'd tossed and turned, couldn't stop thinking about the woman Rocky and Pete had brought to his laboratory. He didn't care for the way those goons handled her. He tried to stay away from personally meeting the patients who were brought in the Comstock Medical Facility. He preferred to be the faceless administrator and scientist. Getting involved only made his job harder.

But he'd met Rhonda Jenkins. She was blind and because of that, he felt safe with her. Besides, he liked talking to her because most everyone else he talked to in Comstock was ignorant about medical issues.

She'd wanted know how he became interested in studying Alzheimer's. He'd been honest with her, only because the information would soon be of little value to her. He'd told her he'd gotten into Zelint's AZ-1166 study late in the final stages of the investigation, but it had still been a wonderful opportunity to have the time and equipment to delve into his personal scientific research.

But Rhonda Jenkins is merely a test subject, no more, no less. No different than a chimpanzee, or a rhesus monkey. I couldn't let her humanity in any way influence my mission to search out critical answers. Some things are much more important than being fuzzy and warm.

Question upon question continued to plague him. They never stopped.

Could a decaying brain heal itself, or at least regain function with the right catalyst? What made cells already damaged by Alzheimer's regenerate in neural tissue?

What in AZ-1166 allowed an Alzheimer's subject's depleted neuron forest to take up increased function again? Regain normalcy?

Was it a different pathway of regeneration? Fewer neurons, with greater or increased cell-to-cell transmission power?

Super neurons?

He thought about that possibility a lot. He always liked the sound of it.

But neurons were only one part of the equation. He knew the only real cure for Alzheimer's would be at the cellular level. That was the part of the puzzle that kept eluding and fascinating him.

There were times even he wondered why he preferred to be so detached and clinical. He'd come to accept that he simply wasn't a herd animal like most of his human counterparts … and that in itself defied reason.

He came from an average family and he'd loved his parents and his brother. But somehow he never bonded with any of the men or women who passed through his life. He felt little need for companionship. He lived inside his intellect.

Ethan looked around the lab. Just being there made him feel at home. He yanked open the bottom desk drawer and pulled out a brand new flash drive. He shoved it into a slot in his PC, next to the one already there. He would finally download everything onto that extra drive, then sleep a whole lot better. He hit the download key and waited for it to finish, and then pulled out the extra drive, and stared at it for a moment before placing it back into his bottom desk drawer.

Life would be so much easier if he could have a tech assistant. Having to do everything himself was starting to wear him down.

Maybe I could train Pete or Rocky?

I really must be tired to even consider trusting anyone in this facility, especially them.

There were way too many people involved already. After having given it much thought, he still wasn't sure how his relationship with any of the existing personnel would end.

But he knew he'd have to think about it and finish it sooner rather than later. The study was at an end and shutting down. All that remained was the FDA approval. Then Zelint could launch the marketing program.

Final dispensation for the personnel would have to be determined very soon.

* * *

Gina unlocked the unit's narcotic box and pulled out Meperidine. She filled a syringe with the narcotic, matched it with Derek Kopek's med card, and set it on a tray, ready to be injected. Hopefully, this would take away his discomfort.

Discomfort?

Yeah, sure!

This med isn't going to bring Derek anywhere near comfortable. Saying that to him is almost laughable. He, of all people, would know better, especially after a lifetime of working in pharmaceuticals.

The guy can barely breathe, so his oral pain meds, along with jabbing him with a needle and pumping him with the smallest dose of happy juice, is not going to do it for him. He's going to keep on suffering because there is no real relief for him.

Is there a single word for suffering? I don't think so. I don't know how to describe the crushing, grinding sensation that can turn someone into a frenzied, mindless creature.

And all I have to offer him are empty words.

Rocky held out the phone for her. "A call for you."

144

"Put it on hold, please." She shoved the unit's supply of narcotics back into the lock box, put the keys in her pocket, and then picked up the phone.

Rocky looked up as she answered, made no attempt to hide the fact he would be listening to her conversation. She walked away as far as the cord would take her, but although she didn't want him listening in, she also needed to keep her eyes on the man to make sure he stayed away from the narcotic-filled syringe sitting on the tray.

"This is Gina Mazzio."

"Hi, doll. Can you talk?"

"Not really."

"Just listen, then. It looks like we can stop wondering which patient was in the basement last night. Rhonda Jenkins is gone."

Gina turned to a patient pushing a walker with shuffling steps. The woman went up to Rocky. "My dresser drawer won't open, Rocky." She gave him a big smile. "Will you come fix it for me?"

Gina could tell it was the last thing Rocky wanted to do, but he had no choice but to go with the woman.

"Are you sure it was Rhonda Jenkins?"

"Are you missing anyone on *your* unit?"

"No ... we have the same census as yesterday." Her heart sank. She'd wanted to be mistaken about the whole basement affair. Hoped there was no patient involved.

"Then she has to be the one."

"Isn't she the blind woman you told me about?"

"Yeah." Harry's voice was throaty. "I questioned Pete, but he played dumb. He gave me one of his infuriating business-as-usual shrugs. The thing is, her chart has already been deleted from the files for the unit's current census; I can't even bring her up on the computer."

"That was pretty fast," Gina said. "What about her room? Are her belongings gone?"

"Not one sign that anyone ever lived there. I went through everything to make sure there wasn't something that I could follow up on. Not only that, someone new is scheduled to arrive this afternoon."

Gina paused to think. "There must be some kind of master file that gives the names of everyone in the study, at least everyone who flows through this facility. We need to look for it."

"Yeah! It's probably in the same place as the exit interviews that were a part of the consent package. I still can't locate that section either."

"That's where they talk about any symptoms they've had while on AZ-1166?"

"That's it. Somehow we've got to get our hands on all that information. And the only place it could be is with Ethan Dayton."

There was a beat before Gina answered, "Oh."

Chapter 22

What has happened to Rhonda Jenkins?

The name kept running through Gina's mind. She tried to remember what else, if anything, she might have heard in the basement corridor the night before. Everything had turned into such a blur. She needed time to think about it, time to disentangle her fears from what she'd actually heard.

The rest of the morning Rocky kept close to her until he finally disappeared for his lunch break. Gina sat down at the desk and mentally walked through everything from the time she left their apartment, to the repositioning of the security cameras so she wouldn't be seen, to the moment she got cat-clawed.

Yes! There was a scream ... just as the cat's claw ripped into me. I'm sure of it. Was that Rhonda Jenkins down there screaming?

She remembered hearing Pete and Rocky walking in her direction, talking in their usual macho lingo, and that's when Ethan called out to them. It was definitely Ethan.

She reached for the phone to talk to Harry again, but Rocky strutted into the station, back from his lunch break.

"Your turn, nurse."

That low-life really knew how to get her Bronx up. She wanted to wipe that smug smile from his face, kick him a good one smack between the legs. Instead, she acted as though she was unconcerned about him and walked off the unit.

Out the door, she checked her watch. The jerk had taken forty minutes for lunch instead of the allotted thirty. Once inside the elevator, she took her ID card off her neck and slid it into the basement slot under the blank square on the board. When the door snapped open—her stomach clenched and she jumped back.

Under her breath, "Cut it out! Don't be such a wuss."

147

She poked her head out into the dimly lit basement corridor and listened.

Nothing.

Stepping out, she began to walk to the right, following the path she'd taken the night before.

Not afraid ... not afraid.

Shaking, she forced one foot in front of the other until she came to a huge outcrop of rock. She wondered if this was a portion of one of the above ground boulders she'd seen.

It was very quiet. No sign of the cat that had caused her so much grief the night before. Right now she was sorry it wasn't here—at least it would have been company.

The farther she went, the dimmer the lights became. Shadows turned from gray to black. She searched for some place to hide if she had to, but there was nothing—only the dimly-lit corridor with its granite walls. Everything felt smaller and tighter.

She squinted at her watch. Couldn't really make out the exact time, yet she felt she'd been gone about ten minutes.

And then, the pathway abruptly ended. Gina was smack up against another huge outcrop of rock that blocked her way.

Now she really felt trapped. She took short and painful breaths as claustrophobia became a rope that yanked at her neck.

"No!"

Her heart was beating wildly. The world was closing in ... closing up.

She needed to get away, to return to the elevator. She spun around and pressed her back against the cold, massive boulder ... a rock stabbed into her shoulders. Everything seemed smaller, tighter. She stared back into the corridor; the near-darkness became a moving wall edging its way toward her.

She clenched her eyelids shut until her scalp was tingling.

Oh God, if you get me through this I promise to be a better person. I promise, I promise...

Buzzzzz.

The sound was loud. It sliced through her panic like a scalpel

What?

She jumped away from the boulder.

Buzzzz.

The noise was coming from the rock.

Her fingers roamed across the section she'd just pressed against. What she thought was a rock stabbing into her was really an oversize metal button-switch.

She lightly touched the button. Nothing happened ... only the buzz.

She leaned hard on the button with the heel of her hand. A click, then a section of stone snapped out and away.

How about that?

She stepped into the continuing corridor, walking as if on broken glass. The silence was so profound; she jumped when the rock entrance suddenly clunked shut behind her.

The dimly-lit corridor finally ended at an unlit doorway. She stepped through and felt for a light switch, found one, and covered her eyes against the sudden blinding light.

The strong smell of formaldehyde was like a smack in the face. And there was something else, something metallic. She could almost taste it.

Blood!

As her eyes adjusted, she saw large glass containers sitting on shelves lining the entire room. Each container was filled with clear fluid ... and floating specimens. She stepped closer, put her hand on one of the heavy glass jars and peered at the contents. It looked like ...

"Oh, my God!" Her hand pulled back like it had a life of its own; her voice startled her. She glanced at the containers on the right and left.

"Human brains!"

The nearest cerebrum looked like firm jelly—almost within the norm. She moved slowly along the length of the shelf, looking at other dissected brain specimens. In many, the cortex was shriveled. and the ventricles had separated, leaving huge empty spaces in between.

Diseased brains.

Her neck started to tingle; her mouth turned so dry she could barely swallow.

Each and every fluid-filled container in the room held either a whole brain or some part of brain tissue.

And then she was shivering so hard her teeth were chattering.

They're staring back at me ... watching me.

She'd seen practically every horrible procedure you could imagine. But looking at those floating brains was making her light-headed.

She turned away and studied the room. In the center was a large stainless steel table—it was set up as though it was in a morgue's autopsy room.

Why is there a residue of blood encircling the drain and a burgundy splatter on the scale?

Close to the table were several trays of instruments, and an array of bloody medical saws. The only thing missing in the room was ... a body.

Where is the body that blood came from? Was it Rhonda Jenkins in here with Ethan? It must have been her that I heard screaming.

As she turned to leave, she saw a small desk; the bottom drawer was cracked open. She *had* to pull the drawer open, look inside.

There was a notebook, laptop computer, and a loose flash drive. She yanked out the notebook and flipped through the pages. It was all about planned cerebral experiments.

Yuck!

She quickly tossed the notebook back in the drawer, and grabbed the flash drive, shoving the small storage device into her pocket. She left the drawer cracked open, just as she'd first found it.

A glance at her watch told her she had ten minutes left to her break. She had to get out of there now.

Buzzz.

Oh, shit!

Someone was coming in.

Her senses were firing at top speed—she could hear every sound, could smell her own terror-filled sweat, and could feel a cold draft on her legs.

The air was coming from under one of the shelves behind her. She bent down, saw a three-foot-high door under the lowest specimen shelf.

Was it a closet? Could she fit in there?

She dropped to her knees, pulled at the handle, crawled into the darkness, and reached behind her to shut herself in.

* * *

Ethan walked into the lab.

Why are the lights on? Did I leave them on last night? Must have.

He stared at the stainless steel table with the remaining tell-tale traces of blood.

God, what a mess! Rhonda Jenkins half awake, looking at me with those empty eyes.

When he'd told Pete and Rocky to lay her on the table, she'd screamed his name—*Ethan! Ethan! Is that you? Help me! These men are going to kill me.*

He told himself that she was only an AZ-1166 statistic. That was her real value. The drug should have turned her Alzheimer's remission into a legitimate positive statistic, but because of her side effects, along with too many others like her, she was here at Comstock. They wouldn't let people like her, and all the rest of them who had gone through Comstock, ruin everything for him … for Zelint.

151

He looked around the room at all his specimens. He was certain each one held a key, an answer. He just hadn't found it yet.

Bottom line—he'd needed Rhonda's brain. That's all. It wasn't personal. Her particular side effects to AZ-1166 had to be studied.

But this time it bothered him.

Ethan had given her the IV med to put her out, but she was still awake when he cut her scalp. Her screams were unbearable; they didn't stop until he was ready with the cranial saw.

He walked to the desk, opened the bottom drawer, and started to pull out his laptop, then he changed his mind and kicked the drawer shut again.

He looked carefully around the lab one last time. Everything seemed in order, except that bloody mess.

Pete will have to clean it up.

He nodded, turned off the light, and left.

* * *

Gina saw the spill-over light from the cracks around the small door disappear. She was in total darkness, wedged into the opening. Her neck was crimped, her legs were cramped, and she wanted to scream. She forced herself to wait until she thought it had been five minutes, then she pushed at the door with her feet. It wouldn't budge.

No!

This was her worst nightmare—she was buried alive.

She took a deep breath, made a fist, and reached back, driving it into the door.

It still wouldn't open.

Chapter 23

Harry couldn't remember ever being this agitated on a job. The uncertainty of Rhonda Jenkins's fate left him feeling puzzled and off-balance. He was accustomed to arriving at a new job loaded with confidence, backed up with a healthy inventory of know-how. But this place was not like any other facility he'd ever worked at—it was totally understaffed and patient care was more custodial than anything else. For some reason, human storage kept popping into his head. It wasn't an image he liked.

His nurses' agency usually provided better pickings.

He couldn't stop thinking about Rhonda. Her sudden disappearance tapped into his insecurities.

Was she really the one Gina heard screaming in the basement?

He and Pete had just now finished handing out lunch trays when the orderly, hands on his hips, mouth spread into a wide smile, said, "So what made you become a girly nurse?"

Some kind of electricity spiked through Harry. Without a word, he reached out and grabbed a fistful of hair and yanked the jerk's head back, exposing his neck; his other hand was poised to chop into his throat. The sleazy smile melted.

Harry couldn't explain why he attacked the guy. Throughout his career he'd been thrown every possible kind of sly, mean-spirited remark about being a male registered nurse. After he decided he couldn't afford medical school and took up nursing, even his parents gave him a bad time about it. Most of the insults seemed like senseless slams against not only him, but against an honorable profession.

He usually let it slide, but this morning Pete had pressed the wrong button.

Harry gave the idiot a long, hard look. It took tremendous self-control to let go of his grip on Pete and back away.

"I'm going to lunch, but before I do, I'll tell you this: one more insult out of you and you'll be flat on your ass ... for days."

Pete ran his hands through his hair, looked Harry square in the eye and said, "Fuck you."

* * *

Harry knew he had to get out of this place. He was feeling what Gina complained about when she was scared, like her world was suffocating her. No, he wasn't scared. But he was uneasy and suspicious.

When he was out the front door, he walked to their rental Jeep, still parked where they'd left it, alongside the building. He took a lap around it, studying the tires, the canvas top; everything looked fine.

He was finally calming down, but now he was angry for losing his temper with such a fool like Pete. He didn't like the guy, or his buddy Rocky. Their being here didn't make sense. Why would Ethan hire two obviously untrained losers to work with sick people?

He walked around to the back of the facility and gave the out-of-place gray boulders a once-over. He didn't see anything suspicious. A little farther on, there was a rift between the rocks. He ambled toward it, found a pathway, and kept walking. After a short time, the foot path ended and he was staring at an eight-foot-high door.

It was definitely an old mining era door, with elaborate tendrils of curled, rusted iron decoration affixed to a solid wooden frame that was held in place by modern heavy metal hinges. A no-nonsense hasp was secured with a large, new padlock.

Harry stepped back. Someone had recently sealed this entrance to a mine.

He pulled at the padlock, hoping it would somehow spring open, but it was firmly clamped shut.

Probably the only way to keep out unwanted visitors ... like me.

Harry turned and pushed on into the open desert, past hump after hump of mine tailings, more evidence of mine activity. Looking up when he should have been looking down, he tumbled over a half-buried door. He kneeled down, touched the lacey, rusted-out metal. The door had been ripped off its hinges and was covered with ragged holes. Finding this second door convinced him there was a mine somewhere beneath his feet. He started making wider and wider perimeters around the area of the two doors, but found nothing else.

He noticed that the sun was getting lower and lower; soon it would be hidden behind the boulders. A sudden chill hit him. Someone was walking across his grave. He couldn't explain why that kind of kid's talk popped into his head. For a moment he did feel weird. He scanned the area. Nothing but desert, mine tailings, and the strange boulders.

He threw his head back and laughed.

What's so unusual about any of this? These mines helped the North finance the Civil War ... provided most of the funds to build San Francisco. Nothing weird here.

I need to get my ass back to the unit.

Still, he wasn't looking forward to spending the rest of the day with Pete after their little encounter.

It took him longer to return than he'd anticipated. He'd wandered out farther than he intended.

Back at the unit, he walked up to Pete the first thing.

"Hey, man, you kind of pushed my buttons earlier. I apologize for taking off on you like that."

Pete hard-stared him and said, "You have no idea just how sorry you're gonna be."

Bette Golden Lamb & J. J. Lamb

Chapter 24

Gina tried to catch her breath, but she sounded like a dying animal.

"Why won't you open?" she screamed.

She couldn't feel her legs anymore, and although there was cold air coming from whatever there was in the space in front of her, sweat trickled down between her breasts.

She tried to punch at the door again, but couldn't really do much with an underhanded back swing, and her legs felt dead and caught in something. She was growing weaker and weaker, could barely hear the thump of her fist as it hit the door. Tears filled her eyes; her sobs surrounded her.

It was getting colder and colder.

Gina had to face it—she was jammed into a hole in the ground. She couldn't go back the way she'd come; and there was nothing but dirt and darkness in front of her.

One part of her brain wanted her to go to sleep, escape all the terror she was feeling. The other part told her that if she didn't do something soon, she wouldn't be able to move or breathe; the blackness would swallow her.

Her mind spun, spitting out little green dots that bounced all around her.

"Let me out!"

Nothing in response.

She screamed it again, "Let me out!"

You're such a wimp, sis.

"What?"

You heard me.

"Vinnie? What are you doing here?"

Wimp!

"Vinnie, don't talk to me like that, you little brat."

Whadda you gonna do about it?

"I'm gonna beat the shit out of you ... like always."

Yeah, sure! You ain't goin' nowhere, big sister. And you sure as hell ain't gonna beat on me.

"Sez who?"

Gina tried to bring her fists in front of her but her arms lay lifeless at her sides, they wouldn't move.

Sez me, said a different voice, deep and hard. She cringed. It was her ex-husband.

"Get out of here, Dominick!" she shouted. "Leave me alone!"

Her heart was racing. He'd kill her this time ... said he would when he got out of jail.

"If you touch me, you'll go back to prison. You'll rot there. That's what the judge told you would happen if you touched me again."

Ain't no judge gonna find you in this hole, Gina girl. No one will find you, you bitch!"

Dominick was coming; his voice was there in the tunnel in front of her. She could feel his cold breath on her face.

"No!" she screamed. She slammed back into the door with both fists; did it over and over and over until there was nothing to hit. The door was gone.

She moved an inch at a time as she backed through the wall. When her knees landed on the lab floor she collapsed.

Chapter 25

Gina lay prostrate on the lab floor. It was a long, long time before she could muster the strength to stand, and make her way out of the lab. Every fiber in her body ached. She didn't dare take the elevator and risk exposing herself. But as she walked up the stairs, she had to cling to the banister to keep from slipping back down. When she finally arrived at the unit, it took all of her will power not to drop her head onto the desk and weep.

Sensing a kill, Rocky had given her nothing but lip for coming back a half hour late. She didn't take the bait even though he was relentless in hounding her with every possible dig. She was too empty inside to respond. She was cold and stiff, her mind constantly drawing a blank. She did what had to be done, working only on auto-pilot.

All she could think about was being trapped in that hole in the ground and never coming out … no one would ever find her.

And Harry? He probably would never know what happened to me.

Her heart sped up, tears trickled down her cheek. Would he think she'd just run away? Would he really think that?

Everything was wrong in this place, had been from the very start.

They'd barely arrived at Comstock, her very first traveling nurse assignment, and instead of the big adventure she expected, the administrator and staff were disgusting. And now, she'd almost died!

* * *

Harry plopped down on the sofa beside her.

"Harry! Don't do that!"

"Do what?"

"Sneak up on me like that! I almost went through the ceiling."

"Sorry, doll, I just sort of collapsed."

Gina looked into his eyes, saw her own misery reflected there. "What is it, Harry? What's wrong?"

"I almost killed Pete today ... I mean *really* kill him."

She reached for his hand. "What happened?"

"I don't know," he said. "He wasn't anymore asinine than usual. I think Rhonda's sudden disappearance got to me. The fool opened his mouth and said one wrong thing too many. I snapped."

"Oh, Harry, I'm so sorry."

"I saw a side of me that I don't ever want to see again." He kissed her on the forehead, looked into her eyes. "Hey, doll, you look totally washed out. What a jerk, laying all this on you."

"It seems we've both had a horrible day." Before she could say anything else, a sob tore out of her. And then she couldn't stop.

"Hey, hey!" He pulled her into his arms. "Tell me about it."

"It was so horrible, Harry. Blackness closing in all around me. I couldn't move ... my arms, my legs were paralyzed."

"Whoa! Back up, Gina. What blackness? Where?"

"I went to the basement again on my lunch break ... found an underground laboratory."

"No!" Harry held her at arms length. "You said you wouldn't go there again. You promised."

"It was because of Rhonda. I had to know..." She was shaking so hard, Harry grabbed a comforter from the back of the sofa and wrapped them both in it and squeezed them together until she stopped shivering.

"The lab. It was so grotesque ... walls covered with jars of floating brains."

"Probably part of the Alzheimer's study. Ethan must be analyzing the brains of the patients who died here at Comstock."

"I tried to tell myself that, too, Harry. I mean, at the time it seemed not only logical, but essential for the study."

"The only way to see what damage AZ-1166 might have caused; how it worked on the brain."

"I could understand that, and even go along with it. But it was something else that got to me. I mean, being in a lab or even an autopsy area is no big thing for me. Been there, done that. But that place, not only smelled of formaldehyde, it smelled of fear."

"You think they cut up Rhonda while she was still alive. That she was the one you heard screaming?"

She squeezed his hand and nodded.

Was it her fear I smelled in that horrible place, or was it my own?

"Rhonda Jenkins shouldn't have been down there," Harry said. "Maybe she couldn't see, "but she wasn't ill … she certainly wasn't dying. Besides, screams are not what you usually hear at an autopsy."

"When Ethan … it must have been Ethan, was coming into the lab, and there was no place to hide, I forced my body through a small floor-level opening in the wall. Maybe it was an opening to an old mine."

"Hey, you were lucky you found any hiding place at all."

"Yeah, but when Ethan left the lab, I tried to back myself out and got jammed in there. It was like being buried alive."

* * *

Gina sat at the tiny dining room table, her hands encircling a cup of hot mint tea. She breathed in the warm steamy mist. It was reassuring to hear Harry moving around in the shower. She'd practically singed herself trying to warm up before him with the shower's hot water. Now, she was feeling better. But she still was racked with sudden chills that shook her from head to toe.

She visualized all the containers of floating brains lined up on shelf after shelf along every wall. It was the perfect setting for a horror flick about a mad scientist, but certainly not something you ever wanted to see in real life.

When Harry came in from the bathroom, he was wearing a Nautilus warm-up suit and running sneakers. His hair was still wet and it glistened with tight, black curls that clung to his head. He pulled a chair close to her, sat down, and kissed the palm of her hand.

"Hey, Ms. Mazzio. Why don't we get out of here and drive up to Virginia City, grab some dinner, and just hang out? Sort of leave this place behind to simmer in its own polluted juices."

"It's kind of late, isn't it?"

She looked into his soft eyes; saw nothing but trust. He believed in her so completely. She was glad she'd told him everything that had happened.

Well, almost everything.

Maybe he was right. Just do something real, something normal.

"Come on, babe. Let's just do it, get away from this place for a while."

Once she made up her mind to go she was up like a shot; it took her only five minutes to slip into jeans, sweat shirt, add a touch of makeup, and grab a jacket.

* * *

It was dark, but lights dotted the hills when they climbed through the pass to Virginia City. When they entered the town's main area, old-time saloons lined both sides of the street. Sounds of rinky-dink piano music floated through the air and Gina was having fun walking on the boardwalk—it felt quaint, like she was the star of an old Western movie.

They'd parked the Jeep down a ways from a twentieth-century Denny's-style restaurant. Gina didn't think the place brought any visions of what the original mining town would have looked like in the 1800s—but it was food and she was suddenly ravenous.

Once inside the restaurant, they slid into a booth; a waitress was immediately at the table with the menus. She was somewhere in her fifties, with a bright smile; it was obvious her feet were killing her.

"Hi, there. Welcome to VC."

"Been a long day?" Gina said.

"Bet your boots on that." She shifted from one foot to another. "It'll be this way until the snow makes it too tough for tourists to get through the pass to Sun Mountain." She took a moment to stretch her neck from side to side. "You folks staying in town?"

"No," Harry said. "We're nurses. We work at the Comstock Medical Facility, about ten miles down the road."

"Don't know that place … mmmm; wait a minute now … is that the place near all those big boulders, way back in the hills?"

"That's the place," Gina said.

"Yeah, I remember them bringing in those rocks. Seems to me that was two or three years ago. Rocks came in sections, as I recall. Folks around here thought it was kind of weird, putting rocks together like that. especially since we're not all that shy of rocks around here in the first place. But we don't pay much attention to outsiders if they don't bring business to the town. If you get my meaning."

"Why do you think they brought them in?" Harry said, laughing.

"Only thing we could figure, it had to do with all the empty mines in the area." The waitress shifted feet again. "The old timers said that piece of land was riddled with shafts going off in all directions. Maybe they wanted the rocks so they could seal off some of them."

Gina was up to her neck with rocks and Comstock. She read the name on the waitress' pin. "Well, Rosa, I think I'll have a nice thick hamburger with everything you can think of jammed inside. Also, I'll have a Caesar salad instead of French fries." She handed the menu back.

"Cost you two bucks extra for the salad."

"Done deal."

"I'll have the same," Harry said, "except I'll take the fries." He laughed. "Two bucks is two bucks."

"Coming right up." The waitress limped a few steps before she caught herself and straightened out her gait.

"Rosa is right about the mines," he said. "During my lunch break I wandered around out back and there were plenty of signs of old mining activity."

"Let's forget the mines." Gina reached across the table and squeezed Harry's hand. "Thank you for getting me out of that place, even if it's only for a couple of hours."

"I know my gal." He scooted around to sit next to her; leaned over, and kissed her on the neck. "Something still on your mind, doll?"

She shook her head.

"Hey, it's me. You can tell me anything."

"No, no, Harry. I just don't like the job or any of the personnel who work there. I wish we'd never come."

"I feel exactly the same way." He started toying with the silverware, moving a fork back and forth. "I've taken on many assignments over the years... some have been boring, some really challenging, but never one that felt ... shady." Harry watched the waitress step their way with their dinners.

"Yeah, that's the right word. Shady," Gina said.

"Are you up for finding out what it is?"

She was silent for a long moment. "You know I'd like to just run away. But I'm willing to stay a little longer and see how it plays out."

Harry took her hand and squeezed it.

Rosa placed the food in front of them, pulled a big bottle of catsup out of her pocket and set it on the table.

"Thank you, Rosa," Harry said. "Can't eat fries without the red stuff." He gave her a big smile.

* * *

Dinner had been great. They'd laughed a lot and there was nothing like a hamburger to make things feel right again.

They were walking down the boardwalk over the rickety wooden planks when Harry pulled her toward the doorway of a bar called The Silver Stope.

"Let's get a nightcap before we head back."

"Hey you!" Gina said, "we've got to get up early tomorrow. Maybe we ought to leave now."

"Oh, come on. A drink will relax us both." Harry pulled her inside. They slid up onto bar stools and Harry put some bills on the counter.

The place was dimly lit; long split logs with a layer of rocks jammed behind covered both the ceiling and the walls. It immediately gave her a bad feeling, reminding her of the mine she'd been in with Harry.

A white-haired guy was hunched over an ancient upright piano playing some Scott Joplin. The counter top was covered with Lucite, but underneath, perfectly aligned, were silver dollars from one end to the other.

"Man, that's something else," Gina said. "Must have invested a load to get this fantastic bar top."

The bartender, a grizzled man with large square shoulders laughed. "Nah, tourists donated their dollars just to get their name planted on a bar top in Virginia City." The man had a cynical smirk on his face. "Ain't anything dumber than a tourist."

The other customers laughed out loud.

"Yep, you got it … nothing dumber than a tourist," said the man at the end of the bar, "…'ceptin' another tourist."

The four other customers really thought that was something. Gina and Harry were the only ones not laughing.

"What'll you two have to drink?" The man behind the bar put two cocktail napkins in front of them. "And we don't make Grasshoppers or Brandy Alexanders in this establishment."

Gina was uncomfortable. She was the only woman in the place and none of the men were nice, or even looked clean. "Harry, it's really late. I think we should go."

"We'll have two Stolies, straight up."

Gina squeezed his thigh.

The man at the end of the bar ambled down and slid onto the stool next to Gina. "Well, now, it looks like we have a couple of sports here. Hey, man, how about buying a round for the rest of us?"

Harry looked the guy straight in the eyes. "Not me. Maybe you can hit on the next dumb tourist who wanders in here."

The man looked up at the ceiling, spoke through the side of his mouth, "Now you sound darn-right unfriendly, dude."

Harry was riled. Gina could tell by his right eyebrow working its way up to his forehead; that didn't happen very often.

He said, "The friendly thing to do would be to buy a couple of strangers a drink." Harry ended his comment with a big, unnatural smile.

The bartender set the shots in front of them. Gina and Harry reached in unison and downed the drinks in one gulp. Gina thought her head would burst, but she pretended like she drank straight vodka every day.

The room was deadly silent. Even the piano player seemed to lose his way on the keys.

"Hit us again," Harry said.

The bartender lifted the bills from the bar. "You ain't got enough here to cover it."

Staring straight ahead Harry pulled more bills from his pocket and plunked them on the bar. "That cover it?"

The bartender poured two more vodka shots.

Harry said to Gina, "What do you say we drink up and blow this fire trap, doll?"

"Let's do it."

Gina didn't recognize either of their voices. They sounded like people from a B movie. Before she could move, the man next to her downed *her* drink and roughly grabbed onto her breast.

Gina was stunned at first, but then she hauled back and slapped him hard in the face. Harry followed up by popping him solidly in the jaw. The man fell like a stone.

The others moved toward them. Gina reached into her purse and brought out a switch blade, pressed the button, and six-inches of glistening steel flicked out.

Harry stood beside her. "Any of you take one more step…" he pointed to the man on the floor… "and she'll slice him open like a dead stag."

The men stopped, looked at each other, and stepped back. Harry reached over and downed the shot of booze. Then they backed out of The Silver Stope.

They ran to the car, spilled in and were pulling away when the bar patrons ran out onto the boardwalk, shouting lost words at them.

"Well, I guess we can add Virginia City to the places we won't go back to," Harry said.

"Who wants to?" Gina said, feeling strangely whole again. "But it was a damn good hamburger."

They both burst out laughing.

* * *

They drove down the hill, the Jeep radio blasting away. Gina leaned out the window, looked up at the night sky aglitter with stars like scattered diamonds. She sang out into the night.

"The hill-ll-ll-lls are alive with the sound of music!"

She didn't even try to hit the right notes.

Harry laughed at her screeching voice. "Whoever said you could sing was stone deaf."

The air was crisp and she was happy again. She turned away from the window, nuzzled Harry's neck, and wrapped her arms around him. "Am I disturbing you?"

"That doesn't quite cover it," he said, hanging on to the steering wheel.

"I can do better." She ran her tongue into his ear and slid her hands down into his jeans.

"Hey, you she-devil, are you trying to get us killed?"

She wouldn't let go of him; when they made it back to the Comstock driveway, the minute he parked the Jeep they were in each other's arms. His fingertips slid across her back and unhooked her bra; his mouth traveled down her neck.

167

"Baby, I really love you."

The drinks had made her feel lighthearted and happy—happy for this moment, happy to be with him. She whispered, "How come we never do this in the Fiat." They both burst out laughing again.

"I can almost visualize that ... but not quite," he said. "Besides, we tried that ... once. I say, let's get out of here and crawl into our bed."

"No-o-o. Being here makes me feel like a teenager again. You're just spoiled."

"And guess who spoiled me?"

They jumped out of the Jeep and Gina ran straight into Pete. Rocky stood next to him. Both of them had wide, nasty smiles on their faces.

"What's so funny," Gina said.

"For a minute I thought we was in for a beaver show," Rocky said. "Hell, there's nothing like watching two people fucking to heat your blood. Not that mine isn't hot enough already."

Harry came around the car. "All right, you two, get lost."

Pete grabbed onto Gina's arm, pulled her to him. "Why don't you get lost, little man, so's we can have some private time with this here little nurse?" His sour breath, laced with alcohol fumes, spilled over her.

"Get your hands off me, you pig," she said.

He laughed at her. She drew back and punched him hard in the nose.

Pete let go, covered his face with his hands. Blood gushed between his fingers and ran down his mouth and chin.

"Bitch," Pete screamed.

Harry lunged at Pete and kneed him in the groin, then chopped hard into his neck. The orderly went down, sprawled in the dirt.

Gina turned, ready for a possible attack by Rocky. But he was bent over laughing.

Pete yelled up at Rocky, "Some friend you turned out to be."

168

"Oh, don't you worry, Petey. They'll get theirs."

Harry grabbed Gina's hand and they hurried to the front entrance. At the doorway, she turned to see if the orderlies were following.

They were gone.

Bette Golden Lamb & J. J. Lamb

Chapter 26

Rocky sat at the bar, still pissed at that goddamn nurse and her boyfriend making out in the Jeep. He'd wanted to grab her, smash her face, fuck her up really bad.

He watched Pete toss back his beer like he hadn't had a drink in a coon's age.

Dude's a boozer. Friggin' fool would cut off his dick for a drink.

Idiots like Pete were easy to control. He learned that lesson when they planted him in some dumbass foster home because his Mom drank herself to death.

His foster parents also chug-a-lugged—beer, wine, the hard stuff—every evening of every single day until they passed out.

He watched Pete take another huge gulp of his fresh suds.

Damn! If the jerk isn't downing another one. That's his last—after that we're out of here. I'm getting laid tonight ... that's for sure. And it's gonna be hot and fast.

Rocky needed to get over this rotten mood—felt like slamming someone hard against the brass bar railing.

Someone's bitch. That's what that male nurse did to Pete. Caught him off guard and made him his bitch.

We ain't nobody's bitch. Nooobooody.

Rocky knew his face had turned bright red—he could feel the blood pounding in his head.

"Hey, dude! Drink 'er up and let's go get laid."

"Not yet, man. I'm just getting warmed up."

"What you're getting is wasted, you jerk."

"Be a buddy; lemme finish this."

Rocky turned away, looked around the room. He played with his half-filled glass of beer, twisted it one way, then another. Typical VC dive—old wooden floors, six-shooters snug in their holsters hanging on the walls next to phony wanted posters, and old Juliette Bulette whorehouse flyers, whoever the hell she was. And there were the mounted stags, their big-time racks on their heads, glassy eyes staring right at him. Stupid, dead animals.

The drinking action was pretty slow, but there were a couple of women giving him the eye, he could feel himself getting hard thinking about doing them.

"Come on, you stupid boozer, down it. We're out of here, hear me?"

* * *

It took them about twenty minutes to get to the whorehouse, Rocky driving a full ninety with the pedal to the metal, windows wide open; Pete was dozing, snoring and snorting every other minute. Otherwise it was only the sound of the wind blasting through the truck. Without the radio on, it was soothing, almost like pretending to fly in the night, like he used to do when he was a kid.

Rocky thought about that ranch he'd been dumped on. His foster parents worked his ass off all day, but after belting their drinks they'd soon quit their screaming at the kids and each other, and fall into bed. He and Pete would sneak out, climb up into a big granddaddy tree and listen to the wind as it whistled through the limbs and in his ear.

Flying like an eagle.

He looked over at Pete. Even back then he was stealing booze and getting high, getting wasted. Rocky liked his booze, but nothing was going to mess with his game. He was in charge of his life, not some fuckin' bottle of booze.

He thought about Harry Lucke again.

Friggin' nurse!

When they finally arrived at the whorehouse, they drove through the gate in the middle of a wire fence that surrounded a trio of connecting house trailers. Bright floodlights and ground light cut through the pitch black night and bounced off the desert floor. Rocky spotted two Dobermans, their flashing green eyes watching intently. They weren't going anywhere while chained to an iron link in the ground, and they weren't anywhere near the pathway to the door, but their presence sent its own message.

There were several cars and trucks in the parking lot, and a big mother-fucker of a bouncer waiting for them at the door.

It looked like business wasn't great, but it wasn't bad either.

Rocky got out of the truck, saw a large six-foot sign posted right outside the first trailer.

NELLIE'S NOOK
THIS IS THE STARLIGHT RANCH
IT'S NOT A HOUSE—NOT A HOME
PAY UP
DO YOUR THING
MOVE ON

Bet they think they're pretty damn funny.

He'd heard a lot of rumors about the place, but he'd never been inside. He knew their prices were high and they had a reputation for good, clean girls.

Hell, I'm just going to fuck them, not marry them.

He elbowed Pete and got him out of the truck. The bouncer watched them move toward the front door. Pete was stumbling and Rocky had to hold him up.

"Maybe you better wait in the car, you loser."

"Hell, no! I'm getting me some action, big brother."

Rocky hated when Pete called him that. Yeah, they'd been together for a long time, but Rocky had no family and he didn't want one. Family let you down even quicker and harder than the average bear.

"You looking for a good time?" the bouncer said at the entrance.

Pete answered, laughing like a hyena, "Whadda you think, we're here for, a seminar?"

173

Rocky threw an arm around his shoulder. "Don't listen to this fool. What we're lookin' for is to get laid."

"Not me. I want a blow job," Pete said, punching Rocky in the arm, laughing his fool head off.

"We don't allow no guns inside. I'm gonna have to pat you down."

"We're not carrying, but go ahead."

"You touch my junk and you're a dead man," Pete said.

The bouncer looked him square in the eye. "The last thing I want to touch is your fuckin' junk, asshole."

"Hey, just ignore the jerk and do what you gotta do," Rocky said.

A police special tucked in a shoulder holster peeked from under the big man's jacket when he squatted down and did his search. He finally nodded them through.

Inside, the lights were dim, sexy music played in the background, and the furnishings were run down and spotted— could have used a real fixing up. Four men sat in covered arm chairs, staring at six girls hoofing past them, wearing skimpy costumes. It was hard to tell the whores' ages, but they were all young enough to make Rocky definitely want to fuck them.

Rocky's gaze flew past two in parochial school uniforms, a skinny broad dressed as a Raggedy Ann doll, a Snow White, a belly dancer, and one in a nurse's uniform.

Now that's what I call accommodating. Even looks a little like that Mazzio bitch—tall, with black Dago hair.

The madam, a woman in her fifties, if she was a day, hovered over the men ahead of them. "This isn't a hotel fashion show. Take your pick and get on with it."

Two of the men stood and smiled at Nellie, if that *was* her name. They each had gaps in their front teeth and looked grungy, with sweat-stained underarms. The madam held out her hand and they filled her fist with bills before each took the hand of a *school girl*. The men sure as hell weren't first timers because they pulled the girls down one of the hallways like they knew exactly where to go.

Pete dozed on and off; Rocky waited, trying to ignore the pressure building in his groin.

Two more girls came wandering out to join the others. They each wore short nighties and Rocky could tell they were already done in by their pale faces and phony smiles. They must have been favorites because the two men in front of Rocky and Pete immediately jumped up and grabbed the girl's hands like they were late for a date.

The madam was quick to block Rocky and Pete from going farther into the waiting room.

"Now hold on a second, you two. No cookie, no nookie." She thought she was pretty damn funny because she cackled as she grabbed their money and let then move on.

"You boys know what you want, yet?"

"Yeah, we'll take the nurse." Pete sat up and looked around.

"You both taking one?"

"You got some house rule against that?" Rocky said.

The madam didn't seem to like Rocky's attitude. She stiffened, thrust a hand into her pocket, and glared at them. He knew she was probably packin' some kind of pea shooter. They always were.

"For you and your buddy, it'll cost triple … and don't you go thinking you're gonna pull any wise ass shit on me or my girls, 'cause I'll ream your ass with a pole. You won't be sittin' so good, but your mouth will be a lot more respec'ful. Get it?"

"All I want is a blow job," Pete whined.

Rocky raised both hands. "I didn't mean anything disrespectful, ma'am."

"Yeah, well that'll still be three hundred bucks." She held her hand out, palm up.

Once the madam was paid, the *nurse* took them to a small room that was almost filled with a king-size bed. Rocky had seen better, but he'd seen worse, too. Pete just stood there staring at the girl's mouth as she sucked one finger.

"What'll make you happy, baby?" she said to Pete.

Pete looked at Rocky. "You go first."

"Nah, I like to watch." He nodded at the woman, who sidled up to Pete and ran her hands up and down the front of his jeans.

Pete's eyes were at half-mast, but he had a stupid, shit-eating grin on his face as she pulled down his fly. The woman pushed him onto the bed, took a wash cloth from a small side table, yanked out his cock, and washed him down. Then she ran her hands under his balls while her lips and tongue rode the length of him. She couldn't have been at it a full minute when he twitched a couple of times and blew his wad.

"Fool! See what the booze does for you? You aint got no stamina."

Pete looked at Rocky with the same silly-assed grin on his face; he rolled over and immediately went to sleep.

Rocky slid his buddy off the bed and stared at the *nurse*. She had moved to the center of the bed, pulled her dress up around her hips and was running her fingers around and inside herself, pumping with her ass, tonguing her lips.

"What do you want, baby?"

Rocky had a boner that wouldn't quit; he bulged painfully inside his jeans. He looked at the uniform and the cardboard nurse's cap pinned to her head.

"Take off the fuckin' dumb hat."

She lifted it away and tossed it on the small side table. He looked her up and down. "Get the rest off, you piece of shit."

Her expression changed, like a fast moving storm. She was scared. He could see her eyeing the door, but she'd have to go through him to get to it. She carefully took off the grungy white uniform-like dress, freeing her small boobs. He could see the Mazzio broad in his head—tall, skinny, black hair, just like this bitch.

It felt like all his blood had drained from the rest of his body and pooled in his cock—a volcano filled and ready to blow.

He undid his pants, crawled onto the bed, straddled her, and rested his hands on her breasts. Rocky waited, but she didn't move; he tossed her legs over his shoulders, thrust himself inside her and plunged in and out, over and over and over.

Nothing! No relief.

His cock grew tighter, bigger; stretched, hurt. But he couldn't climax.

Fucking nurse's fault. That fucking bitch!

"You whore!" he screamed. His hand balled into a fist and he slammed her in the mouth, again and again, beating on her until blood was all over the pillows and spread, smeared across her face, arms, and breasts.

Rocky laughed as her screams bounced off the walls.

When they grabbed him, he roared even louder as a geyser of spunk sprayed out across the bed.

Chapter 27

Rocky looked through the steel bars at Pete in the adjoining cell. He was sitting on the floor, his long legs stretched out in front of him. The jerk was finally sober after heaving all over himself and the squad car; he never stopped barfing during the twenty-minute ride from the whorehouse to the police station. Rocky was disgusted; he couldn't seem to get away from the stink of the mess all over the idiot's shirt and pants; he might as well have been sitting on top of him.

Made the cops mad, that's for damn sure.

He chuckled, knowing the pigs had to clean up the gunk.

Pete was doing it again, picking at his face. It really pissed Rocky off he had to sit in this godforsaken cell and watch that boob stab at the mole on his face.

Pick, pick, pick.

How many times have I told the dork to stop doing that? It'll only give him trouble. Not supposed to pick at those things. What a damn fool.

Rocky looked over at the large clock on the opposite wall. His gaze latched onto the moving hand, traveling to each second where it would pause with a click before moving on. It was almost three in the morning. They'd been in the slammer for two hours.

"When's Ethan gonna come get us, huh?" Pete said, digging deeper into his face.

"Leave that goddam thing alone, for chrissakes."

Pete ignored him, kept on pick, pick, picking.

"When's he gonna get here?"

"Stop your whining. He'll be here soon enough … not gonna let us off work. So shut up and wait."

"It smells bad in here. I don't like it."

"Well, it wouldn't stink if you hadn't puked all over everything, you jerk."

"I'm not the jerk who beat up the whore. Why'd you have to do that, anyway?"

Rocky sat on the floor, brought his legs up. "She looked like that friggin' nurse at the Comstock. It set me off."

"Mazzio? Nah, she don't look nothin' like her. Besides, that whore gave me a good blow job." Pete grinned.

"How would you know? You were stinkin' drunk."

"So you say—"

They were interrupted by a guard, who first unlocked Pete's cell, then Rocky's. "You made bail, you losers."

Pete was out of the cell like a shot, but Rocky took his own sweet time, strolling like he was taking a walk in the park.

* * *

Ethan watched the two men leave the police station and walk toward the SUV. He was fuming, tapping a shoe on the floor in an erratic rhythm.

Looking at those two cretins had his stomach shooting sparks.

Bribing the madam of Nellie's Nook, along with the sheriff *and* his deputies, had cost him a bundle of money. And all of it was coming out of his own pocket. David Zelint would go through the ceiling if he even got wind of any of this.

All so he could get those two freaks out of jail.

You'd think two ex-cons would have more sense than to get into this kind of mess and get thrown back in jail.

Pete wouldn't look Ethan in the eye, but Rocky wore his cowboy hat low, the rim hanging over wraparounds, exaggerating the arrogant sneer on his lips.

Three in the morning, just bailed out of jail, and he's still trying to look like a punk movie star.

Rocky never lost his pace as he slid into the front passenger side, slamming the door. Pete melted into the back seat on the driver's side, closing the door with a quiet click.

Ethan turned to glare at Rocky—security flood lights posted around the station lot shone on the man's face.

"What the hell did you think you were doing?"

Silence.

"Did you hear me?"

Silence.

"If you want to get your rocks off in a whorehouse, that's fine. But beating up a woman is insane. What on earth could she have done to make you slam her in the face so hard you fractured her nose and cheekbones? She's going to need extensive facial reconstruction." Ethan paused. "And who the hell do you think is going to pay for that?"

"You are, Ethan." Rocky's steely voice promised more trouble to come. It made Ethan's skin prickle.

"Why the hell should Comstock pay for your after-hours problems?"

Ethan glanced at Pete in the rearview mirror. He could tell Pete didn't like Rocky making trouble.

"Do I have to spell it out for you?" Rocky said.

"Put your cards on the table right now, so we know where we stand," Ethan said, leaning into Rocky's space.

"In case you haven't noticed, you've been cutting out people's brains."

"I'm a pathologist. That's what I do! Examining brains is a big part of our study. This is all about science and the study we're involved in. Not that I expect you to understand." Ethan sat back, threw his hands up in exasperation. "God, you're dumb!"

"Not dumb enough." Rocky gave him an evil grin. "Not half as dumb as you think we are."

He's right. I'm the stupid one, letting him get the upper hand.

Ethan had gotten comfortable, not only with the whole AZ-1166 operation, but with the extra time it gave him to research his own projects, meet his own goals.

I took these goons for granted; thought money was enough to keep them silent until I was ready to deal with them.

"You think anyone is going to listen to you two jailbirds?"

181

"When we tell 'em how Petey and me bring those dudes into your lab alive, and when you're through with them, they're dead, how do you think that'll sit? Yeah, I think they'll listen ... even if we are two jailbirds."

How did I let these lowlifes corner me? This changes everything.

"Are those cards good enough, Doc?"

Ethan sat up, ignored the question and closed his fingers around the steering wheel.

"Hey, boss man; don't forget to stop at the whorehouse so we can get the truck." Rocky sneered at him. "You know where that is, don't ya?"

"Why did you have to bring attention to yourselves?" Ethan turned the key in the ignition and the engine caught.

Pete piped in, "The whore was dressed in a nurse's getup. Made Rocky think of Mazzio ... the new nurse. He don't like her."

"So that's a reason to beat this woman beyond recognition?"

The edge of a smile tugged at Rocky's lips. "Reason enough, far as I'm concerned."

Chapter 28

David Zelint's phone vibrated in his pants pocket, startling him. He didn't like these meetings; it was all he could do to sit still in his seat and listen to the same questions being tossed at him time after time.

He looked around the conference table at his brother and the three other board members to see if any of them had heard the distracting buzz. No one even looked his way. He slid out his smartphone, checked the screen, saw it was a call from Ethan Dayton.

What now?

It seemed as though he'd been on the phone with that man every single day. Right now Dayton was the last person he wanted to hear from. David had made it clear that he wanted no part of the Comstock operation. That was their agreement. Dealing with the FDA, their manufacturing facility, and the processing of Zelint's final data of AZ-1166 was difficult enough. But Dayton wouldn't let him be. David slid the phone back into his pocket.

Well, he'll just have to wait.

"David, for the umpteenth time, when is the FDA going to look at our stats?" Saul's words sounded impatient, but his brother's face was simply benign and questioning.

"They're supposed to be going over them in the next few days. After that, they'll decide if we can go to market."

Two of the other board members wore distrustful expressions; a third shifted nervously in his seat.

What are they worried about? I'm the one who's neck-high in strategic manipulations to make everything gel.

"What's taking the FDA so long to review our data?" Saul said, placing a hand on his arm. "I don't get it—how many companies are as far along as we are? Can't they see this is a miracle drug?"

"You'd be surprised," David said. "There are more companies than you can imagine trying to be the first one off the mark. Every company involved in this kind of R & D is hoping for its own AZ-1166. It will probably be the drug of the century. It's not only great for humanity, but the amount of money that can be made is off the charts."

"Speaking of marks," one of the board members said, "how are our current Good Manufacturing Practices? Will the plants meet the quality standards?"

Again and again and again.

"Oh, come on!" David said. "The FDA has been all over our operations with a fine tooth comb—you can be sure our cGMPs are A-One. Do you really think at this late stage we would allow ourselves to trip over that kind of nonsense?"

Saul smiled. "He's only asking what has to be asked, David."

"I guess you're right. And I hope you'll forgive me if I get miffed when I have to repeat the same information at every meeting since we started our clinical trials. Questions about our current good manufacturing practices is coming a little late in the game. cGMPs are pretty basic and I've answered these same questions too many times not to be a little teed off. I've been working with AZ-1166 from its inception; I have too many years into this to make those kinds of slipups." David took a long sip of water. "Do you think I don't know that we've been sinking all of our money into this ... that it's win or lose for Zelint? *Everyone* at this table knows that."

"What if the FDA doesn't look favorably on AZ-1166?" another board member said.

"You already know the answer to that. But I'm betting that won't happen," David said. "In fact, I'm hoping they'll agree that our drug is so effective, they'll go along with our stopping the clinical trials immediately and give AZ-1166 to all participants—

even the ones who have been on placebos. After that, we should be out in the market in a year ... or less."

* * *

David paced back and forth behind his desk. He was so agitated he could barely put his thoughts together.

Just a bunch of slugs. Even Saul seems out of the loop.

He finally sat down at his desk and began to take long, even breaths. He'd almost reached a level of calmness when the phone vibrated in his pocket again.

He knew who it was and the screen confirmed it.

"What do you want, Ethan? Calling me constantly like this is downright irritating. Enough is enough!"

"We've got some real problems out here, David."

"Oh, for chrissakes just lay it on me before I hang up on you."

"You might stop to realize I'm your only ally here. No one else knows what you're up to except me ... well, me, Rocky, and Pete."

It took David a moment to really focus on what was being said. "Rocky and Pete? The two orderlies?"

"Exactly!"

"Well, what about them?"

"I've needed them and I've let them get too close to the operation. They've managed to see too much."

"Like?"

"Like, they know where all the bodies are buried."

"Get to the point!"

Ethan paused. "Well, they know ... everything."

David was trapped. Ethan hadn't kept his word, hadn't kept him out of the messy Comstock operations.

"Ethan, don't you think it's time you completed your exit strategy?"

"Yes. I guess it is."

"That's always been your end of the deal... so do it!"

185

Bette Golden Lamb & J. J. Lamb

Chapter 29

Tuva Goldmich finagled an early lunch so she could get to the OCI offices before noon—that's when their lunch hour began. She rushed out the door of the building, her legs stretching out into long strides. She was determined to walk the ten blocks to avoid spending money on a cab, that is, if she could have even flagged one down.

Money was real tight and she refused to use her credit cards anymore except for emergencies. Her landlord had agreed to wait a couple of weeks for the rent, but she could see the wheels turning in his head, like: *Is this tenant going to turn into a problem?*

She'd lived in the apartment for three years and hadn't been late once with her rent, let alone miss a payment. But she knew businessmen had a whole set of different rules. Money was money—pay the rent or you're out.

She thought about her new job, really a replica of the old one. Another sweat shop, with her being low shmo on the totem pole. But the place did pay better, and the people were much nicer. Plus, all of the other artists were noticeably relieved she'd come on the job—the work backlog was tremendous. She saw the situation as a real plus; there would be lots of overtime in her future. And if all went well, in three or four months she'd be back on the right financial track.

She tried to walk even faster, but her body held back. She still wasn't sleeping well. She was too worried about her mom, and exhausted easily.

Why doesn't Mom answer my letters? It's not like her to ignore me. Something is definitely wrong!

Tuva glanced at her watch—like it or not, she needed to nab a taxi. She walked to the curb, waved, and, wonder of wonders, a taxi immediately pulled up alongside of her.

Now there's s a first!

She slid inside, gave the cabbie the address, and they were on the move before she'd solidly closed the door.

* * *

Carl Krueger was in a terrific mood. He'd called in some favors from his former FBI unit and it looked like he might be able to have his old job back. It had taken days and days of hanging on the phone, talking to just about everyone he knew. Of course, that made his work schedule a real mess, but it looked like his persistence was going to pay off.

Finally, he would get back to the West Coast.

He leaned back into his desk chair—it would take a lot of sweet talk to bring his wife over to his side, especially now that she was going to be interviewed for a new marketing position at Bloomingdales.

She knows how unhappy I am here. She'll understand ... I hope.

His phone buzzed. The caller info window showed that it was reception.

Hell with it. Maybe if I ignore it, she'll try to get someone else.

The call light went out.

He took a deep breath, leaned back, and allowed himself to daydream for a moment. He'd barely pictured a pristine Hawaiian beach, with palm trees gently swaying when the phone did its thing again.

"Oh, shit!' He reached out and picked up the receiver.

"There's a Tuva Goldmich here to see you, Mr. Kreuger."

"Can't you get someone else to handle it, please?"

"No, she won't see anyone else ... says it has to be you. What do you want me to do?"

"Throw her out the back door." He could imagine the receptionist rolling her eyes, barely tolerating him.

Finally she said, "I'm waiting, sir."

The way she said "sir" was definitely a sarcastic slam. "Tell her to grab a seat. I'll be out to get her in a minute."

His Tuva/Emma Goldmich notes sat there staring at him from the corner of his desk, the same place they'd rested since Tuva Goldmich's brief telephone call. The only thing he'd done was print the computer file. Something inside of him had refused to pack it away in his cabinet of active files.

He opened the folder, fingered the papers. Yeah, the Alzheimer's study. As if he didn't know.

Even if there's nothing to it, why the hell haven't I gotten in touch with the LA regional office to look into this Comstock facility?

He knew the answer: It would take too damn much time. First there would be the telephone calls, then multiple e-mail communications, and last, but not least, the razzing he would get for even initiating an unnecessary investigation. The draconian budget cuts was reason enough right there.

He'd had a lot to deal with. Setting himself up for getting back to LA being his first priority. Life was too short … and would be even shorter if he didn't get out of New York soon.

* * *

Carl brought the Goldmich woman into his office, pulled out a chair for her. But she just stood there glaring at him.

I fucking don't like the look on her face … she's the kind of broad who thinks she's better … smarter than me.

"Mr. Kreuger, you swore you'd follow up on my mother's case."

Damn princess. That's what she is.

She was still standing there.

"Ms. Goldmich, you know all of this takes time. And it doesn't help when you continue to badger me." He went around the desk and sat down in his chair and looked up at her.

"Badger you? I'm worried about my mother, Mr. Kreuger. I thought you'd help me. Don't you get it? There's something

189

wrong. My mother would never ignore my letters. *Never!*" She finally dropped heavily into the chair opposite him.

"Have you tried calling her?"

"Haven't we gone over this before? Of course I have. But when I call, they say it's too late, or it's too early ... or she's in treatment ... or she's sleeping. There's always a reason why I can't speak to her. They won't even give a good time for me to call. At least when she was in a facility here in New York, I was able to visit her, talk to her almost anytime."

Carl felt the pangs of guilt sitting right in the middle of his chest. He also felt pretty stupid for getting a burr up his ass about a woman who was simply worried about her mother. He leaned across the desk and looked at Tuva Goldmich's worried face. Her eyes were wide open. She was really scared.

"I promise, I will speak to the LA office as soon as you leave."

"So, you *haven't* called them yet?" Tears trickled down her cheeks.

"I'm really sorry. My caseload has been unusually heavy; I just haven't gotten to it." He stood and walked around the desk and held out his hand. "But I promise, I will call right away."

She looked up at him for a moment, then placed her hand in his.

After Tuva Goldmich closed the door behind her, he turned to his wife's picture on the edge of the desk. She seemed to be looking at him with accusing eyes.

Yeah, I know. I'm a boob for a lot of reasons.

He tapped into the computer address book for the OCI offices and found the telephone number he was looking for.

* * *

Outside the building, Tuva started walking down the street in the direction of her office. She couldn't remember the last time she'd felt so alone, so scared. At one point she reached for her cell phone and was about to call her best friend when she remembered

190

Nadia was vacationing in Europe and wouldn't be back for two weeks. She folded the cell and shoved it back into her purse.

Without thinking about it, she sidetracked and climbed part way up the steps of the Metropolitan Museum. It was a beautiful day and the steps were crowded with people eating their lunch; two people scooted over so she could sit down. She was already late getting back to her job, but she couldn't focus enough to even act, much less hurry.

Tuva glanced at the trees that bordered the sidewalk outside Central Park. The leaves sparkled in the sun. They had a transitional look that told her they would soon turn to the red-orange autumn foliage she loved. Then they would fall and it would end their cycle of life.

Was it time to stop obsessing about her mother? Was it time to let her go and get on with her own future, especially now that she had a new job and things were really happening for her?

She stood and climbed the rest of the museum steps, pulled her pass out, and walked through one of her favorite places in New York City. How many times had she come here just to wander around and study the different styles and expressions of art?

It was peaceful and beautiful.

When things were out of whack, when she was troubled or perplexed, like now, she would head for the Egyptian exhibits. In this section of the museum she knew her problems or questions would somehow be subliminally dealt with. She imagined herself back in a time and place when the mysteries of the universe must have seemed uncomplicated and orderly. Life and death were a simple equation; it was either one or the other.

She strolled through the tomb replicas, her fingers trailing along the walls, sweeping over the hieroglyphics. Behind closed eyes she imagined herself in Egypt under starlit skies. The gods were reaching down to protect her.

When she opened her eyes again, she smiled.

* * *

Tuva returned to the office a half an hour late. Her good mood disappeared when she saw her manager waiting in her office, sitting on the edge of her chair, tapping one index finger on the acrylic top of her desk.

"I'm sorry I'm late, Susan."

"I took a real chance on you, Tuva. You know that, don't you?"

"I do. But *some* things are even more important than a job."

Susan was smartly dressed but wasn't into designer outfits. There was nothing phony about her; she was a working woman and she dressed that way. Tuva liked her direct approach and felt she would be a friend worth having. She pulled a work stool from the corner of the office, sat down and prepared for the worst.

"You're not going to like what I have to say," Tuva said. "In fact, there's a good chance you're going to fire me."

"I'm already flirting with *that* idea."

"My mother's in trouble." She wanted to scream the words, but she was just too tired.

"Oh, please, don't pull the sick mother card on me. Most people have the decency today not to use their family as an excuse for their lack of professionalism."

Tuva bowed her head, covered her face. She could hear her manager shifting in the only comfortable chair in the office; her voice had been filled with exasperation. But at least she was giving Tuva a chance to talk. Not like the manager at her last job.

"My mother has early Alzheimer's … she's been in a national study for a new medication … and it was working. She was so much better, then…"

Tuva dropped her hands into her lap and looked directly at her manager. "…then she suddenly became crippled by severe arthritis, and was moved to a facility in Nevada for treatment. I haven't been able to speak to her since."

"How long has it been?" the manager asked.

"Three weeks." Tuva barely recognized her own voice.

"I see."

Then the words poured from Tuva's mouth. She couldn't stop to even think about what she was saying.

"I've done everything I can, Susan. I went to the FDA's office of criminal investigation to have them look into it ... I've tried to wait ... be patient ... but I know something's wrong ... she's in trouble ... she needs me ... you have to understand ... I would never make this up ... I have to go to her ... she needs me. ... she needs me—"

"Okay," her manager said. "I think I see the problem now, Tuva. It's just that I barely know you and the last company you worked for was not throwing accolades in your corner. It's hard to ignore that."

"I can't stay here and do nothing about my mother."

"What do you want me to do?" Susan's voice had softened and her eyes were kind, but the set of her shoulders were still firm.

"I have to go to Nevada ... find out what's happened to my mother. I have to do it. Don't you see?"

Susan rose, walked over and rested a hand gently on her shoulder. "I do understand. And if there's anything I can do, please let me know."

"My job?"

"I'll hold it for you ... for as long as I can."

Chapter 30

Carl Kreuger placed the telephone receiver back in its holder and glanced at the work schedule taped to the frame of the computer screen. The damn piece of paper fluttered with the slightest breeze or movement, constantly attracting his attention. Every single item on that piece of paper had to be tied up—one way or another—before he could move his butt back to his old FBI job on the West Coast.

He turned away from the jumble of words on the list and tried to get the Goldmich call to LA out of his head. It kept interfering with his focus.

Dammit. Why can't I stop thinking about Tuva Goldmich and that Zelint- Comstock Medical business?

He clenched his thinking pencil, the one with teeth marks and chunks of missing wood, tapped the graphite point lightly on the desk.

Connecting with the OCI regional office in LA had left him unsatisfied. Like his office, they were understaffed and overworked. Only a few words into his conversation with one of their agents told him that Tuva Goldmich's mother was headed for a trip to the bottom of someone else's work stash.

He shifted in his chair, tried to get comfortable. But the seat felt too small no matter where he slid his rump.

Well, I kept my damn promise and made the call.

His wife's picture kept staring at him. She still seemed to have a disappointed turn to her mouth.

Everyone was disappointed in him: his wife, because he didn't love New York the way she did; the Goldmich woman, because he wasn't giving enough attention to her mother; his supervisor, because he wasn't diminishing his backlog of case files.

He tried again to push the whole Goldmich business from his mind. He'd done what he promised to do.

That should be the end of it!

But he knew that wasn't the end of it; *he* wasn't satisfied that someone would soon get around to that mother and daughter's problem in the near future.

He couldn't explain why, but that truly bothered him.

A lot.

He envisioned his work pile escalating with every blink. He really needed to get on the stick. Instead, he picked up his pencil and started tapping again.

In a flash, he tore the work list off the screen, put it in his top drawer, and slammed the drawer shut. Then he hit the keys of his computer and brought up Zelint Pharmaceutical's website. Staring back at him was a picture of the twin brothers who owned the pharmaceutical company. Their home office was in Reno, Nevada. As expected, the company praised their business operations and their dedication to humanity. It was obviously set up to woo potential investors, although there was the usual disclaimer to that notion.

No surprise there.

He cleared the screen and hit into OCI's file on the company and its facilities.

LA's regional office had very few consumer complaints regarding Comstock.

All small stuff.

That in itself would guarantee the overworked staff wouldn't be checking into Zelint in any hurry. He also saw a recent updated bulletin: AZ-1166, the Alzheimer's treatment medication was pending a Class IV drug status.

Tuva Goldmich's sad face flashed into his head. Against his better judgment, he continued to be drawn to this woman who refused to let go of her mother.

196

He picked up the phone and called Zelint's offices, asked to be put through to David Zelint, the listed contact for the company. It took more than a few minutes of dancing through a chorus line of assistants before he actually reached the man.

"David Zelint, here."

"Mr. Zelint, this is Carl Kreuger from OCI in New York City."

There was a pause. "Yes, of course. I've read about you. You're a branch of the FDA. Right?"

"Yes, we're the investigative arm of the agency."

"I see," Zelint said. "What can I do to help you?" An uneasy chuckle followed. "Are we under investigation?"

"Well, of course you are, sir. You have applied for Class IV, FDA status." Carl didn't like the tingling at the base of his neck. Something was off about the man's responses.

"What can I do to help you?"

"I'm sorry to say we've had a complaint about one of your facilities—Comstock Medical." Carl could have sworn Zelint was holding his breath.

"Complaint?"

"Yes. It seems you have a woman by the name of Emma Goldmich at Comstock. Her daughter, Tuva Goldmich, has filed a complaint at our offices. She states she has not been able to reach her mother by mail or telephone. She's extremely concerned."

"I'll look into it immediately, Mr. Kreuger. May I have your telephone number so I can get back to you?"

Carl gave him the information.

"You said you're in the New York City office of OCI?"

"That's correct."

"Aren't we somewhat outside your sphere of operations?"

"Normally, but Ms. Goldmich's complaint was filed here. However, I've also relayed the information to our LA office, which handles your region."

"We'll take care of everything at our end, Mr. Kreuger, rest assured."

"Thank you. I appreciate that. I'll expect your call." Carl hung up, but he was less than satisfied.

* * *

Ethan's smartphone vibrated in his pocket. It startled him, even more so when he saw David Zelint's name in the window. Of late, every time he'd tried to reach the man, all he'd gotten was grief. Ethan allowed it to ring for a few times before answering.

"David! You're calling *me* for a change?"

"I call when it's necessary."

"What can I do for you?"

"For one thing, you can take care of business, like you're supposed to do." David Zelint usually raised his voice and almost shouted when they talked. Now, his tone was low and menacing.

Ethan sat down at his desk and waited for his heart to stop racing.

Bad! This sounds bad.

"What do you mean? I've taken care of everything."

"Really? What about Emma Goldmich? What about Emma Goldmich's daughter, Tuva? Does any of this jar your memory, Ethan?"

He immediately pictured the woman's file, remembered that if it hadn't been for a foul-up, she would have been out of their hair some time ago.

"Yes, I know who you're talking about."

"The daughter has filed a complaint with the OCI. Claims she can't get in touch with her mother. Not by mail, not by telephone. Why is this happening?"

"OCI?"

"Remember them? We've had conversations about them before. That's the FDA's police force. The F-D-A. Do you get the picture now?"

Ethan's mouth was frozen. Raw fear roiled in his gut.

198

"You get this taken care of," David growled. "Fix it. Now!"

Chapter 31

Emma lay in bed, staring at the ceiling. Every part of her, from the top of her head to the tip of her toes, was hurting. When she tried to move or change positions, it became a roller-coaster of screaming pain. The medicine Delores had given her two hours ago had worn off—they all wore off so quickly now—leaving her breathless.

She pressed her bedside call button once, twice. When nothing happened, she pushed it over and over. She watched her bedside clock lose fifteen minutes before the nurse finally appeared.

"Yes, Emma, what can I do for you?"

"I would like to use my cell phone so I can call my daughter. It's been three weeks since I've spoken to her."

Delores frowned with annoyance. "I told you, we don't have cell phone reception here. It's the mountains."

"Then I want to call her from the nurses' station." Emma could hear the shrill in her voice. "Please! I have a right to talk to my girl."

Delores made a point of looking at her watch. "Your daughter is probably in bed sound asleep. It's late in New York. You wouldn't want to wake her up … would you?"

"Yes! I want to wake her."

"Well, I can't let you do that. Besides, the phones are for medical personnel only." Delores turned around and started to leave.

"Delores, please help me."

The nurse swung around to face Emma again. "It's too early to give you more meds for your pain, Emma. And you know that."

"No, it's not the pain." Emma held onto her bedside table, tried to raise herself, but she couldn't. "Please, Delores! Help me call my daughter. You could do that if you really cared."

Delores's face turned a bright red. "We have our rules, Emma. I have to follow instructions."

"What are those instructions?"

Delores raised her voice. "You know what they are. You can't use our telephones to call your daughter. Every single day I tell you the same thing. Over and over. I've had enough!"

"What did you do with my cell phone?" Emma screamed. "Whether I can use it or not … it's mine! I want it back!"

Delores stepped to the bed and pounded her fists on the mattress; the violent movement caused Emma stabbing pain, like electrical fingers crawling all over her.

"You listen to me, you … you … Emma! Your cell phone is useless, and that's not going to change." Delores thrust her face inches from hers. "Get it! Now don't ask me again."

Delores returned to the doorway and swung around to glare at her before she left. "Why don't you accept it? Your daughter doesn't give a damn about you."

Emma bit back the screams that kept welling up inside. Delores would hurt her again if even one of them escaped her lips.

* * *

Ethan sat at his laboratory desk, brought up Emma Goldmich's file. He remembered how the woman had been scheduled out. Then the arrival of the two new nurses had delayed the finalization.

The patient should have been gone from the equation. She should be dead. Just a brain floating in a glass specimen container.

Then there would be no complaint from David Zelint; no complaints from anyone.

David's angry face was there every time Ethan closed his eyes, and every time he saw that face, a glob of fear would stick in his throat.

He looked around the room at all the preserved brain specimens. He'd done hundreds of dissections … and to what end?

No conclusions! No supportable theories. All he had was garbage, and brains floating in jars.

He turned back to the computer and in a frenzy he began to review the data and observations he'd carefully documented. He moved to his paper files and compared all his notes, as well. Frustrated, he threw the papers up in the air and let them fly everywhere.

"Where is the *pattern*?" he screamed at the brains. "Where is the logic, the harmony, the progression of scientific thought?"

He'd had all the advantages of studying living tissue. What did he learn? What definitive information had it given him? Where did it take him?

Nowhere. Only down dark, empty alleys.

He scrolled his computer files, tried to make sense out of his observations. But the more he searched, the more it all turned into gibberish.

He scratched at his arms until there were tracks of blood. Where had he gone wrong?

"I was supposed to be a pioneer," he said to the specimens. "I was to create new pathways for others to follow, to find new information about the functions of a living brain. I was to create maps for future explorations."

He'd not succeeded in his quest, had not answered any of the vital questions.

Ethan pulled up the original platform for his personal research, the one he'd used to convince David Zelint that it was worth the money to purchase special equipment for Comstock.

How does AZ-1166 actually affect the functioning of the brain?

Do the fewer nerve cells and synapses in Alzheimer's patients cause the remaining neurological survivors to morph into superhero status? Become superhero cells by taking on more responsibility? Does AZ-1166 help accomplish that, or do all brain cells try to compensate in the same manner?

Could there actually be brain tissue regeneration?

"I've learned nothing!" he shouted at the room.

He jumped up, paced around the lab, scanned the collection of brains that surrounded him. Yes, they were *his*. He remembered every single one of these subjects.

"You were all willing participants."

Jar after jar of brain matter seemed to stare back at him.

"You were supposed to be a part of world-shattering discoveries!" he yelled at the jars.

He surveyed every container, each carefully labeled with the name of the donor, the date and time it was received.

Derek Kopek was floating next to Rhonda Jenkins.

He rested a finger on an empty slot on one shelf.

Emma Goldmich should be right here.

Kicking at the remaining research papers on the floor, he returned to his desk chair and brought up a separate file that gave the actual results of AZ-1166. Not the altered one the FDA received.

After testing 1,200 subjects, in 151 neurogenic national centers, it was determined that the spread of Alzheimer's could be stopped in Stage I participants using a well-tolerated, oral therapy. However, an unacceptably large number of subjects also experienced the acceleration of age-related diseases. A very small percentage even slid back into Alzheimer's. (Note: See patient's question and answer sheets.)

David had laid out the situation to Ethan when he hired him.

The FDA would never allow them to continue on to Stage IV if the actual percentage of side effects to AZ-1166 participants was reported.

The immediate problem was that it could take years of research to weed out the negative aging results. In that time, some other company might succeed where Zelint had failed. They would be the companies that would reap all the massive profits.

Derek Kopek's brain stared at him. Some of his blood was still caked on the floor near the head of the autopsy table.

Ethan tried to block out the memories of Derek's screams and struggles. No matter how much he drugged him, the man stayed wide awake until Ethan finally severed his brain stem to shut him up.

I should never have agreed to hide the truth. Should never have agreed to juggle the numbers of participants with unacceptable side effects, make those statistics disappear.

Ethan continued to pace around the room, wondering all the time why he ever got into this mess.

It's not my fault. I didn't lay down the rules. I wasn't even here at the beginning. I didn't create the pit. It wasn't my idea to get rid of those subjects.

He collapsed into his desk chair again.

A scapegoat. That's how he would end up. David would claim he knew nothing about what was going on at Comstock. He would claim that as far as he knew patients were getting all the necessary treatments for their side effects before being discharged.

Ethan laid his head on his desk. He would have to cover his tracks or take the fall, possibly go to prison for the rest of his life. They might even execute him. The thought of that made his stomach drop.

That's not going to happen!

Ethan started shaking. It was time to prepare for his escape.

He had plenty of money—enough to live in South America for the rest of his life.

Like the Nazis.

Is that the way the scientific community would think of him? He looked around the room at his brain specimens … knew the answer.

He brought up the copies of the real informed consents he'd deleted from all the patients' charts. The regular consent forms and the question and answer sheets would have to be altered and placed back in their charts.

He quickly read through one of the signed forms. There was hardly a mention of the possible age-related conditions the test drug could cause—heart disease, congestive heart failure, osteoporosis, blindness from cataracts, crippling arthritis, incapacitating strokes.

He then programmed the computer to add all the specific potential side effects to the master consent form and pasted in the paragraph for every study participant, going back to the time the study was launched. It would now look as though each patient had *really* been informed about AZ-1166.

Almost 1,200 participants. By the time he finished, he was exhausted.

Ethan stood on a wooden chair and disconnected the smoke alarm. He had to burn several bags of letters stored in the corner of the lab—both patient letters that were never mailed; letters to patients that were never delivered. There were very few of the latter.

It had always been in Zelint's favor that families quickly lost interest in elderly Alzheimer's patients when they left home. Comstock just made it even easier by eliminating all communications between them.

He scooped up his hand-written laboratory notes that he'd scattered around the lab and started feeding them into a paper shredder.

After emptying the shredded ribbons of paper into a deep lab sink, he set them on fire. When the flames started to die down, he tossed in all of the patient/family letters. The flames roared again.

Soon everything was consumed.

Perspiration ran down his face and his clothes were soaked. He held his shaking hands out in front of him.

If he were to get away, he would have to figure out every possible avenue of discovery.

Bone Pit

He was not going to be *anyone's* scapegoat.

Bette Golden Lamb & J. J. Lamb

Chapter 32

This brief encounter with Comstock had been enough of a trial balloon for Gina. She would never do travel nursing again, no matter how much Harry assured her that this wasn't a typical assignment.

Give it another chance?

No way!

Gina wasn't cut out for this kind of nursing. She missed the hospital environment, missed the excitement of new concepts floating around her, missed the interchange of ideas with colleagues. And most of all, she missed the friends she'd made at Ridgewood Hospital; it was amazing how a supposedly cold, indifferent institution could turn into a second home. And San Francisco had become a safe haven away from New York ... and Dominick.

Harry had a different take on things.

He'd been a travel nurse for too many years to just turn his back on any one job. His flawless record had always been a real plus; he could pick and choose almost any assignment he wanted. Not completing an assignment, especially without giving decent notice? Well, that would really screw things up for him.

She'd allowed him to talk her into staying, but for the only reason that really meant anything—leaving her patients exposed to a danger that she couldn't even pinpoint would gnaw at her long after she'd gone.

Well, she'd suck it up, do her job, and find a way to protect these patients. Wasn't that what nurses were supposed to do?

Again, when she arrived on the unit, Delores didn't bother to give her a patient status or any other kind of report; she silently passed the narcotic keys to Gina and walked away.

She tried to avoid Rocky's cruel, piercing eyes, eyes that shredded her clothes away, from neck to ankles. The worst thing was not that she felt naked, but that she was really scared of him. In the same way that she was scared of her ex-husband.

She forced herself to stare Rocky down. "Why don't you get your mind out of the gutter?" she said. "Move your ass and do your job! Get the vitals and start getting everyone ready for breakfast while I put together the pain medications. Can you do that?"

He slowly rose from the desk. Standing, he pretended to enter notes in the computer.

Why doesn't Ethan toss him? Why do he and that clod, Pete get such special treatment?

She tapped into the computer and brought up the patient census. Someone was missing.

Derek Kopek. He was gone!

She called out to Rocky, who had finally started down the hall. "What happened to Derek Kopek?"

Rocky kept on walking. "He was transferred out."

Gina tried to bring up the Kopek's file, but his name and everything about him had been deleted. The same thing had happened to Rhonda Jenkins, Harry's patient.

She grabbed the phone. "Harry, another patient is gone."

"What do you mean, *gone*?"

"I can't find any sign of him, or of what happened to him. All I got from Rocky was that he was supposedly transferred out."

"Do you think he died?"

"I think the grim reaper would be a different kind of transfer. Wouldn't that jerk Rocky just say that's what happened?"

"How ill was he?"

Gina thought about Derek, pictured him barely able to breathe, yet still smoking. "Very sick. Stage IV, CHF."

"It sounds like he might have died. I'm really sorry, babe."

She hung up the phone, got back to setting up her treatment tray. When everything was ready, she carried the tray from room to room, spending a few minutes with each patient. Most of them only wanted to talk about the constant pain they were having. Every single patient on the unit had an aura of defeat. It made Gina feel ill.

When she got to Derek's empty room, she stepped inside. There was nothing to indicate he'd ever been there other than the faint odor of cigarette smoke. She tiptoed through the room, trying to visualize Derek in the last place she'd seen him—sitting in the chair near the window.

What happened to you, Derek?

She walked to the chair, tried to conjure some kind of clue, something ethereal that might have been left behind.

There was nothing.

Gina made her way back toward the nurses' station. Emma Goldmich was the last to receive her meds. As she walked to the bedside, Emma looked back at her with sunken eyes.

All of these patients are suffering the death throes from every other aging disease.

"Emma, you look exhausted. What's the matter?"

She turned away. "Nothing."

"You can talk to me." She sat down on the edge of the bed, but the movement of the mattress made Emma wince with pain.

Gina lifted up from the bed slowly. "Let's give you your meds. It will help … at least for a little while."

She gave Emma a shot and gently took her hand. "I know there's something's wrong. Please tell me. I promise I'll try to help."

"Will you let me use your cell phone to call my daughter?"

"I don't have it with me, Emma. No sense carrying it around when there's no reception up here in the mountains."

Gina could see Emma didn't believe her. "I'll go get it from my room, if you want. But you really can't get a signal ... and I've tried, believe me!"

Emma shook her head, turned soulful eyes on Gina. "It doesn't matter. My daughter doesn't love me anymore." Tears trickled down her cheeks. "I wish I were dead."

Gina could almost feel the suffering deeply etched into every line in Emma's face. Gina reached for a tissue from the bedside table and gently wiped away her tears.

"Why do you think your daughter doesn't love you?"

"I haven't heard from her in three weeks ... three weeks!"

"Oh, Emma," I'm so sorry."

* * *

It was lunch time and Gina couldn't stand one more minute inside the building.

Emma's unhappiness stayed with her all morning. It was like heavy fingers pressing on her shoulders. When she walked out the front door, a stiff, blast of fresh air blew through her hair, making her feel better—it was enough to finally lighten her spirits.

She strolled down the long driveway, but stayed exactly in the center of the road, remembering that the rattlesnakes hid in the crevices of these roadside rocks.

Not this time, you monsters. I know you're hiding in there.

She tried to empty her mind; she didn't want to think about anything. When she approached the end of the long driveway and Comstock was finally out of sight, she could finally breathe freely again.

She was about to turn around when a jeep pulled into the driveway and stopped. Bold lettering on the driver's door said: CAPITAL COURIERS.

She smiled and waved at the driver.

He had a worried look on his face and he stuck his head out of the window.

"Hi, are you one of the nurses here?

"Yep, unfortunately."

The courier gave her a weird look, then said, "I hate to ask you, but would you do me a favor and take the mail up to the administrator? I'm really way behind and it would be a big help."

Gina smiled. "Oh, sure. Glad to."

The man reached behind his seat and pulled out a small bundle of mail.

"Is that all?" Gina asked.

"Yeah, they never get much." He stepped out of the Jeep and handed the mail to her. "You sure you don't mind?"

Gina grasped the bundle. "No, of course not."

He gave her a wide smile. "Thanks a million." He jumped back into the vehicle, backed out onto the road, and was gone.

Gina started back up the driveway. She fingered the corners of the letters—most looked like bills and were addressed to Ethan Dayton.

Dull, boring.

She'd been so busy with the mail, she walked right into a depression in the road; the mail flew into the air and scattered on the ground. In addition, it felt like she might have sprained her ankle.

"Dammit!"

She gingerly tested her foot; except for the pain, it seemed okay. She stood and scooped up all the pieces of mail. Among the bills to Ethan was a letter addressed to Emma Goldmich. The return address showed it was from Tuva Goldmich.

"Yahoo!" Despite her injured ankle, she danced in a circle, jumped up and down, and then ran all the way back to the building.

Bette Golden Lamb & J. J. Lamb

Chapter 33

Gina was ecstatic. She actually had something tangible to offer Emma, something that could bring real hope—mail from her daughter. She shoved the letter deep into her pocket.

When she pushed through the front door of the building and headed for Ethan's office, she was breathless with excitement.

His door was wide open. She started to walk in, but he looked up at her with stony eyes—it was like a slap in the face; it stopped her in her tracks. Stunned, she remained at the threshold waiting, but he stayed on the telephone and dismissed her with a wave of his hand.

Administrators!

In Gina's opinion, most health care executives lived in the upper stratosphere, not in the real world of patients with their complex emotional needs. And what they knew about nurses could be written on the thumbnail of a newborn.

At least she and the administrator at Ridgewood Hospital had reached an uneasy truce when she'd tried unsuccessfully to help find his murdered niece. He'd even surprised her by asking her not to leave when she agreed to take on the travel assignment.

But she was never going to come to terms with this man. There was something sinister about Ethan Dayton and his laboratory of floating brains.

She stepped outside his office, leaned against the wall, the letter burning a hole in her pocket. She wouldn't let Ethan's attitude get her down. She was going to bring a spark of joy into Emma's eyes. Gina could almost visualize the woman's smile.

It wasn't enough.

She was wasting her time at Comstock. Lack of staffing and minimal patient care left little room for any professional highs. Until the letter for Emma, job satisfaction was hovering near zip.

She zeroed in on the buzz of Ethan's conversation and tried to hear what he was saying. While she couldn't make out his words, his tone of voice surprised her.

Her experience told her that he rarely lost his cool, that his emotions were held intact with an iron grip. He was all about the business at hand.

Today, he sounded erratic, his voice running the gamut of emotions, almost out of control.

She checked her watch and knew if she didn't get this over with soon, she would be late in getting back to the unit. She heard Ethan shout out, "That's all, goddam it," followed by the loud slam down of the phone.

She moved from the wall and looked into his office.

His gray eyes took her in. She reluctantly unclenched the bundle of mail she had pressed to her chest, and walked up to his desk.

"The courier was in a rush so he asked me to drop off the mail." She placed the small bundle on the edge and started to turn away.

"Why you? The courier company has specific instructions that the mail and all other parcels are to be delivered to me and to me only." Ethan's voice was tight, demanding. He looked like he would have strangled her had she been close enough.

"The driver said he was running late."

What's up with this? Why the hassle? He actually looks worried. Worried? Could Comstock be keeping the patients' mail from them?

"*What*," Ethan said, "were you doing out there in the first place?" His voice was menacing.

"Hey, it was *my* lunch hour. I went for a walk." He'd really pushed her *I hate administrators* button; her internal volcano begin to roil. "Don't tell me I have to account for my off time, too."

With that, Gina turned and strolled out of his office without looking back. The letter remained in her pocket like a bomb ready to explode. When she was out of his sight, she could still feel his hostility reaching out, trying to encircle her before she got away.

She could have used the stairs, but she deliberately waited for the elevator to take her one floor up to the unit. She wanted whoever was viewing, or reviewing, the security cameras to see her looking as casual and unconcerned as possible. She entered her ID card and rode the short distance, examining her fingernails all the way. She even faked a yawn.

"You can go to lunch now," she said to Rocky when she arrived back on the unit.

He looked creepier than usual. Or was she imagining even more trouble from someone who already meant trouble by his mere existence?

"I'll go when I'm ready!"

The lummox seemed to be hanging around a lot longer than usual when it was time for his break; much less his lunch time.

"Well, *get* ready!" she said, hands on hips. He glared, turned around, and headed down the hallway. As soon as he was gone, she rushed off to Emma's room and closed the door behind her.

Emma lay prostrate, staring at the ceiling. She had ignored her lunch tray—tomato juice was coagulating on the sides of a glass, and a cheese sandwich was looking old and stale.

Gina took a deep breath and blurted out, "Emma! I have a letter from your daughter."

Emma turned her head slowly and looked at Gina; her eyes went from sad to just the hint of sparkle; she smiled tentatively. "You do?"

"Yes! It's from Tuva."

Emma began to cry, then sob. Deep moans shook her body.

Gina's throat was tight as she fought back her own tears. She stepped closer to the bed and held out the letter.

Emma started to reach for it, but her hands were shaking so much that she gave up and said, "Please read it to me." Her eyes were still wary, as if Gina might be playing some kind of cruel joke on her.

"Of course!" Gina ripped open the envelope, removed the letter, and began to read.

Dear Mom,

>*I'm so worried about you. Why don't you answer my letters? I've written to you every day and have yet to hear from you. I've even tried to call but I can't get through to you on your cell and the office there won't let me talk to you.*

>*Our doctor tries to reassure me, says not to worry. But I can't help it. I'm very scared. I only have one mother.*

>*I really miss you, Mom. I have no one to talk to about my art, especially since*

>*Nadia is in Europe. And besides, you're the only one who really* gets *my paintings.*

>*I can't wait for you to come home.*

>*Love you.*

Tuva

Gina folded the letter and put it back in the envelope. She reached out and gently took Emma's hand. "I don't know why you haven't gotten your letters before, Emma, but I think it might be safer if I kept this for you. Just for now."

"I don't understand. Why won't they let me talk to my Tuva? Why have they kept her letters from me? Why?"

"I wish I had an answer for you, and I *will* try to find out why. But for now, what say we keep this letter our little secret?"

Emma squeezed her hand. "Thank you."

When Gina opened the door to leave, Rocky was standing there.

"Why was the door closed?" he demanded.

"Getouddahere, you miserable S-O-B! I don't have to answer to you about patient care … or anything else, for that matter."

He stayed in place, like a huge immovable barricade. She stuck out her chin, let a deep breath fill out her 5-10 body, and stared straight into his eyes.

"Man, you better get out of my way, and I mean right now." She started moving into his space, with no intention of stopping.

He jerked away. "We're not finished with this."

"Damn straight!"

* * *

Gina and Harry hurried out the front door like convicts escaping from a prison. They climbed into the Jeep and immediately dug into a couple of stale sandwiches they'd bought from the lunchroom vending machine.

"I told you things were screwy here," Gina said. "Now I find out that Ethan has been holding back the patients' mail."

"As usual, you were the first one to pick up on all the weirdness," Harry said. "Where does that sixth sense of yours comes from?"

"From always running for my life as a kid." Gina said, "At least I got *something* out of that."

She took a huge bite out of her ham and cheese sandwich. The bread was stale and she had to chew and chew before she could swallow it. It made her think of the soggy sandwich she'd seen in Emma's room.

"And Emma!" she said between bites. "I can't even begin to imagine what it's like to feel so abandoned."

"Lots of people are neglected by their families." Harry looked out the window. "You just can't make people love you. Either they do or they don't."

"Well, I'm glad Emma has someone in her life who does." Gina fanned herself with her hand. "Man, I had to get out of that place and breathe some fresh air even if all I get to look at are those flipping boulders."

"I miss not having my computer," Harry said. "You were right—we should have never turned them in. If I could at least do some more research, we might get to the bottom of this whole setup and—"

"Harry?"

"I'd at least feel like we were doing—"

"Harry?"

"something. We're so isolated out here—"

"Harry!"

"What is it, doll? I mean, I feel like someone's cut off my right arm."

"Harry Lucke!" she yelled. "Will you please be quiet for a moment?"

"I'm sorry." He drew an imaginary zipper across his mouth, sealing his lips, but he was smiling at her in the next breath.

"I still have my tablet."

"You have what, your tablet? He … he ordered us to hand over our computers."

"He didn't say anything about tablets, did he?"

At first he looked at her with round and startled eyes, then reached out and crushed her tight against him. Both their sandwiches went flying.

"God, I love you, Gina Mazzio!"

She whispered in his ear, "We can also download the flash drive I snatched from Ethan's desk in the lab."

He held her at arms length and looked straight into her eyes. "You didn't?"

"Oh, yes I did."

Chapter 34

Gina dragged through the rest of the shift, forcing herself to stay focused on the patients. Throughout the day, Rocky had virtually stood on top of her, tailing her, watching her every move. She'd dealt with creeps before, but there was something not only weird, but sadistic about the man. And the way he treated the patients was hair-raising—more like they were things rather than people who needed help.

If she was working in a hospital, there would be places to get away from him, places to hide, places to disappear into. But there was no place here to blend in or become wallpaper. Not at Comstock.

Their apartment was the only safe place inside the building. *If* it was safe.

Have to face it: nothing is private or off-limits.

When she finally finished the shift, she walked to the elevator, where Harry was waiting for her.

"Where did you—"

Gina tugged down hard on his hand and frowned at him. He nodded, pulled her close, and said nothing

When the door to their apartment clicked shut, Harry said, "Okay, where did you—"

She clamped a hand over his mouth, then went to the pantry, pushed aside stacks of food cans, and pulled out a large cereal box. Inside were the tablet, charger, and Ethan's flash drive. She took his arm and led him to the bathroom, where she turned the shower and wash basin faucets on full blast.

"This is what people do in the movies," she whispered in his ear. "Like when they don't want anyone to hear them."

"Smart move! I'm not used to all this cloak and dagger stuff."

"You may be smart, Harry, but you'd make a horrible spy."

"I didn't go into nursing to become a spy. If I'd wanted that kind of life, I would have hooked up with the CIA, and I'll bet they pay a helluva lot more money." He gave her a big fake smile, showing lots of teeth.

"It's strange. In the beginning I didn't really hide the tablet from Ethan ... I just forgot it was in my purse."

"Ah, yes! The bottomless pit."

"Call it what you want, I don't leave home without it."

"If you really think our apartment is bugged, this is way too late to be taking precautions."

She gave him a *who-knew* gesture with her hands and squinched up her face as they sat down on the floor. Gina plugged the flash drive into a USB connector, the connector into the tablet, and began downloading the stored files.

"Everything's gone wrong so quickly, babe. And it's my fault. I should have been sharper. I'll never forgive myself if anything happens to you."

"Forget it! We walked into a bad situation, that's all. Heck, maybe the gods got up on the wrong side of the bed and forgot we were the good guys."

"I hope they remember soon," Harry said, "because I'm as spooked as you are."

"Let's see what's on that flash drive."

The screen filled quickly with a long string of saved files.

"There!" Harry said, pointing to the top of screen.

Consent Forms A & Consent Forms B

"Two different consent packages?" Gina said.

They opened the files and compared the two sets. Each listed possible side effects for those taking part in the clinical trial of AZ-1166.

Gina tapped the screen. "Only one set lists severe upswings of age related diseases ... crap ... even increased dementia?"

"They weren't taking any chances. It was probably a lot easier to get them to consent to the one that gave the less serious and more common complications."

"I'll bet you the Fiat," Gina said, "that the non-specific forms will be deleted at some point. That way, anyone investigating will think everyone was properly informed."

"Did you notice the paragraph about all bodily remains becoming the property of Zelint Pharmaceuticals for further study? And the final disposal ... cremation."

"Yeah. That was in both consent forms," Gina said.

"Sure as hell would make it difficult for any outside agency to check up on the real cause of death."

"What's the point of all the lies?" Gina said. "They either have a clinically sound drug, or they don't."

"The point, doll? Money."

"But that drug is hurting people," Gina said, "Making them sicker."

"Never let the truth get in the way of making a buck."

"That's pretty sick."

"Remember that whole lecture from Ethan about industrial espionage?" Harry said.

"Who could forget?"

"It keeps coming back to me," he said. "Especially since every patient in this facility is no longer on the drug."

"I've got to admit, it did make being here kind of exciting for a few minutes."

"Exactly. It was nothing but a come-on ... he wanted us to think this *was* a really exotic, important job."

"Why go to all that trouble?"

"To keep us interested," Harry said, "to keep us from walking away from the exhausting job that it is."

"Yeah, a prison with a backbreaking load, terrible hours, and dismal working conditions, plus Rocky and Pete, the cherries on top."

"The large sum of money was supposed to be the clincher," Harry said. "And we fell for it."

"Hook, line, and sinker. Let's just finish what we started." She scrolled through the file and stopped at:

(Non FDA) AZ-1166 Side Effects.

After a few minutes of reading, they turned to each other. Harry's expression reflected how she felt. "The results of this study are awful. Look at those numbers … a huge percentage of the participants have had devastating outcomes—increased dementia, acceleration of heart disease, crippling arthritis, pulmonary failure, osteoporosis, stroke, and on and on. If they turn this into the FDA, they'll never get the go-ahead to market it."

"See if you can bring up individual outcomes," Harry said. "Tap in Rhonda Jenkins' name."

Gina brought up *(FDA) Study Participants*. It was a simplified, quick scan list. Strictly the name of the participant and the outcome.

Rhonda Jenkins: Patient discharged, slight change in vision, Alzheimer's in remission.

"I guess you can call blindness a slight change in vision," Harry said.

Derek Kopek: Patient discharged, CHF, status quo, Alzheimer's in remission.

"This diagnosis is a sham," she said. "His congestive heart failure had gone to Stage IV almost immediately from the day he arrived at Comstock. He was in terrible shape, could barely breathe. They did absolutely nothing for him."

Gina's eye was doing the twitch thing double time. If she didn't know it already, it told her just how horrified she really was. "None of these outcomes match the real results of taking the drug."

"The FDA will only see what Ethan and Zelint Pharmaceuticals want them to see," Harry said. "They'll get some kind of fictional report, with statistics that favor Zelint's new miracle product. Damn!"

"Let's see if Emma Goldmich is on that list."

"She's still an in-patient," Harry said.

"I'm just curious."

Emma Goldmich: Patient discharge; minor increase of arthritis; Alzheimer's in remission.

"Can you believe it? Minor increase of arthritis? Is that nuts or what?" Gina was ready to pull her hair out.

"Maybe she was supposed to be discharged."

"Hit on *Research*; I'll bet those are Ethan's notes about his laboratory procedures."

"Look at that!" Harry said. "Derek and Rhonda are listed under *Live Brain Studies.*"

Gina's throat was so dry she could barely speak. "All those jars of brains in his laboratory … does that mean he took brain samples from them and kept them alive … or … oh, my God! Do you think he removed their brains while they were alive?"

Harry's features sagged. "Either way, he was working with living tissue, trying to find out why their other diseases escalated with Zelint's drug."

She covered her face. "No one was ever discharged. These patients were brought here to die. He butchered them, didn't he?"

He was silent.

"Answer me!" Gina's heart was pounding in her ears. "Do you think he experimented on *everyone* who came to Comstock?"

"I don't know for sure, but where else did he get those brain specimens? Looks like all the study's problem patients were brought here solely for experimentation and termination."

"Did they think they could get away with this? Get away with murder? I mean, any of the nurses or orderlies could bring them down."

"You don't think Delores, Rocky, or Pete is going to stand in their way, do you?"

"But, Harry, what about you and me?"

"I wish you hadn't asked that question."

He shut down the tablet and disconnected the flash drive. "Let's get the hell out of here, babe. We need to get this information to the FDA, the police, or someone who can help these patients. We're way out of our league."

Gina stuffed the tablet and flash drive into her traveling purse, and headed for the elevator. At the first floor they nervously waited for the door to open, then rushed from the building and ran to the Jeep. Harry pulled out the keys, unlocked the door, and they piled in.

"This is how you make a quick exit, doll." He gave her a huge smile and turned the ignition.

Nothing.

He turned the key again.

Nothing.

"Someone's been messing with our Jeep."

"Oh, my God, Harry! What now?"

He jammed the keys back into his pocket. "We'd better find a place to stash the tablet and flash drive. This may be our only chance."

Chapter 35

When Gina and Harry walked back into the Comstock, the trio of Ethan, Rocky, and Pete seemed to appear out of nowhere.

The two orderlies stood on either side of Ethan, hands at their side, wide smiles on their faces.

"There's no escape for the two of you," Ethan said.

"Ain't it the truth," Rocky added with a sneer.

Ethan looked directly at Gina. "Why the hell couldn't you just leave things alone? All you had to do was perform your job, then whiz out with a bundle of money."

"What are you talking about?" Gina said. She looked at them with wide eyes, trying to play the innocent.

"You were right, Ms. Mazzio." Ethan's voice turned low and menacing. "We did bug your apartment and we know about your mini-laptop, or whatever it is. In fact, we know about everything." He gave them a sardonic laugh. "And as far as the movies go … watch a better quality of films. We heard every word you said in that bathroom. Maybe you should have gotten *into* the shower." Ethan nodded to Rocky, who grabbed her purse, opened it, and swiped a hand all around inside of it.

"No computer," Rocky announced. "Nothing here but a lot of female junk."

"Hey, give that back to me, you creep." She reached out and tried to pull it away from him.

Rocky held the purse at arms length. "Not in charge now, are you?"

"Why bother to listen to our conversations?" Harry asked. "Just a couple of nurses who are beat from a day slaving away on your units."

Ethan smiled and pointed to Gina. "We didn't … at least not until *you* brought in the mail and had your little talk with Emma

Goldmich. Obviously you found a letter from her daughter, Tuva, who writes to her mother practically every day. You must have pulled it out of the bundle the courier gave you." He moved in closer to Gina. "But you never said a word about it to me, did you? From then on, I knew you both needed to be watched a lot closer."

"Okay, so we're fired," Harry said, holding out a hand to Gina. "We'll go pack up our things and get out of here."

"It's *ouddahere*," Gina said, her phony laugh sounding weird even to her. She snatched her purse out of Rocky's grip. "Why can't I ever seem to teach you to talk like a real New Yorker, Harry, no matter how hard I try?" She turned to Ethan. "You know what? We'll send for our things later." Gina grabbed Harry's hand and they started for the door.

"Pretty cute, big city girl," Rocky said, moving to block their way. "Did you plan on hoofing it? You ain't going nowhere with that dead car of yours."

"That's enough!" Ethan's voice cut like steel through the back and forth taunts. "Where is the tablet, my flash drive? Give them to me right now and I'll let you go."

"That's bullshit, Ethan!" Harry pointed at the administrator. "You have no intention of letting us walk out of here."

Pete stepped forward, poked a finger into Harry's chest. "That's right! And I owe you big time, smart ass. I'm gonna get a big piece of you … chew you up, and spit you out. This is where your luck runs out, Lucke."

"Oh, fuck you, Pete. People have been telling me that my whole life, and I'm still here."

Rocky pointed at Pete. "He doesn't know what having a piece is, but I sure as hell do." He leered at Gina.

"That's enough, I said!" Ethan shouted. "This isn't a playground … just get rid of them!"

Harry leaped up and jump-kicked Pete in the chest, knocking him backwards, turned and bashed Rocky solidly in the jaw with his fist. Both orderlies went to the floor in rapid succession.

"Run, Gina!"

"Not without you."

As Rocky started to push himself up, Gina kicked him in the face.

"Let's move it!" Harry grabbed her by the hand.

They both started running for the door when a shot cut through the moment like a cannon.

"Far enough!" Ethan said. "Both of you come back over here."

Gina and Harry turned, looked first at Ethan, then at each other. They saw the administrator waving his pistol at them, first at one, then the other.

Ethan glanced down at Rocky and Pete, who were getting to their feet. "You're the most stupid, inept idiots I've ever had to deal with in my whole career."

"When I get through messing them up," Rocky said, "they'll give up that computer stuff. You can bet your ass on that."

"Who cares?" Ethan said with a sneer. "Once we get rid of them, it won't matter." He waved the gun again. "Can you possibly manage the rest of this without my help?"

"We'll take care of it," Rocky said, grabbing Gina's arm while Pete clamped a hand on the nape of Harry's neck. "Lookin' forward to it."

* * *

"You two are gonna regret the day you were born," Rocky said, as he tightened his grip on Gina's arm. His other hand rubbed his jaw where Harry had bashed him.

Riding down in the elevator, Rocky and Pete briefly whispered to each other. When they stepped out into the basement, they began moving toward the tunnel. The path became narrower and narrower until they were forced to walk single file. She could hear Pete still bad-mouthing Harry. She tried to look back, but all she got was a quick glimpse of Rocky's hate filled face.

They're going to kill us ... they have to. We know way too much about how the study's been rigged. Ethan made it plain— they can't take a chance on our getting damaging evidence out of here.

Rocky let go of her arm and began slapping her on the behind with an open hand, trying to get her to move faster.

"You better cut that out," she yelled, turning around to face him, balled up fists at her sides.

"Or you'll do what?" He squeezed her neck until she thought he would strangle her, or crack her vertebrae.

* * *

What she'd guessed was a tunnel, or corridor, was really a mine shaft. The ceiling was shored up with timbers and the side walls were bulging with mine tailings that poked through the rough-hewn boards. Plenty of rock and soil had already fallen from the ceiling. Gina wondered just how stable the whole place was. It made her queasy.

The mine floor was very uneven and she kept tripping over loose rocks. When they came to a Y, Rocky shoved her off to the right.

"Harry, are you there?"

There was no answer.

"Shut your mouth, bitch!"

Her legs were shaking and it was difficult to see—the light bulbs that lined the mine were not only dim, they were few and far between. Moving from light to light, she began to sense a horrible blackness closing in around her. She could barely breathe.

Rocky kept shoving her forward.

The deeper they went, more and more of the ceiling of dirt and rocks had collapsed. Some of it had been removed so they could walk through, but a lot of the debris was still in the way.

The path even narrowed more as they started on a sharp slant downward. She tried to control her breathing, but she was starting to pant; it felt like someone was sitting on her chest.

Where's Harry? Did Pete take him the other way at the Y?

She stopped in her tracks and turned to face Rocky, her anger and fear a hot coal inside. "Where's Harry?" she screamed in his face. "Do you hear me? Where's Harry, you big ape?"

He punched her in the mouth. Her purse went flying and she fell to the ground, teeth biting deep into her tongue. The metallic taste of blood filled her mouth and she tried to wipe it away; tears filled her eyes.

"I've fucking had enough of you, city girl."

She stared up at him hovering over her. Even in the dim light she could see a mean smile slashing across his face.

She'd been cornered like this before and knew what was coming. He pulled down his fly, reached into his pants. She jolted up and turned to run. He grabbed her, nails clawing her arm. He swung her around and threw her hard against the wall. Rocks tore into her shoulders and back.

"When I'm through with you, you won't give a shit about Harry … or anything else."

His cock was out of his pants and he was starting to yank her scrubs down. She kneed him in the groin as hard as she could. When he pulled away, she kicked his balls, once, then again. He fell like a bag of rice, lying across the pathway, blocking the exit. Croaking sounds filled the shaft.

She reached to scoop up her purse lying next to him, but he rolled over and his fingers encircled her ankle. She kicked out, then stomped on his hand over and over until she heard the snap of bones. His screams followed her as she grabbed her purse and ran deeper into the mine.

"I'll kill you, you bitch! I'll kill you!"

* * *

Harry was certain that Pete intended to follow Ethan's orders ... kill him.

The bastard kept stick-poking him in the back every time he tried to lessen the pace so he could slow everything down and think his way out of the situation.

But Pete was big and had a lot more heft and muscle than Harry. Even if he'd worked out day and night, he still wouldn't have been able to match the man's muscle mass and hitting power.

Harry tried to visualize the terrain above them—form some idea where they might be.

Probably behind Comstock where I scouted out before.

There was only one thing in Harry's favor—Pete was a slow thinker.

When they came to a Y, Pete shoved him to the left. He listened carefully, but he only heard Gina call out once.

Then there was nothing.

* * *

Gina ran fast and hard, but the rough terrain kept her tripping over rocks and broken pieces of timbers. She couldn't go back; Rocky would be there waiting for her. She'd gotten away once, but she knew it wasn't going to happen a second time.

The air was stale as she ran deeper and deeper into the mine shaft.

Should have listened to Harry when he was trying to teach me about the mines.

Harry! Where are you?

She was breathless, had to stop, had no idea how long she'd been running. She leaned over and rested her hands on her thighs while she tried to slow her breathing. It didn't help; she continued to gasp for air. It was useless, she couldn't take another step.

An eternity later she started moving again, slowly, drifting from one side of the mine shaft to the other, banging into the walls, not knowing where she was or what to do next. Her muscles were cramping; pain was stabbing every part of her.

The light bulbs were getting farther and farther apart until suddenly there was only the dimmest of light around her … and only blackness ahead.

Exhausted, she slumped to her knees, fell against the wall.

Chapter 36

Tuva was squeezed into the window seat of a 767. The plane was jam-packed; everyone was inhaling and exhaling the same stale air. Babies were screaming, and the kid behind her wouldn't stop kicking her seat.

It's like being in steerage ... the real designation of economy fare. Just once in my life I'd like to fly first class.

She clutched a book she'd bought at a Kennedy International kiosk. Why she ever thought she could read when she hated to fly was beyond her. Margaret Lucke's *House of Whispers* deserved more than sweaty fingers practically tearing off the cover with each air bump, large or small.

The plane began to bounce up and down, roll from side to side. The woman in the seat next to Tuva looked at her with sympathy. "It'll stop, dear, as soon as we get past the mountains."

"It would have been easier if I could have flown direct. Once up, once down. " She grabbed onto the armrests with both hands. "Stupid to be so freaked out, huh?"

The woman was somewhere in her fifties and had the brightest red hair Tuva had ever seen. "I used to be exactly the same way," she said.

"You look like you have it together now."

"Well, a really smart old lady told me something once and I've been fine with flying ever since."

Tuva laughed, but her heart was in her throat and she gave the book another sweaty squeeze. She couldn't help it. The lurching plane reminded her of another of her worst nightmares—roller coasters.

"What did she say?"

"When your time's up ... it's up." The woman chuckled and patted Tuva's hand. "It sounds corny, but one day you'll see the wisdom of it."

"I suppose." But right now she didn't. Nor did she think that old phrase was funny or terribly wise. "I'll have to think about that," she said, not wanting to be impolite. She turned back to the window and watched the layer of clouds below her, hiding any sign of land.

I must be crazy to just drop out of a new job and load up my credit card to run to Nevada.

But she kept staring out the window at the empty sky above, and the blob of clouds below.

No, there's something's wrong. I have to do this, find out for sure whether Mom is okay.

* * *

Tuva whizzed through the Reno airport, her carry-on rolling close behind her.

When she got to the Avis counter, one of the hottest guys she'd ever seen was handling customer requests. When it was her turn, she stepped up and almost fainted when the most gorgeous pair of aqua eyes met hers.

"Good morning. Welcome to Reno."

Her tongue felt fuzzy. It wouldn't move.

"Too much air time, huh?"

"Yeah. I've pretty much had it."

"Are you here on business?"

"No, it's a personal matter. I'll going to Carson City."

A look of disappointment crossed his face. "Well, let's get you out and moving. What kind of car do you have in mind, Ms. Goldmich?"

"Cheap."

Man, are those the whitest teeth in the universe, or what?

"I think I have just the car for you. How about a Ford Fiesta? Easy on the pocketbook but a decent ride." He laughed and she felt as though rainbows had fallen all over her. "I bet you'll love the bright red color."

They did all the paperwork. He gave her the keys and directions for picking up the car, and as she turned to go, he pulled out a business card. "If you end up spending any time in Reno, I'd love to hear from you."

"Thanks," she said, finally looking away from his face and taking in his name tag for the first time. "Carlos ... don't be surprised if I call."

"I'm counting on it."

* * *

Driving from Reno to Carson City was spectacular with the fall array of colors on the trees scattered throughout Washoe Valley. It made her realize how fantastic the West was, with its combination of empty spaces and hovering mountains. Then guilt hit her. Here she was enjoying herself when she should have been back at her drafting table in New York.

Carlos had suggested a reasonable motel at the edge of town and he'd called ahead for her. She drove into the Happy Sleeper parking lot and registered for three days. They let her into her room even though she was an early check-in. She rolled in her small suitcase, set it in the corner, and after tossing off her shoes, dove onto the bed.

She was awakened by the hot sunlight coming in through the window and shining on her face. She sat up with a start and looked at the clock-radio on the bed stand.

"Oh, my God! It's three o'clock already."

She jumped up and headed for the bathroom.

Half an hour later, she was in her car and on the way. The map showed Virginia City clearly, and she knew Comstock Medical was only a short distance before that.

But she drove past the turnoff and had to make a 180 when she reached the sign welcoming her to VC. Within a short time she found the actual road and wondered why the sign was so tiny and obscure for a supposedly major medical facility.

Moving down the entry road, she passed a continuous line of large boulders that seemed to absorb all the light and brightness from the sky. An uneasy feeling began to weigh down on her shoulders.

She parked in one of the three designated *Visitor* spaces in front of the building.

Looks like they didn't plan on too many people dropping by.

The building was far smaller than she'd expected. She had assumed it would be like a large hospital or institutional-type of building instead of this three-story structure.

She locked up the car and stared up at the second floor windows.

Bars?

As she stepped inside, she was sure she heard a buzz nearby. There was no reception desk.

She stood there trying to figure out what to do next when a man came out of an office down the hall and walked up to her.

"Is there something I can do for you, Miss? I'm Ethan Dayton, the Comstock administrator." His smile never touched his eyes and her first instinct was to turn around and leave as fast as she could.

"I'm Tuva Goldmich," she said just as formally. "I've come to see my mother, Emma Goldmich."

Ethan's face turned lead white. "Oh, yes!" He held out a hand.

"Why don't we go into my office?" He pointed down the hallway. "This *is* rather strange; I was just working on your mother's discharge papers. How fortuitous that you came here just now. Probably saved us a lot of back and forth telephone calls."

When she was seated in his office, he said, "Allow me a few minutes and I'll take you up to see her. I know she'll be happy to have you here."

After the administrator stepped out, Tuva exhaled all of her anxieties. She hadn't eaten much in the last 24 hours; it was probably what was making her jumpy.

It's going to be all right.

She smiled as she started planning her mom's temporary living arrangements—her mother would take the bedroom, Tuva would sleep on the couch. It would only be that way until she could work out a more permanent solution.

Tuva was happy and relaxed for the first time after three weeks of uncertainty and worry.

Life's pretty funny ... if I'd waited just a few more days, Mr. Dayton would have called me.

Oh, well. I'm glad I'm here.

She closed her eyes, but she was really high, couldn't wait for everything to come together, to finally see her mom after three long weeks.

As she opened her eyes, a fist slammed into her face and a large hand smashed against her nose and mouth. She fought to push it away, but it was useless; the person was too strong. She couldn't catch her breath... there was no air. Spots of red exploded in her head.

Help!

Her arm was yanked out, a stabbing pain jolted her.

Help! Can't breathe!

A jack hammer was drilling into her head; her heart was exploding.

Spinning ... spinning ... spinning ... turning black ... blacker.

Helpmehelpmehelpme!

Bette Golden Lamb & J. J. Lamb

Chapter 37

Carl Krueger and his wife Annie zoomed along the two-lane Geiger Grade in a Porsche Boxster. This is what he missed living in New York City—owning a car that hugged the curves like two lovers in a swelling climax.

Man, this is living.

The rental cost for the low-slung roadster was exorbitant, but Carl didn't care … the glorious drive up the twisting mountain grade made it worth every penny. Too bad he couldn't put the Porsche on his expense account. It would have been nice, but when you got right down to it, it didn't matter much—a great ride was a great ride.

The view as they circled the mountain?

Nothing to knock yourself out over. Just a bleak panorama of dried-up shrubs and scattered rocks of every conceivable size and shape.

Annie had barely spoken during the plane ride from New York to Reno. She'd just begun to indulge in monosyllabic conversation, but a big frown rode her forehead every time she looked at him.

"Sorry to drag you away," Carl said, "but there's something we have to talk about—"

"We can't talk in New York?"

"I don't think so. Actually, there're a couple of issues—"

"Uh hum."

"Anyway, I think you're going to like the Ore House in Virginia City. It's supposed to be a great little hotel from what I've read, and the meals are about as gourmet as they come in this part of the world."

241

He could see she wasn't buying into any of his limp preliminaries. When they came to a flat open area, he pulled off to the side of the road and turned to her. "Okay, Annie, let's talk."

She turned to face him. "About time, don't you think? Why I ever married a law officer is beyond me … silent … uptight. I've been sitting here wondering how long it would take you to just spill it out. Heck, I guess I'm lucky you didn't take me to Alaska."

Is she yanking my chain, or what?

He felt indignant, but was trying to avoid a fight so he let her comment ride.

"Annie?"

"Oh, for God's sake will you please say what you need to say? You've been impossible the past two weeks." She reached for his hand. "What is it, Carl?"

He let it all fall out like a big cow plop. "I've transferred out of OCI to go back to my old FBI unit in LA." He was wincing so hard he could feel his face scrunching as he waited for the hammer to fall. "I mean, I feel really bad. I know you love New York—"

She held her hand up to stop him. Her fair skin was blanched, if that was possible, or was it the sun shining on her face?

"You think I don't know you, Carlie?"

"Well … yeah, I guess you do after all these years."

"I knew New York and I were living on borrowed time. An LA brat like you can't live without his car and the beach."

"But what about you, Annie?"

She leaned over and kissed him on the cheek. "I like New York a lot better than you do. But I've done all the museums; Central Parked myself silly; and shopped all the stores. There was no sense my really getting involved in a job since I knew sooner or later we were going to end up back in California. I was beginning to get tired waiting for the hammer to fall, so I started looking around for a job and got that appointment for an interview at Bloomingdales."

"But, baby, I thought you really loved being there."

"Well, yeah. I like New York; the people are a kick; and its energy is a real turn-on." She threw her arms around his neck. "But I'm as much an LA kook as you are. And besides, I want you to be happy. I can work anywhere."

* * *

They unpacked the few pieces of clothing they'd brought and Annie sprawled out on the bed.

"There's more to it, isn't there, Carl?"

He'd poured them each a glass of the complimentary Zinfandel and took a sip. "Man this is pretty damn good."

She gave him that look that always made his heart almost stop.

I swear, the woman's a witch.

He told her about Tuva Goldmich.

"Don't try to kid a kidder, Carl. That would never be enough to get you on a plane to come to Nevada. Especially since you don't gamble."

"You're right, Annie. I mean, I feel for the woman but that whole business with clinical trials is pretty well regulated. There's probably a good reason she hasn't heard from her mom."

"Well, what is it then?"

"I spoke to one of the partners at Zelint Pharmaceuticals, the company behind the trials. And, I swear, there's something *off* with that operation."

"Something *off?* Merely from a telephone call?" Annie smiled at him.

"Yeah, I know, that's pretty lame."

"Did you call the regional office of OCI before dragging us half way across the country?"

"I did, but they're so backed up with cases they'll never get to it. Besides, I promised Tuva Goldmich I would follow up. I don't know what's the matter with me, but I don't want to let that woman down."

"Aren't you the one who told me to never make promises you can't keep?"

"I think that's why I dragged us out here."

But she wasn't listening anymore. She laid back, brought her arms overhead, and gave him that look again. This time it sucked his mouth dry. He slid onto the bed next to her, barely able to breathe. When she lifted his shirt, goose bumps trailed behind her nails as they rode up and down his back; his hand wandered across her smooth skin, found its way to her inner thigh.

"Have I told you lately that you're the love of my life?"

"Never often enough, Carlie."

* * *

Carl and Annie had walked themselves out traveling up and down the boardwalk in Virginia City when Carl came to a stop in front of a small gun shop. It was tucked in between two much larger buildings; he'd almost missed it.

"Let's go inside and poke around," he said, pulling her in with him.

"You men and your guns. You have your service revolver and that teeny thing you wear on your ankle at home. Why are we looking at more guns?"

"Because I've always wanted to own one of those western six-shooters."

The shop was even smaller than it appeared on the outside. The man behind the counter wore a large western hat and his jacket and shirt had cowboy cuts; a bolo tie held a large, mottled turquoise stone in the center.

The man's fingers were large and meaty; all but the thumbs were encircled with silver rings set with turquoise stones, rings like the ones in the showcase where his hands rested. Along side the display of rings was an impressive array of beautiful beaded and turquoise Indian bracelets and necklaces.

Carl could see Annie admiring all the exclusive Indian artifacts, while he was eying the hefty prices attached to them.

His gaze traveled up the walls that were covered with antique Colts of every description and condition, mostly excellent.

"Help you?" the man said in a quiet voice. Carl could sense he was probably the kind of man who never bluffed at poker, and rarely lied.

"Interesting store you have here."

"I like it."

"Where do you get all these old-timers?" Carl said, pointing at the guns.

"Oh, I travel from show to show throughout the Southwest. Pick up one piece here and another there." He gave Carl a half-smile. "People inherit them … got no use for them … sell their collections to me. I love them old guns."

"What's the price range?" Annie asked.

He could see the man didn't much like a woman butting in. Carl wrapped an arm around her waist and kissed her on the cheek to let the owner know where things stood.

"Well now, I could sell you a Colt SAA. 44 S&W, pre-war, single-action Army revolver for about $75,000 bucks." His quote was accompanied by something that could be called a dry laugh. "But I'll have to go into the vault for that one."

"Ah, save yourself the trip," Carl said. "That's way out of my league."

"Is this your first antique Western?"

"Yep! Always wanted one."

"Well, why don't we start you with a 1917 Colt double action 38?"

"What are you asking?" Carl asked, holding his breath.

"Let's see: polished stainless, no pitting, bore is clean, action is tight, and it's firm overall. A nice piece." As he spoke, he reached under the counter and brought out a clean-looking pistol with pearl grips "I'll let you have it for six hundred and fifty."

Carl picked up the pistol, cocked the trigger, and spun the empty barrel. "Action feels good, like you said." He could afford the money and he really wanted it.

"Why don't I throw in a box of ammo?"

Carl carefully uncocked the hammer, set the pistol down on the counter. "You got yourself a deal. And while you're at it," he pointed to a turquoise and red-beaded bracelet that Annie had been eyeing, "let's have a look at that, too."

Annie's smile was like a beautiful sunrise.

As they were leaving the shop, Carl turned around and said to the owner, "Say, have you heard of the Comstock Medical facility? It's supposed to be around here someplace."

"Yeah, I heard."

Carl waited, gave him the time he needed to come up with more of an answer. It took him a few moments.

"If I were you … I wouldn't send anyone I knew up there." And there was that dry laugh again.

"Oh? Anything else?"

"Thanks for the business. Come back when you're ready to add another piece to your collection."

Chapter 38

Gina blinked, rubbed hard at her eyes, blinked again. She saw only the emptiness of being totally blind in the dark.

Confused, she jolted to a sitting position and groped out in front of her.

What happened? I must have passed out.

A stale smell of mold settled around her as the memory of where she was hit home.

"Oh, my God!" She remembered she was in this creepy inkiness below the ground. Buried in a mine, deep in the earth.

How do I get out of here?

She started to shiver, rocked back and forth. Her sobs echoed throughout the heavy silence.

Don't think about it, Mazzio. Move! Just keep moving!

Move where? I can't see a thing.

She was panting, her breaths a loud rasp that came faster and faster until she grew faint. She was so light headed she knew her erratic breathing had to normalize or she would pass out again.

Stop it! Get a grip!

She forced herself to breathe slowly, deeply. She pushed herself up onto her knees, and ran her fingers across the dirt. Her purse had to be somewhere nearby, didn't it?

A frantic 360 sweep brought nothing but silt that rose up and made her choke—it hung in the air all around her, clogging her nose and throat. And there was nothing else on the ground but a scattering of rocks that bruised her searching fingers.

Standing on shaking legs, she reached out to steady herself, touched the mine wall. and felt something crawl across her wrist.

"Oh God!" She was surprised to hear her voice resound around her. She shook away whatever the creature was and stepped back. At least it hadn't bitten her.

She muttered, "Forget that! Concentrate on getting out of here."

With baby steps, she shuffled toward the other side—her toe side-swiped something. She crouched and swept a hand across the floor again. Her purse! She clutched it to her chest for a moment before frantically rummaging inside.

Where is it? Where is that damn little flashlight, that stupid gift they gave us on Nurses Appreciation Day?

She'd kept meaning to throw the thing away but like most things that went into her purse, it never came out.

Her hand closed over her cell phone.

"Thank God!"

She flipped it open and it gave up just enough light to tell her that the battery was dying. As if she didn't already know, it advised her that there was *No Service*. Then it gave up the ghost altogether. The light went out. Blackness quickly surrounded her again.

Why do I keep forgetting to turn that thing off?

She rummaged through her purse again, fingers digging into every corner, finding emery boards, keys, lipsticks, a small rock, paper clips and every other useless item you could think of. Then, there it was, the tiny flashlight. She yanked it out and pressed hard on the end of it.

Nothing.

Her heart almost stopped.

What was she going to do without light? Blind, she could only wander aimlessly until she died, if not from fright, from dehydration.

She closed her eyes and envisioned the metallic red gizmo in her hand. Then she remembered—you have to twist it in the middle for it to function. The moment she did that, a small powerful beam of halogen light slashed through the darkness.

She wanted to kiss it.

Holding the light to the ground, she could see where her footprints came from, where she'd fallen.

If she could only turn around and go back, find Harry, and run away. But that wasn't going to happen. Rocky would be waiting for her. He'd kill her on the spot.

She couldn't take the chance.

Even if he was gone, he could have locked her in the tunnel. She would still have to find a new way out.

Gina started moving in the same direction she'd been going.

* * *

Pete hustled Harry along with the stick, constantly poking him in the back. He knew it wouldn't be long before the orderly made his move. Probably first beat the shit out of him just for the joy of it, then kill him. Or maybe knock him out, lock him up, and leave him to rot. Either way, he was going to be dead.

Pete's Maglite led the way, giving off enough light to allow them to move rapidly through the tunnel. Harry tried to study the path, get a sense of where he was being taken. But his mind kept picturing Gina trapped somewhere underground. Every time he thought of her, he wanted to shout out her name. But he knew she couldn't hear him.

The Maglite's beam bounced off the walls, the ceiling, the ground. The mine was in terrible shape. Every step sent up a cloud of powdery dirt. He could see the deterioration of the splintered shoring in the ceiling and realized how close to collapse the passage must be. This was an old, old mine. It would be a miracle if it didn't disintegrate around them just from the vibrations of their voices or their stomping around.

The orderly was slowing down and Harry spotted another Y in the distance. One of the entrances was only about three feet high. This had to be where Pete was taking him. He'd probably shove him in that hole and leave him. There was no more time to save himself. This was it?

In one fluid motion, Harry spun around, yanked the stick from Pete's grip, and aimed the pointed end at his trachea. Pete's legs gave way; a look of disbelief distorted his face. He tried to talk, but only high whistling sounds rode his rapid breath.

Harry had crushed his larynx.

Jeez, the guy's an ox. What are you waiting for? Hit him again before he gets it together and kills you.

Harry looked at Pete's stricken face.

Do it!

Pete was clutching the front of his neck, his eyes wide and terrified. He tried to get up, his high-pitched squeaks filling the tunnel with each attempt. But he couldn't make it; he kept falling back. Harry knew the man would soon starve for oxygen and die; he was never going anywhere again.

Harry grabbed the Maglite from Pete's hand, held it like a bat, and aimed for the orderly's neck, thinking to finish him off with a final blow.

But he couldn't do it. Couldn't look in the man's eyes. Couldn't straight out kill him.

Instead, he grasped the flashlight and walked away.

Chapter 39

The pain in Rocky's hand was vibrating up his arm; his groin felt as though someone had castrated him.

He limped back to the Y where the tunnels had split, slammed shut a heavy ceiling-to-floor metal gate on the right side and secured it with a heavy-duty padlock that was hanging open in the hasp. That would take care of the Mazzio bitch.

He started to limp away, but stopped and went back to the other branch of the Y; the one Pete had taken Harry down.

"Petey, are you in there?"

There was only an echo.

He slammed the rusted gate shut and locked it, too, but he screamed with pain from the jarring movements.

Gotta get outta here. Get some help.

The trip back to the elevator and up to Ethan's office was excruciating. He limped into the room.

"What happened to you?" Ethan said, sitting at his desk.

Likin' this, aren't you? Nasty fucker.

Rocky held up his damaged hand. Ethan eyed the two misshapen, discolored fingers.

"You mean a woman did that to you?"

Rocky wanted to smash him in the mouth, but he'd probably end up with both hands fucked up.

"Forget about those two nurses," Rocky said. "They're finished. I locked the mine down. Ain't no one coming out or going in without this." He reached into his pocket with his good hand and pulled out a key.

"Where's Pete?"

"Fuck Pete. My hand needs fixin'. Now!"

Ethan gave him a measured look—like he was buying a bull for breeding. "Maybe we better do that … fix those fingers before they swell up anymore. Or, if you want, I'll take you down to the hospital in Carson." Ethan shrugged. "It's up to you."

"God dammit! Do something *now*. Can't you see I'm dying?"

* * *

"Why do we have to do it here?" Rocky said, looking around the lab. "All those things in the jars ... nothing but weird shit."

"This is where all the medical supplies are stored ... don't think it would be a good idea for the two of us to go puttering around in one of the second-floor units." He raised Rocky's injured hand. "Sit still and keep that arm elevated so your fingers don't swell up anymore."

"I'd like it better on one of the units. I don't like lookin' at those things ... they give me the creeps."

Ethan laughed, but he had that same indifferent look he'd had in the office. Rocky didn't trust him.

Ethan pointed at the disgusting organs in the jars. "Think of it as a different sort of beauty all around us. The brain and its parts have an almost poetic, lyrical, rhythm of their own. Cerebellum ... medulla oblongata ... pons varolii. Don't you think those words are almost musical?"

"Nothing pretty about that stuff ... or those doctor words. I don't wanna think about it." Rocky looked away from the jars; he'd seen too much already. He sniffed at the air. "Smells like there was a fire in here."

"I had to put out a fire. I was burning some papers and the flames almost got away from me." Ethan was now rummaging through his small medicine cabinet. "But it worked out all right."

He seemed to find what he was looking for, sat down, and pulled bottle of bourbon from a drawer. He poured a water glass half full, opened the bottle of pills, and dumped most of them into the liquor.

"What's that? You ain't planning on poisoning me, are you?"

"It will help the pain when I set your fingers."

"Listen, old man: I'm not taking just anything *you* give me. Let me see that bottle! I don't want you putting me down like you did all the others."

Ethan brought the bottle of pills and held it up so Rocky could see the label: Morphine Sulfate 200 mgs. Rocky smiled when he read it.

"Awright! That ought to do it. And I could sure use a shot of booze, too, right about now anyways."

"So what happened to Pete? I haven't seen him since he took that male nurse away." Ethan opened one of the drawers and brought out several tongue depressors and tape. "I'm worried about him."

"Petey can take care of himself." He was getting tired of holding his hand up, but it did seem to ease the throbbing. "That puny man-nurse ain't gonna give him much trouble."

"Did you say you locked up the mine shaft where he took Harry?"

Rocky was starting to have second thoughts about having locked down that mine. "I called out ... he didn't answer."

Ethan was looking at him in that funny way again. "Do you suppose you locked him in?"

Rocky thought about it. "Oh, shit! I was hurting so damn much, guess I didn't think it out."

Ethan nodded. "It will only take a short time to fix those two fingers. So let's clean your hand first, then we'll go check on Pete."

"Ain't you gonna give me that morphine? Shit! I really need it, man."

"As soon as we clean your hand," Ethan said.

Rocky was really worried now. He needed to get back to that mine and let Pete out if he was locked in.

Ethan finished washing off his hand.

"How about that drink now?" Rocky said, motioning at the glass with his head.

"Let me just get everything ready." Ethan moved the supplies to a tray, rolled it next to Rocky, and handed him the morphine concoction. "Down the hatch, Rocky."

The pills had dissolved; Rocky swallowed the mixture in two huge gulps. It seared its way down his throat, and landed like lava in his stomach.

Ethan moved very quickly now. He pressed the two injured fingers together and splinted both sides with the tongue blades, then wrapped tape around them. It couldn't have taken him more than a couple of minutes. His fingers felt like he was in a cast.

"How's that? Better?" Ethan said.

Rocky's hand still hurt like hell—the morphine hadn't kicked in yet. He got up from the chair, but his legs were weak and he was lightheaded.

"Let's go find Pete," Ethan said.

Chapter 40

Emma Goldmich was filled with hope. The nurse, Gina, had brought her only child back into her life. Now, if only she could live to see her one more time.

Where is she? How is she doing? Will I hear from her again soon?

It was difficult to focus on anything else.

She fingered her locket, the one with Tuva's picture inside; just touching it made her feel better. She opened it and looked at her daughter's image, then closed it again. Open, close, open, close.

For the first time she noticed that the hospital floor seemed unusually quiet. On most days, Rocky would come in and out of her room to taunt her with nasty, hate-filled words about old people.

Old ... useless. Why don't you just die, you old bitch?

Mean words that always made her feel less than human. But even he wasn't around today. Now that she thought about it, she hadn't seen him all day. Not that she missed him, but the silence was strange, disorienting.

She was starting to lose focus again. She repeated her name over and over, tried to make herself think constructively.

Emma, Emma, Emma.

She forced herself to roll from side to side on her bed; repeated her name again.

Emma, Emma, Emma, Emma.

The movement caused terrible pain, but the more she moved, the better she felt. After a while, the pain eased.

Had she only imagined that Gina brought a letter from her daughter? Had Tuva *really* written to her? Had it *really* happened?

Was it true that the administrator had kept Tuva's letters from her? Why would he do such a terrible thing? Questions and more questions.

Delores was talking outside her room. She was talking to someone whose voice Emma didn't recognize.

"Something's going on," Delores said. "The administrator doesn't usually poke his head in here."

"Heck," the stranger's voice said, "anyplace I've ever worked, we usually can't get rid of them."

"Well," Delores said, "we better give these shots. This ought to knock them out. They'll all sleep pretty good after this."

Emma didn't like Delores, but she especially didn't like the way she was talking tonight. Emma wasn't going to take a shot. She'd refuse. No matter how much pain she had, she wouldn't take it.

Then Delores was next to her bed.

"Time for your shot, Emma."

"I don't want it! Leave me alone." Emma started scooting away from the nurse to the other side of the bed. She kept her rump flat against the mattress.

"Now I don't want to be mean to you, Emma, but you're getting this shot … like it or not!"

She grabbed Emma's arm, pulled her back near her, roughly pushed aside her clothes, and jabbed hard with the needle.

"You'll get a good sleep, Emma." And with that, the nurse left the room.

Tears rolled down Emma's face. She refused to think about Delores. Instead, she closed her eyes and visualized her daughter. In a few minutes she started to doze and was floating away, doing things with Tuva.

The two of them were in a narrow hallway and it was very, very dark. She could barely see where they were going. Tuva's movements were slow and sluggish. She was in trouble. Some kind of trouble.

"Stop! Don't go there! Tuva! We have to go back!"

Tuva let out a piercing scream and fell into a black hole. She watched from above and saw herself drop down after her daughter.

She sat up in bed; her body screamed in pain from the sudden movement.

"Help my daughter! Someone help her!"

* * *

Tuva groaned and tried to turn but she couldn't move—some invisible force kept her flat on her back.

Snippets of visions came and went, along with shadowy people who appeared and disappeared as they floated through her head.

One time she was in a hospital, lying on a stretcher. Harsh male voices were above and around her. They kept speaking her name, talking back and forth about her. She could see herself, half awake, trying to catch a glimpse of them. But her head became heavy and she fell back. The men became blurry phantoms again. She needed to concentrate, but each time she almost grabbed onto what the men were saying, even understand a sentence, she'd drift off and the scene would change. Now, in a new vision, the same people, with the same voices, were pushing, shoving her around. When they lifted her and carried her, every part of her body ached.

With a suddenness that made her head spin, she was tossed into the air, then landed hard on her back.

She screamed as something stabbed into her flesh.

Then everything went black.

* * *

Tuva opened her eyes. She was wide awake now; she tried to remember what had happened to her. She'd come into the building where her mother was supposed to be and the administrator had taken her into his office. He'd stepped out and someone grabbed her from behind, covered her face, A strong-smelling chemical

257

had burned its way through her nose and mouth. After that, everything went blank until she woke up here.

Now every inch of her body felt beaten.

She couldn't see very well, was still trying to adjust to the very dim light. She rubbed hard at her eyes, turned to look around, and stared into two empty eye sockets, and a gaping hole where a nose should have been.

Tuva screamed, then over and over until no sound escaped her mouth.

She tried to back away, move away from those empty eyes, but kept sinking lower with every movement. Dead people kept closing in until she was caught between shifting bodies and splintered bones. She was trapped in a huge pit ... a pit with sheered-off walls, and a top that was way, way above her.

Frantic, she tried to sit up, but pieces of decapitated skulls kept rolling onto and over her. Everything was moving like an ocean wave filled with putrid, rotting bodies. Soon she would go down and drown in this terrible pit.

She yelled at the top of her lungs.

"Let me out! I have to get out! Please let me out!"

She took a step and started to fall. Then the lights blinked and went out.

Chapter 41

By the time they got to the tunnel, Rocky was stumbling; his legs didn't want to work right; they got heavier and heavier. Ethan was poking at him, shouldering him to keep him upright and going.

Man, that morphine's strong. Can't even feel my feet no more. Shit! Ain't complaining. At least the fuckin' pain's gone.

Rocky's mind kept wandering, thinking back. He saw himself in Montana … the sky a pretty blue. He hadn't thought about that for a long time. It distracted him and he stopped to look at his fingers. They looked strange. Blue fingers? Well, the tips were blue … or were they purple? Couldn't see the rest. They were wrapped with those flat sticks and tape. Oh, yeah, tongue blades.

Tongue blades on fingers don't seem right.

Blades of green grass. That's where blades belonged.

Blades of grass.

He was runnin' across a grassy meadow, Petey was right behind him … they were little boys. And there was that big hill comin' … their legs were pumping, they were panting so hard.

Stop it, Petey! Stop pushing me!

He turned.

"Ethan?"

"Keep moving, Rocky!"

Ethan was panting in his ear, working hard to hold Rocky up. "You know, Rocky … haven't really had a chance to thank you … and Pete … for everything you've done for me … without the two of you … I'd never have been able … to bring this whole thing off."

Rocky thought those were strange sounding words. "What thing off?"

"You know, taking care of the patients … making sure the nurses stayed in line."

259

"You mean bumping off them half-dead suckers?" Rocky barked out a laugh. "Ain't much different from killin' a chicken."

Made Rocky think how he wanted to do a thing or two to Ethan. The man kept forcing him along when all he wanted to do was crash for a while.

As soon as I get Petey out of the mine, we'll take care of the bastard. Hell, maybe I didn't even lock my buddy Petey in there. Maybe he's out front waiting for me right now, waiting to go get a brewsky.

"Ha." He wanted to laugh, but it turned into a soft mutter. Petey go back without him? Nah, he'd have to carry on about takin' out the male nurse, making a big thing out of it, especially since that nurse almost beat the shit out of him.

Yeah, I must have locked him in. Damn!

He stopped and started laughing, an uncontrollable roar. It *was* pretty funny. "I locked Petey in the mine. Wow! What a fuckin' stupid thing to do. He's really gonna be pissed at me."

"Yes, I suppose he will be," Ethan said.

Rocky's head felt funny, like it was lifting off his shoulders. He was pretty damn high—so high, his heart was trying to fight its way out of his chest, sweat was dripping off his hands.

I'm sweating like a pig.

He continued laughing, going on and on until he couldn't stop.

"What's so funny," Ethan asked, but kept nudging him forward.

"Sweating like a pig." Rocky kept laughing, laughing so hard he could barely get the words out. "Don't you hear it? Sweating like…" Then he couldn't remember why that was so funny.

Ethan was shoving him hard, and Rocky was having trouble getting his legs to move. He couldn't see real well in the dim light and the mine floor seemed to be changing like the rippling waves at the beach. He kept stumbling over rocks as he tried to squeeze through the narrowing walls of the mine.

He needed to sit down, rest a while.

"Come on, Rocky. We're almost there."

"Goddam, my chest hurts … there ain't enough air in here."

"Look ahead, see, there's the Y. See it? And there's the mine gate." Ethan slipped a hand in Rocky's pants pocket and took out the key.

"I'm gonna just sit for a while. You go ahead and let Petey out."

"Are you sure he didn't go back to the units?"

"No! Not without me. Not Petey. We were going to meet here after takin' care of those stupid nurses. He wouldn't go back without me. Not Petey." Did he say that before? His words trailed off … not without …"

Ethan grabbed him under his arms and dragged him to the Y.

"Hey, whadda … you..." Rocky didn't think that sounded right, but his mouth didn't want to move like it should.

He was sprawled in the dirt; he watched Ethan open the iron gate part way on the left side. The loud, rasping sound echoed in Rocky's head. His brain was on fire, flashes of red burned behind his eyes.

"Are you sure this is the mine he went into?"

"Yazz."

Ethan came back for him, pulled him into the mine shaft. Silt clogged his nose until he could barely grab a breath.

Rocky wanted to lift his arms, wanted to stop Ethan.

Gonna beat the mothafuckin' bastard.

But every part of him felt like lead—heavy and dead.

"Like I said, you and Pete have helped me a lot, but at the same time the two of you have been nothing but … as *you* would say, fuckups. And you're both very stupid not to see this coming. Someone with the brains of a snake could see you'd need to be taken care of at some point. And by the way, Rocky, that amount of morphine and liquor you had, would probably have brought down a Clydesdale … you know, those giant horses? Consider the booze a farewell gift."

"Hey, whadda … you—"

Ethan leaned over him. "Don't bother, Rocky. It's all too difficult for you. Just close your eyes and it'll all be over in a few minutes."

Ethan started to lock the huge gate, and as it almost clanked shut, he said, "Thanks for saving me the job of having to take care of your buddy Pete."

Flashes of red fireworks attacked Rocky's burning brain. It was like the fires of hell, whipping at him in the near darkness. He could barely hear, or even understand Ethan's last words.

"Rocky, my boy, you're a scholar and a gentleman."

But the laugh that followed was loud and clear.

* * *

Getting the gate in position again almost did Ethan in. It was very heavy; Ethan's grunts were loud as he shoved it closed, sealing Rocky inside—alone in the dark for the last moments of his life.

He wasn't a bit sorry for the fool. Given the chance, Rocky would have snuffed Ethan out without a moment's hesitation. Ethan's only regret was the lost opportunity to examine the Neanderthal's brain tissue under the electronic microscope. He might have been good for *something*.

The thought amused him.

He was still panting hard. Exhaustion was starting to seep into every part of his body; he could barely move his legs. He leaned on the wall and inched back down the passageway to the laboratory.

He would have to get his computer—it held all of his personal research notes, plus each and every step of the AZ-1166 drug study, both the unofficial record for the FDA, and the actual data.

His mind drifted; it was difficult to concentrate.

Where on earth could the two travel nurses have hidden his flash drive?

Forget it. What difference does it make? Both of them are dead, along with everyone else that knew the truth.

262

Truth?

The truth was, he needed to move faster. Even with all of his machinations, he knew there was only a small window of time for escape. Sooner or later it would all come out. He was betting he had at least enough time to get out of the country.

* * *

When Ethan finally walked into the lab, he cringed at the sight of the mess he'd left while cleaning Rocky's hand. Dirty 4x4s, broken tongue depressors, the empty glass that had held the killing dose of morphine.

He carefully put everything back in its place—unused dressings into the small cabinet, the few pills left of morphine in the medicine cabinet. He couldn't seem to help himself—he even compulsively cleaned the table where Rocky had rested his hands to have his fingers fixed.

Why was he doing all of this?

He sat down again, too weak to move on.

He thought about the two orderlies.

Both men had been psychotic and every one of the nurses knew it—none of them ever stayed more than three months. Every last one of them, except Delores, left after complaining about Rocky and Peter.

Especially Rocky.

The man was violent to women from the day Ethan hired him. He'd had to pay large sums of money to squash rape charges that otherwise would have been brought against not only Rocky, but Comstock; maybe even Zelint.

When he once asked Rocky why he couldn't stop hurting women, the orderly looked at Ethan like he was an idiot.

"I don't like 'em … don't trust 'em, and the only thing they're good for is fuckin'."

Well, Gina Mazzio didn't have big muscles like Rocky and Pete, but she did have a brain and knew how to use it. They were both done in because of a woman.

There's some kind of poetic justice there, if I was willing to search for it. Too tired to care.

Ethan stood, grabbed the printed confirmation of his plane ticket and put it in his jacket pocket. The first leg would take him from Reno to San Francisco, then on to Buenos Aires. At least that city had a huge population. They would have many subjects for his future studies.

A whole new world of opportunity.

He'd hardly done any traveling. Becoming an MD and practicing his specialty had taken up a good chunk of his life. The rest of his time always seemed to be about his job and the fascination of research. Over the years all that hard work and no play, no wife to spend his money, had made him a very rich man. He had enough money to go anywhere in the world.

A sudden dizziness caused him to stumble to the desk. He held on until the room stopped spinning and he could ease himself into the chair again.

Done in.

He needed time to regain the strength he'd lost lugging Rocky into the mine. Ethan massaged his aching shoulders and at the same time forced himself to take deep, deep breaths. But he knew it wasn't only the exertion of dealing with the orderly exhausting him. For weeks he'd been working double time getting ready to wrap up the Comstock facility for Zelint. They were right down to the wire, terminating patients at break-neck speed. He wanted every one of those subjects so he could study their brains. But it had been too much work and it was destroying him.

David Zelint had become a frantic reminder of how it was all closing down. The man had started plaguing Ethan, insisting that he tidy things up before the pending FDA hearing.

Yes, they'd finally gotten a real presentation date.

"No loose ends," were the very words David had used. And the way he'd said it had rankled Ethan.

No loose ends? Tidying up? Cleaning up? All euphemisms that David used for killing off the rest of the patients on the units. David expected Ethan to dispose of them. That man didn't care about the answers to the burning questions that seared Ethan's mind. No, he sat in his pristine office and expected Ethan to do all the dirty work, clean up the final mess at Comstock; clean up everything that could sink AX-1166 and the company that created it.

Did I tie up all the loose ends? Yes, David, I tied up the loose ends.

Gina Mazzio, Harry Lucke, Tuva Goldmich, the two orderlies. That part was tied up. All of them gone.

And they were lost opportunities; human material that might have provided answers to the burning questions about Alzheimer's. Brains that Ethan would never get his hands on now.

He reached into the second desk drawer and lifted out two boxes of his prepared slides—all stained specimens from living tissue. Within these very cells, real answers might exist; solutions to uncovering the hidden secrets to the Alzheimer's puzzle.

And all the others? The remaining participants here at Comstock?

Not my problem anymore.

That was one loose end Zelint Pharmaceuticals would have to deal with.

And as far as David Zelint was concerned?

Goodbye

Chapter 42

Harry had always known his mine-hopping hobby would get him into trouble one day—who could imagine it would happen smack in the middle of a nursing assignment? If someone had even hinted at it, well, he would have laughed his head off. Yet, here he was on a new job, locked up in a mine with no way out.

He couldn't help but think about all those stories of people lost in the abandoned hard-rock mines in Alaska, or in mines of the eleven other Western States. He'd heard just about every one of those tales. He believed them, because most unoccupied mines were open and untended—provocative invitations to adventurous thrill-seekers of the mysterious world of the underground.

Once he and his brother were in a huge old mine, could have driven a truck into it. They were on the way out when the mine's ceiling gave way. It was the loudest noise Harry had ever heard. A roar and rumble of sound that blew out enough dust and bad air to keep them coughing for hours afterward. He could still remember the noise of dirt and rock dumping onto a floor that still held the recent imprint of their footsteps.

The four-cell flashlight he'd taken off of Pete was heavier than he was used to, but in the surrounding darkness, it was good to have the greater power. It helped make him feel better, less anxious about the mysterious sounds around him.

He was more than a little uneasy about stepping over the dying Pete. The man's wide-open eyes burned holes in his flesh as they followed Harry's every move. Worse, the whistling in the orderly's throat, from his crushed larynx along with the struggle of his body trying to get a lung-full of air, really spooked Harry. As he moved along, he refused to look back at those eyes. He knew they would follow him while he hurried back to the Y where they'd come into the mine.

Back at the Y, instead of finding the exit he'd expected to find, the opening was blocked by an immovable prison-like iron gate.

Rocky must have locked it ... would he do that to his buddy? Maybe Ethan...

He turned back and had to pass Pete again. This time, the man's eyes were closed. Harry stopped and checked for a pulse even though the air-starved squeak had stopped. He knew Pete wasn't breathing.

Why am I bothering?

Was he feeding a sadistic ogre that lived inside of him? Because, pulse or no pulse, Harry was never going to do a thing to save the bastard's life.

He patted Pete's pockets. There were no keys. Whoever did it probably wanted to keep him from getting out. But what was the rationale for locking in Pete, whether it was Rocky or Ethan?

How many times had he thought about things like that, knowing, accepting that even though he was a nurse who dealt with human beings day after day, he still didn't really understand people? Maybe he never would.

Why did they do such despicable things to each other?

In his job, he'd seen real generosity and sacrifice among family and friends, even strangers stepping forward to help someone they'd never met before. And in the next breath, they would commit hateful acts.

Most days, he tried to have a wait-and-see attitude, and to be the best kind of nurse he could be. The best kind of person. He'd even dared to think his motives were pure.

Yet, he'd just killed a man.

His mouth was bone dry; he tried not to think about dead Pete, tried not to think about Gina alone with Rocky. If he did, those thoughts would crush him quicker than the mine.

Picking up the pace, he walked with a steady stride, broken only by his own clumsiness.

He *would* get out.

Even if the flashlight died, he would crawl out on his hands and knees.

He *would* get out.

He directed the light at the shoring above him, which looked ready to collapse here, too.

An unexplainable chill jolted him. There was something ruffling the mine atmosphere. It was weird, like everything was squeezing, sucking in the air all around him.

He tried to ignore it and continued to walk as the tunnel turned 180-degrees, reversing on itself. Harry assumed he was now facing in the same direction as when they'd originally entered. At least, it felt that way.

His heart was racing and his breath was rapid. A sudden deadly panic drilled into his chest. Then he knew why. That sound—there it was! The sound he'd only heard once before— with his brother.

Not loud at first, more like the creaking or groaning of an old porch. With a shaking hand, he shone the light above, inspected overhead for as far as he could see. Above, the sagging timbers were drooping into a critical point of no return.

"Nooooo!"

He took a deep breath and ran.

He was still running when the roar and rumble of the collapse filled the mine.

The sound of tons of rock and dirt blew through his ears as it fell. A solid wall of debris was at his back, close at his heels, as it entombed the mine behind him and tried to drag him in.

And then it stopped.

Harry kept running, but the silence and his heaving chest finally made him stop. As he looked back, he couldn't help feeling that any quick movements on his part could send some kind of vibration to the collapsed pile. And maybe next time the mine would claim him.

Dazed, he turned and pointed the flashlight down the tunnel at the fallen wall of dirt. As he clutched the Maglite, he saw the dirt shiver, start to move toward him. The rush of dirt was still coming for him.

The racket behind kept him running; the mine was shrinking over his head, pressing closer around him. He ran harder until the shoring was right on top of his head and he had to tuck his arms in close because the walls were squeezing into him. Finally, he was down on his knees, leading with only one shoulder, barely getting through an opening.

He finally stopped.

The silence behind him was deafening. The mine had stopped filling itself in. But he was trapped. There was no place for him to go.

Chapter 43

The deeper Gina moved into the mine, the more a sense of finality, a feeling of doom pressed down on her. She stopped, stood on shaking legs, wondered if she would ever escape from this endless nothingness.

The mine held her in its belly, and it was not silent. Creepy, eerie sounds surrounded her, and she jumped at every one. It was like being in a haunted house, where a suffering unseen entity was taunting her. The groaning, rasping creaks warned that Gina would suffer, would writhe in pain. It told that *this* is where she would die.

Gina had seen her patients die. For some it was a fight to the very end; for others, it was a strange, ethereal acceptance. But her own experiences of almost being murdered remained closeted in the depths of her soul, rarely examined. Had her pounding heart ever crashed in her ears like this? Had every step brought this sense of an unknown that could reach out with strangling tentacles; tighten its grip around her throat?

She tried not to listen as she shone the light on the beams above her head. They looked splintered and weak, ready to let a load of heavy rocks rain down on her, pound her skull to a powdery white residue.

Harry had laughed when he told her that these ancient mines were held together by only a scattering of molecules, a mere thread of substance glued to the memory of once having been whole and strong. It had seemed colorful, even amusing at the time. But that was when they were above ground and he was with her. It wasn't funny now. At any moment those threads could shred and all the dirt and rocks above would crush her, bury her alive.

She started hyperventilating, sure she would be smothered at any moment by her own strangling fears. But she forced herself to stare at the slash of light from the tiny flashlight—her only hope. Without it, she would wander aimlessly though underground passages that went on for miles and miles.

No, it couldn't end that way.

She removed the purse from around her neck, felt inside for her Swiss army knife and was strangely reassured when her fingers touched the bulk of it. The folded knife might not be enough to stab herself to death, but it would sever her veins with very little pain.

Move! You have to keep moving.

She continued to trip, fall over chunks of ore that had dropped into the tunnel over the years; she knew she was breathing in massive amounts of dust that carried toxic elements. It was the purest of luck that she was wearing long pants—it would at least help her avoid open wounds that could further expose her to arsenic, lead, or mercury, or any other contaminants left behind in old deserted mines.

Gina's legs were aching; she kept forcing herself to move through the heaviness. It felt like she'd been going for days, but her watch told her she'd only been in the mine for about two hours.

Two hours! An eternity!

When she couldn't take one more step, her legs folded and she collapsed to the rocky floor.

She shone the flashlight everywhere so she could remember what was all around her. Then she turned off the light—she had to conserve the batteries. If there *were* ghosts in the mine, they would find her whether they could see her or not.

She brought her knees up, rested her head on them; she raked her fingers through her hair and dry-washed the grit away. It seemed to comfort her in the inky blackness.

Harry, where are you? What have they done to you?

Tears welled up; she tried to swallow down her despair. Soon she was moaning and her sobs filled the space around her. She was crying for Harry, her parents, her brother, friends whom she loved, people whom she had cared for. They, too, were all doomed. None of them would live forever. Everyone died.

Everyone!

* * *

Gina awoke with a start. Exhausted, she had dozed off in the darkness. She felt on the ground around her for the flashlight. But there was nothing. It was gone!

Terror cramped her gut. "Where … are … you?"

She tried to stay calm, but was soon clawing at the surrounding dirt until she could barely breathe in the clogged atmosphere.

"Stop!"

She couldn't go on like this. She had to take time to think.

Falling asleep, she must have nudged the flashlight until it rolled away from her.

She remembered walking on a downward slope. Crawling on the floor, she followed the ground, feeling the subtle turn in the path. Her fingers touched it—the flashlight! It had rolled next to the wall. She twisted it and it flicked on; the beam fought its way through the dust. She sat back on her heels, eyes closed in relief.

It was then she thought she heard something, something different. She listened carefully.

Someone crying?

Or was it her imagination? She stood, tilted her head.

"Hello!" She waited. "Any one out there?"

As she started walking, a faint voice answered, "Help me! Please help me."

Gina started walking faster, then running full out. She wrapped the coiled strap from the flashlight around her wrist, leaving her arms free so she could run even faster. The light bounced every which way.

She was suddenly airborne. Her stomach seemed to fall to her knees. She came down hard, rolled, and rolled some more.

* * *

When Gina opened her eyes, a crazed woman was across from her, clutching hard onto … a corpse. Her hand seemed to be deep into the rotting flesh. The putrid stink of decay struck Gina like a fist slamming into her.

"Help me! Please help me!"

She caught the desperation in the woman's voice but Gina turned to stare at piles and piles of corpses in all stages of decay—from the newly dead to the bones of the long dead. She jerked into a sitting position and saw Derek Kopek's face.

"Oh, my God!" she whispered, a chill coursing up and down her spine.

The woman kept crying out to her. "Please! Please help me!"

Gina turned back to her. "What happened? How did you get here?"

"I don't know. I came to see my mother. Someone drugged me and when I woke up I was jammed into this hole with … with all these gross bodies. I can't move. If I let go," she looked at the corpse she was holding onto, "I might slip down even more." She screamed at Gina, "I don't even know if *you're* real." Her voice dropped off to a whisper. "Are you really here?"

Gina swallowed her revulsion and crawled over the bodies separating them. Twice she almost dropped into the open spaces between the corpses before she got to the woman.

"Oh, thank God, you are real!" The woman grabbed onto her hand.

"Yes. My name's Gina Mazzio."

"Help me," the woman said in a quavering voice. "Please help me."

"Who are you?"

"Tuva Goldmich. My name is Tuva."

"You're Emma's daughter?"

274

"You know my mother?"

"I do. But right now we need to get the hell out of here."

The collective souls of the dead watched as she got to her knees and tugged at Tuva's hands. "What are your feet doing?"

"I think there're bones all around my legs; I'm jammed between them."

"Can you wiggle your feet at all?"

"I think so. I think they're hanging free."

"Okay, Tuva." Gina swallowed hard, tried not to vomit from the stink of decay around them. She spoke very softly, tried to focus only on the woman. "Pretend you're climbing a mountain." Tuva's eyes grew wider. "No, listen to me. Close your eyes, hold onto me, and try to find footholds, and climb."

"I can't do that."

"You can, Tuva. Hold my hands and when your feet have a toehold, I'll pull, and you'll climb."

Gina tugged at Tuva's hands.

"It's not working. I can't do it."

"Tuva, listen to me … this is the only way." Gina put some steel into her voice. "Do you understand?"

After a moment Tuva said, "I'll do it. I'll try really hard."

"On three." Gina said, "One … two … three!" Gina yanked hard, could feel the woman moving upward. When Tuva finally emerged, Gina fell back, gasping for air. Tuva fell on top of her; her tears washed across Gina's face.

"You did it!" Gina said. But Tuva had shut down, began to rock back and forth, moaning, lost in a fugue state of despair. She was there, but, at the same time, she was gone.

Gina wrapped her arms around Tuva, hugged her, drew as close to her as she could. "Can you hear me, Tuva?" Gina said, over and over.

Finally, Tuva answered. "Yes." But she still held onto Gina's arms, nails digging deep. "I've been down in this hell-hole for hours … in the dark … with all these dead people. In the dark … the dark … dark—"

"It's all right, Tuva. You're not alone anymore. *We're* not alone. We have each other."

"The bodies kept rolling into me, touching me. There were creatures moving around. I could hear them."

"Tuva, there's nothing alive here … except you and me."

"They rubbed against me. I was so scared." She began to cry again.

Gina turned off the light. A dim glow remained in the pit. The top edge was too far up to reach, but for one ghoulish moment she thought of piling the bodies and bones atop each other to help them climb to the lip of the pit. But she knew she would never have the strength to do it. Even on her best day.

Where was the light coming from?

Tuva let out a blood-curdling scream. "Something touched me again." She clung to Gina. "Help," she screamed in her ear.

"It's all right, Tuva. Let me see what it is."

Gina carefully unwound herself from the squeezing, clutching arms of the terrified woman and tried to see in the dim light, then turned on the halogen flashlight.

The light shone into the luminous eyes of a cat whose fur was streaked with caked gore.

"Look! It's a cat."

Tuva had her eyelids clenched closed and it took her several seconds before she would open them. She pointed where the beam of the light fell. "Oh, my God. Look what they're doing."

Gina followed Tuva's gaze. All around them were cats of all shapes and sizes.

They were feeding off the dead bodies.

Chapter 44

Harry never thought he would die in a mine. When he and his brother went exploring underground, it was an adventure with no real thought of danger, let alone death.

They didn't know what they were looking for deep under the earth, even though they'd found some old relics: pickaxes, gloves, and even a risqué picture of a woman who probably earned her living in a brothel sometime in the late 1800s.

When he wandered in a velvety black universe, he learned a lot about himself and what he considered the important and unimportant things in life.

Petty thoughts were really just that – small and useless. And there seemed to be a lot of that to ignore. What mattered most in life was love and friendship. Those were the reasons to return topside again.

Now, Harry tried not to think about dying. If he allowed himself to do that, he would glom onto the certainty that there was probably only a finite amount of oxygen left in the small outlet he was wedged into. Exactly how much air? It could be days, maybe only minutes. He didn't know and didn't want to know.

One thing was certain: there was no going back. Five feet behind him was an impenetrable wall of dirt and rocks. And the sad truth? The shaft ended right here because it was too narrow to advance any farther. It was a dead end.

This was it.

He focused on the one person he desperately wanted to see one more time.

Gina, I can feel the oxygen in this space dwindling. Sooner or later there'll be no more air to breath. I would give my last breath to have one more moment where the two of us could hold hands and know for sure that nothing else has ever really mattered except being together.

We found each other. I'll always be grateful for that.

You are the love of my life... forever.

It was time for him to close his eyes and let go. If he could do that without panicking, just surrender to his final moments, he would die in peace.

He turned off the Maglite and laid his head down on his arm and stared at a yellow outline in the distance.

Light?

It hadn't been there before.

Can't be real.

But there was an outline of light framing the edges of a square about ten feet in front of him.

He tried to wiggle ahead, force his way. But he just couldn't get through the dirt. He backed up and grabbed hold of the Maglite again. He twisted off the bottom, let the batteries fall into his hand, and tossed them behind him.

Using the open end of the flashlight as a chisel, he started slamming into the earth. Each blow cut deeper and deeper into the soil blocking his way. He hit, hit, hit at it, again and again; grabbed fistfuls of it and shoved it behind him until the lower half of his body was almost buried.

Would his chipping away at the dirt cause enough vibrations to bring the ceiling down and bury him? Sudden fear paralyzed him. His heart raced, he gasped for air.

"Stop it!" The words exploded in his brain, but the sound was muffled, buried in the dirt.

This was his chance to survive. His only chance.

The soil began to drop away in large clumps. The opening grew larger; it began to open up enough for him to squeeze his way through.

He moved ahead, his elbows propelling him forward until he came face-to-face with a square panel of wood. Light seeped around the cracks, coming from what was probably a room on the other side.

Harry listened for a long moment. There was no sound.

He squeezed his knees up to his chest and inched forward. Over and over, he punched hard at the wood until it finally sprang open.

The crash of light blinded him as he pushed through.

When he could finally see, he was staring into the muzzle of a gun.

* * *

"Well, aren't you the clever one," Ethan said, waving the gun in Harry's face.

Ethan held the weapon in one hand and a computer carrying case in the other. The administrator's shirt was mapped with perspiration, his blanched face coated with sweat.

Harry leaped for the gun, but his cramped leg muscles failed him. Ethan easily side- stepped before Harry could snatch the barrel. He fell to the floor.

"You and your girlfriend have caused me enough problems. Get up on that table! Now!"

For the first time Harry looked at the room with its shelved walls holding container after container of floating brains, just as Gina had described it. And in the center of the room was an autopsy table. His heart clawed at his chest. That's where Ethan wanted him to go—onto an autopsy table.

Harry stayed down on the floor, eyed the carrying case. "I don't care what you do, or where you go. Just tell me. Where's Gina?"

"Oh, I'm afraid you're too late to help your girlfriend. She's dead. Now get up on that table!"

"Noooooo!"

Harry grabbed onto the table, pulled himself up, kicked out with one leg, and knocked the gun out of Ethan's hand. It slid across the floor and through the opening into the tunnel he'd just crawled out of.

The two of them stood facing each other.

"Where the fuck is Gina?"

Ethan swung the carrying case into Harry's head.

As he fell, Ethan hit Harry hard again in the ribs.

Everything was shutting down. The last thing he heard was Ethan laughing—the last thing he saw was a smiling Ethan hovering over him.

Chapter 45

Gina swallowed hard. Revulsion turned her stomach as she watched the feral cats feed off of the dead bodies. She held tightly onto Tuva's shaking hand; tears rushed down her cheeks.

All these people came to Comstock for help. Instead, they were murdered, dumped like garbage.

"Is that what those cats are going to do to us?" Tuva could barely get the words out between her chattering teeth.

"Tuva, please don't say that."

A cat rubbed against Gina's arm, then shrieked and leaped away when Gina tried to reach out for it. She directed the light to the top of the pit again. It was so high up she could barely make out the edge.

Nothing's changed. We're still not getting out that way.

"Maybe the cats jumped into the pit," Tuva said. She was quieter now, but continued to shiver.

Tuva wasn't the only one on the edge of hysteria. Gina knew it wouldn't be long before they both flipped out.

"Cats are way too smart to jump down that far," Gina said.

"But then how did they get in here?" Tuva insisted.

Gina shifted, couldn't stop herself from yelping when a corpse pushed against her shoulder, bringing with it the rank stink of decay. She pushed hard at the body, but it was stuck and the slightest movement made it lean back against her.

She directed the flashlight at one of the cats moving from one corpse to another without stopping to eat.

"Tuva! Did you see that?"

"What? What is it?" Alarm made Tuva's voice climb to a shriek.

"One of the cats just disappeared. One minute it was there, the next it was gone." Gina gave the flashlight to Tuva and directed it. "Hold onto this and keep lighting up that area. And for God's sake, don't drop it!"

"Why? What are you going to do?

Gina tried to push herself up, but she kept falling back. Tuva reached out to help her.

"No!" Gina said, "You concentrate on keeping the light on that spot, no matter what happens. I'm going to see what happened to that cat."

"Don't go! What if you fall between ... them ... and can't get out ... I'll be all alone again ... Please don't go!"

"Tuva! Try not to think about that. Just concentrate on our getting out of here. Now hold on tight to that flashlight, okay?"

"How do you know?" Tuva said.

The woman's desperation fired Gina's panic, and it was getting harder and harder to control. "Know what?" she said impatiently.

"That we're going to get out?"

She held Tuva's shoulders, talked to her like a child; at the same time she tried to calm herself. "We have to do this together. Just hold onto the flashlight. That's all you have to think about ... that's all you have to do. Okay?"

Tuva nodded, her head bobbing up and down, up and down.

This time, instead of trying to stand upright, Gina got onto all fours and tried to imitate the cats. She swayed with the shift of the corpses, let the different body parts fold in under her as she balanced and rebalanced herself while moving from spot to spot. She forced herself to think only about following the beam of light.

"Are you all right, Gina?"

"I'm good." But her hands kept digging into soft, decaying flesh. No matter how hard she tried to ignore the disgusting stink, it was so overwhelming it grabbed her by the throat. But as she got closer to the spot where the cat disappeared, there were fewer corpses. Here, all signs of flesh had disappeared; what were left were picked-clean bones.

Soon she was able to stand and walk, her feet pressing down on packed bones.

"Keep the light there, Tuva!" She stopped about three feet from where the beam was directed.

"Gina?"

"It's all right. We both have to be quiet now. Twist the middle, that will turn off the flashlight."

Gina waited for her eyes to adjust; soon she could see this was where the ambient light was coming from.

The cats probably started eating the bodies here and kept working their way farther into the pit as they consumed the food source. Standing still, Gina watched the shadowy cats move through the spaces between and on top of the bones. She didn't even want to imagine how many cats there were.

"Tuva! Turn on the flashlight, hold it with your teeth so you can see, and crawl over here."

"But … but I'll have to go through … the bodies."

"Tuva, I may have found a way out for us."

There was a long pause before Tuva finally said, "I'll try."

"No, Tuva! You can do better than that. Get on all fours the way I did and do it. Do it now!"

Please don't fall in one of the spaces. Please. Please. Please.

After several attempts, Tuva was able to crouch down and move toward Gina. She stopped time and time again to yank the flashlight from her mouth. Every time she did, it squeezed Gina's heart with fear.

When she was almost there, Gina took her hand and helped her over. "That was really something. You were great!"

Tuva gave her a weak smile.

"See the light down below?"

"Yes."

"That's our way out. I'm sure of it." A cat suddenly materialized in front of them, screeched, and jumped back down toward the light.

"Okay, we need to move these stacks of bones over and out of the way," Gina said. "Remember, everything is crushed together, so we'll have to start from the top and move the pieces very carefully."

Like a giant game of Pick-Up-Sticks, they studied each and every bone that was wedged against another, throwing away each free one. They only needed to create a small space between the bones for them to get to where the cats had been entering the pit.

It was slow, tedious work, but as the bones were tossed away, the light became brighter; they finally saw a small opening leading out of the pit.

"Look, Gina!"

Gina reached out and hugged Tuva. "We're almost there."

They'd cleared out a small space, creating a narrow passageway through the maze of bones. They had to move very carefully; if they nudged a bone in the wrong way, they could be impaled by splintered shards. Even a sudden shift could wedge them in, leaving them with no hope of escape.

"There's not much room for both of us and the opening will need some digging, Gina said. "You stay here, let me go ahead, and I'll take care of it."

"No! I'm going with you."

Gina saw Tuva fully for the first time—filthy face and probably dark hair, but so matted with gore and dirt, it was hard to really tell. Her eyes were filled with resolve and Gina knew she wasn't going anywhere without her.

"We'll hold hands and step down onto the layer below. No quick movements. Okay?"

Tuva nodded.

Gina took her hand and they stepped on stack after stack of bones. Gina placed her feet on the long, thicker bones and Tuva followed in her footsteps. Finally, they stood in front of the tiny opening where the cats had been slipping in and out of the pit.

"There's hardly any space for us to get through," Tuva said.

284

Gina searched the piles of bones all around them and grabbed a thigh bone. She used it to carefully poke at the opening—the dirt began to fall away in clumps. Soon there was a hole large enough for them to squiggle through.

"Wait a moment!" Gina said.

Is it safe for us to go out there?

"What's the matter?"

Gina could feel Tuva's eyes boring into her.

Does it really matter? We sure as hell aren't going back into that damn pit.

Gina reached for Tuva's hand. "Let's get out of here."

They walked out of the pit and into the bright light.

Bette Golden Lamb & J. J. Lamb

Chapter 46

Ethan watched Harry fall. He stood over the nurse, adrenalin pulsating, heart pounding.

Pete was supposed to finish off this bastard.

He spoke to Harry's inert body. "Who the hell do you think you are, standing in the way of real genius, someone who's on the verge of finding the answers to the Alzheimer's puzzle?" He toed Harry's shoulder. "What have *you* done for humanity lately?"

Ethan looked around the lab at his huge collection of specimens. They represented all of his research and he was proud of his work. He'd spent hours, days on these brains—cutting, slicing, prepping, staining them. And now it was all going to end.

The loss tore through him. He wanted to cry out his disappointment.

There were still empty shelves, ready and waiting for his future brain specimens … specimens that would never come.

These people are heroes. They gave their lives, gave them to me, so I could find the answers, so others could live … wouldn't suffer.

He kicked Harry's shoulder. "You just wanted to make money. You hear me?" Then he kicked him harder. "Money!"

Harry moaned, but was still out.

Ethan thought about going after the gun; it couldn't have landed too far inside the tunnel. It would be much safer to shoot Harry, get rid of him now.

Look at him. Just a pile of disorganized laundry, his head leaking into a messy puddle of blood on the floor.

Ethan didn't like loose ends any more than David Zelint. As long as Harry was alive, he could get to his hidden copies of evidence. It wouldn't matter where Ethan ran, that loose thread would be out there, waiting to bring him down.

Ethan put down the computer case and moved to the medicine cabinet, pulled out a bottle of injectable morphine sulphate, and filled a large syringe.

"Let's end this right now," he said to the inert nurse. He picked up Harry's arm, looked at it, then let it drop.

I haven't got the goddam time to mess with, or dig for your vein.

He wrapped a hand around Harry's deltoid, jammed the needle in, and pushed the plunger.

It may be a lot slower than a vein; but it's just as sure. We won't be hearing from you anymore. By the time anyone finds you, you'll be just as dead as that little snoop Gina Mazzio. And I'll be high in the sky, free as a bird.

He glanced at his watch. He had to leave this instant, drive down the grade to the Reno airport, and grab his connecting flights to San Francisco and Argentina.

Move! No time to pack. Grab my passport and run!

He picked up the computer carrying case and the box holding all his slides, and then headed for the open lab door and the elevator.

On the first floor, he walked as fast as he could toward his office. Delores was standing in the doorway.

"Not now, Delores. We'll talk later."

"But I need to know who's coming to relieve me. Gina and Harry never showed up this morning and there's no answer at their apartment. Have you called for a temp to relieve me?"

"Get back up there on the unit and take care of things. Let me worry about the rest of it."

Delores was usually meek and compliant around him, but he could see a definite look of suspicion. More than that, a glint of defiance.

He walked past her into his office, reached into his pocket for the key chain with both his keys and the original flash drive. From the bottom drawer, he swooped up his passport, shoved it into his pocket.

She stood there, still not moving.

"Well, what are you waiting for?"

"I need to know who's going to relieve me."

And I need to get the hell out of here!

The look on her face was driving him crazy. "There'll be a huge bonus for you, Delores. But I really need you to get back to the unit. I'll talk to you later."

She was silent for a moment. "Okay," she said, and left his office.

Ethan headed for the front door, but he was breathing so rapidly, he could barely catch his breath.

Slow down.

He eased his pace as he walked out the door. When he got to the van door, he saw a sports car pull into a visitor's parking space. He stopped.

Who the hell is that?

He hesitated for only a moment.

Not my problem. I have a plane to catch.

He got behind the wheel and started the engine.

* * *

Gina and Tuva looked back at the small opening they had just crawled through. It was almost closed off now with fallen dirt. They jumped up and down, hugged each other.

"We did it! We did it!" Gina shouted.

"Look at that gorgeous sky," Tuva cried out.

The sky *was* beautiful. "Look at that blue, Tuva. Did you ever see anything so incredible?" Gina couldn't stop. "And those boulders. I've hated them from the moment I set eyes on them. But now, they're wonderful."

Tuva laughed and threw her hands up in the air.

Gina saw a cat off to the side, sitting on its haunches, waiting for an opportunity to enter the pit. She screamed at it, "Thank you, you beautiful creature."

"Really?" Tuva said softly.

"You can't hate the cats for being survivors. Besides, without them we would have never found a way out of there." Gina looked around; saw the Comstock building off in the distance. Elation was replaced with a sudden feeling of exhaustion ... and dread. It settled deep onto her shoulders, then into the pit of her stomach.

Harry, where are you? Are you still alive?

She took Tuva's hand. "Let's get back now."

"I don't want to go in there again."

"That's up to you, Tuva. But I need to find my fiancé. You can get into your car and leave if you want to, but please, first go to the hospital in Carson City ... they'll take care of that cut on your neck. Tell the nurses what happened. Tell them to send the police. I have to stay here and find Harry."

"My mother's in that building, Gina."

"I know ... but it's still up to you. You have to make up your own mind."

Chapter 47

Gina walked slowly, her purse pulling at her neck muscles. With each step she thought about dropping it, but it had been her lifeline. She doggedly kept the strap wrapped over her arm and around her neck.

She and Tuva leaned heavily on each other as they moved with dragging steps toward the Comstock. It seemed so very far away.

Gina knew they were both suffering from shock and dehydration, and out in the daylight, she could see the terrible bruises spreading across Tuva's face and arms—injuries she hadn't noticed or thought much about in the semi darkness of the pit. A large, serious laceration bisected the side of her neck; it was covered in blood and filth. If they hadn't gotten out of the pit when they did, it wouldn't have been long before a massive infection would have set in and finished her. She would still need serious medical attention; antibiotics to help her heal.

If that cut had penetrated any deeper, it probably would have severed her carotid and she would have bled out.

As that thought flashed through Gina's mind, she resisted the urge to examine Tuva's wound more closely—it would only alarm her, and there was nothing she could do right now.

Tuva started crying. "Why did they do this to me? All I wanted was to see my mother."

"I know," Gina said, taking the petite woman's hand. "But they hadn't been delivering your letters to your mother, and then you show up out of the blue. They probably didn't know what to do with you."

"Why did they keep my letters hidden from my mother?"

"You were too persistent, a big threat to their whole operation. If you started digging into her care, you could have caused them real trouble … brought them down."

"That was never going to happen."

"Why not?"

"I complained to the authorities. You can see how that turned out."

"Who'd you talk to?"

"The man I saw said he would look into it." Tears ran down her cheeks, cutting through a long string of etchings in grime and blood. "He promised."

"And then you came out here?"

"Yes." Her dark eyes were sad. "My mother kept coming to me in my dreams, kept calling for me." Tuva looked away. "I'll bet that sounds really weird. But she was crying for help and it got so I couldn't sleep any more. I *had* to come."

"She's lucky to have someone who loves her so much," Gina said. But she wasn't thinking of Tuva anymore.

Harry? Did they kill you in that tunnel? No! No! Please be alive and safe. I'll do anything. I promise I'll stop trying to run away. I promise I'll marry you. I promise, I promise … promise…

* * *

Someone was calling her. A voice from very far away; she wanted to ignore it. She was so tired. It kept insisting: "Gina! Gina! Wake up! Please wake up!"

She opened her eyes, stared up at Tuva, who was crying and shouting her name, over and over. She felt the hard ground under her, along with pinpoints of broken rock jabbing into her back.

"Tuva?" Gina sat up too quickly; a wave of nausea swept through her. For a moment the sky spun, taking the hills around with it. "What happened?"

"I don't know. You just collapsed."

"Give me a minute … just a minute."

Bone Pit

Her mind was spinning, her body floating. This was the moment she'd always dreaded, that mythical line in the sand. And when she crossed it, she would finally surrender to defeat. It was a time that came to everyone—as certain as death.

The terror in the mine, the horror of the pit had drained her. But the thought that Harry could be dead tore away that inner core of strength that had always been there for her.

"Gina, get up!"

"I can't do it anymore, Tuva. I'm sorry."

Tuva got behind her, tried to lift her.

"Look, Gina, we're almost at the Comstock. We can make it!"

Gina knew she had to get up. She ignored the trembling that made her feel like she'd given the last of her grit, warned that she had to rest, had to wait to go on.

All right, Tuva. Help me up."

Tuva half lifted Gina to her feet, put an arm around her waist and held on tight. As they walked, Gina started to gain momentum. By the time they approached the front of the building, she was holding her own, and so was Tuva.

Chapter 48

Annie Kreuger was getting restless. She glanced at her watch, saw it had been more than ten minutes since Carl had gone into the building after telling her he would only be a minute or so.

Should have gone with him.

She looked over at the entrance door, then at the façade of the building.

Thought he said this had to do with an FDA drug study. So why all the bars on the windows?

She'd barely finished the thought when two filthy, limping women in ripped clothing came around from the side of the building, headed for the front door.

Oh, my God! They look like they're going to keel over.

She flung open the door of the Porsche, ran over, stepped between them, and wrapped an arm around each of their waists. They leaned heavily on her as she tried to keep them on their feet.

"Jesus, what on earth happened to you?"

The tallest one slowly raised one arm, pointed to her mouth. Annie saw the coating around both their lips, could see they were in desperate need of water.

"Okay, let's get you inside, get some water, and find you a place to sit down." She struggled with the door, finally managed to pull it open with the help of the taller woman.

Once they were through the doorway, she saw Carl standing in the foyer, talking to a woman who appeared to be a nurse. They both looked over at the trio, startled.

"Could really use some help here, Carl," Annie said. She felt like she would collapse at any second under the weight of both women.

"Gina! Is that you?" the nurse shouted. "What the hell's going on?"

Carl had reached them; he took the closest woman from Annie's hold and helped her walk to a nearby sofa. As he lowered her down, he got a good look at her face.

"Tuva Goldmich?" His expression was a mixture of surprise, and alarm. The petite woman looked at him, squinted, and nodded.

"Get them some water! Now!" Annie told the nurse, who was still standing there, seemed to be dumbfounded. She guided the one called Gina to the sofa, helped her sit.

The nurse returned from the water cooler, a large cup of water in each hand, and held them out to Tuva and Gina. Tuva started to gulp hers down, but Gina lightly touched her arm; Tuva nodded and slowed herself down.

* * *

Almost from the moment the water touched her tongue, Gina felt better—she knew that she and Tuva desperately needed fluids. With slow, even swallows, she finished the water and was up and out of the sofa, limping to the cooler for a refill before anyone could stop her. She pulled down a fresh cup, filled it for Tuva, and went back to the sofa.

"That's him!" Tuva said. "Carl Kreuger, the man I told you about from New York."

"Well, Mr. Kreuger, at least you're here. That's something."

"And you are?" he asked coolly.

"Gina Mazzio ... the nurse who's been taking care of Tuva's mother."

"I'm going back up to the unit," Delores interrupted. "I came down to answer the doorbell, but I'd better get back."

"Mr. Kreuger, I'd appreciate your coming with me to the basement," Gina said. "There's something there you need to see." She was doing her best to remain calm, but it wouldn't take much to give into the scream working its way up her throat.

"My wife? Can she come?"

"I don't think so." She glanced over at the agent's wife. "But you were great! Thanks for your kindness. Tuva and I were pretty done in when you came to our rescue." She continued to look at the attractive woman.

"I'm Annie," she said. "I'm glad I was there."

"If you don't mind, would you stay behind with Tuva?"

"Of course." Annie stood and went for more water. "Don't you worry; I'll take good care of her."

Gina barely heard Annie's response as she moved to the elevator, Carl Kreuger at her side. "Mr. Kreuger—"

"Carl."

Gina reached into her purse and found her employee card. When they stepped into the elevator, she shoved the card into the slot and sent them down to the basement. That simple action seemed to open up a floodgate of despair; she began to weep. Her sobs filled the elevator.

Carl put his arms around her and tried to comfort her, but all she could visualize was Harry dead. Gone.

She murmured into his shoulder, "Harry … what am … I going to do… without you?"

When she could finally think again, she stepped back and wiped at her wet, gritty face with the back of her hand. Carl's once clean shirt was streaked with black filth.

She pointed to his shoulder. "Sorry!"

"Never mind that. Who is this Harry person?"

"My … my … fiancé."

"Then let's go find your guy."

Chapter 49

With the opening thunk of the elevator door, Gina painfully limped toward the basement's middle corridor. Carl was right behind her.

She switched on the lights and led them through the tunnels, heading straight for the Y where she last saw Harry.

The dimly lit corridors should have frightened her, but her concentration was fixed on finding Harry. Fear kept her mindless and focused at the same time.

"Wouldn't want to get lost in this rat hole," Carl said, "Are you sure this is the way?"

"We're almost there," Gina said, barely getting the words out before the Y loomed ahead.

"Oh, no!" Gina cried out. Both entrances were closed off, blocked by prison-like gates that sealed the tunnels from top to bottom. Gina rattled the metal trying to loosen it. She yanked the lock, but both the bars and the lock were solid.

"Harry!" she screamed, pressing her face against the metal, trying to see into the mine.

All she saw was dirt and scattered rocks on the floor inside. There was no one in sight.

"Harry! Harry!"

Carl gently placed a hand on her shoulder. "I'm sorry, Gina. You did your best."

"No! Ethan must have the keys in his desk drawer in the lab. "They have to be there."

She turned and headed back, hating her body for letting her down, for giving her so much pain. She dragged her leg and no matter how hard she tried, the best she could do was limp slowly. Her body was shutting down and all that remained were broken threads of energy.

I can't stop now. Please, please. I have to keep going. I have to find Harry.

"Here," Carl said, holding out an arm. "Grab onto me ... together we can move a lot faster."

Gina clutched his arm, her only lifeline.

Out of the corridor, they turned toward the laboratory. When they stepped inside the room, they saw Harry on the floor. Blood and sweat had created a huge smear under him.

"Harry!" she screamed and fell to her knees beside him. She grabbed onto his wrist; his pulse was weak and thready. He was barely breathing.

She bent over him. "Harry?"

"I think he's been drugged," Carl said, picking up an empty syringe and a drained vial of morphine sulfate from the autopsy table.

Gina lifted Harry's eyelids; pinpoint pupils stared back at her.

"There's no time to waste." Carl's voice was urgent. "We have to get him to a hospital now!"

"No! He'll be dead before we can get him out the door."

Gina felt the room spinning, an edge of blackness trying to close in. She struggled to her feet, grabbed the phone and called Delores.

"This is Gina. Listen very carefully. I'm in the lab. Harry's been overdosed with morphine. I need you to bring several vials of Narcan down to the lab. Now!"

"What lab?"

"You've never been to the lab?" Gina's head was exploding. "Push your employee card into the bottom slot in the elevator panel. That will take you to the basement, then turn right."

"And you want what, Narcan?"

"Yes, yes—Naloxone hydrochloride ... and some twenty-one-gauge butterfly catheters." She was breathing so hard she could barely get the words out. "Run!"

She opened the medicine cabinet, grabbed a tourniquet, a fist full of alcohol packets and tape. At Harry's side she collapsed to her knees again and made herself slow down. But everything seemed so strange and distorted. She focused on Harry's arm.

"He's shutting down, his veins are collapsing. Carl! See that towel there … stick it under hot water, then bring it to me. Hurry!"

She wrapped Harry's limp arm in the towel. She muttered the words echoing in her head "Harry, don't you dare quit on me. Don't you dare!"

Delores came rushing in, small Narcan vials clutched in one hand, butterfly catheters in the other.

"Gina, maybe you'd better let me do this. You look—"

"Draw up two milligrams! Have it ready! And hurry!"

In one continuous motion, Gina unwrapped the towel, folded it under Harry's arm, and tied the tourniquet. She ran a finger up and down his arm, searching for any sign of a vein. *Any* vein.

There was nothing.

She closed her eyes and gently felt his arm again, then rubbed an alcohol swab on his skin.

The faster she tried to move, the slower everything became. She reached for a butterfly catheter, held the "wings" and carefully poked its needle into his arm. She held her breath, as though air moving in her lungs would steal the needle from his vein.

Just when she thought it wasn't working, blood began to back flow.

My God, I'm in!

Her heart was tearing at her chest; she could barely breathe. She gently pushed the needle farther in.

"Delores, attach the syringe to the tubing and inject the Narcan very slowly."

Gina held the needle steady as she undid the tourniquet.

Come on, baby, don't let me down.

Gina gaze shifted to her watch. It had been two minutes.

"Give him two more milligrams."

Delores nodded and pushed the meds slowly.

Harry stirred, gasped for a breath.

Oh, my God! He's breathing!

Gina smiled, reached for the pulse in his neck, but the room was spinning again and the blackness swallowed her.

Voices zoomed away … far, far away.

Silence.

Chapter 50

Muted voices swept away then returned like the explosive roar of the incoming tide.

Coming. Going.

Softer, louder. Softer, louder.

Timeless. Endless.

Gina turned away from the sound, sank further down into the womb of time where she could hide in mindless nothingness; safe in the endless warp of a peaceful forever.

"Gi-in-n-na-a-a!"

Go away!

"Gi-in-n-a-a-a. Come back!"

That special voice; it thundered through her solitude; rolled into her body, her heart, forced her to turn away from the quiet darkness. She spread her arms, looked up into a shaft of light.

Slowly, she moved up through the deep, inky layers.

Sound exploded around her.

"Gina?"

Her eyelids snapped open. Harry was sitting on the edge of the bed.

"Harry!" She quickly sat up, then fell back, her arms limp and heavy.

"Hey, babe, take it easy." He squeezed her hand. "How are you doing?"

"You're safe!" Tears filled her eyes. "I was so afraid I'd lost you."

"Well, if you hadn't found me when you did … well, let's just say, you're my hero."

"Are you all right?"

"Just a mild concussion from where our buddy Ethan bopped me on the head. Other than feeling weak as a slug, I'm alive, thanks to your quick thinking."

"You're a brave woman." A tall man stepped forward. Gina knew him ... his name was lost somewhere in her head.

She thought a moment. "You're the one who helped me find Harry ... you're ... you're ... Carl, right?"

"That's me."

Gina looked at the woman standing next to him. "And you're Annie, aren't you?" She stepped up to the bed, a big smile spreading across her face. "Thanks for being there when we needed you."

Gina forced herself to her elbows. "Tuva? How is Tuva? Is she all right?"

"She's in a room down the hall," Harry said.

"But how is she?"

"She insisted on seeing her mother before they could load her into the ambulance. The EMTs were not happy with her."

"She was in terrible shape," Gina said.

"When Tuva and her mother were together again, she didn't want to leave her side," Annie said. "It was quite a reunion."

"Tuva went through hell to get to her mom."

"Yeah, she literally went into shock and collapsed before they could get her here," Harry said. "That neck wound of hers is pretty deep and ugly looking. They had to bring in a plastic surgeon to work on her."

"But she'll be all right?"

"Things look good and the prognosis is excellent," Harry said. "Like you, she's covered with bruises, but nothing could match the ones on your hip and knee. You're going to be limping for a while, doll." He leaned over and kissed her on the cheek. "You're lucky you didn't break anything."

"Tuva told us what happened in the pit," Carl said. "If you hadn't come along when you did … well, it's just a good thing you were there for her."

"You not only saved her life, but her sanity," Harry said. "She was really losing it; she's still pretty shook up. "They had to sedate her just to get her to rest."

"What's going to happen to the patients at Comstock?"

"They're all being moved here."

"Here? Where am I?"

"You're at the main Comstock Hospital campus in Carson City."

"Did you have to bring me *here*?"

"Yeah, well," Harry said, "they claim they didn't know anything about *any* of this mess. I think they were taking money under the table for directing personnel to Ethan, but I don't think they were involved any more than that."

"It's hard to know what the truth is," Gina said.

"I think they'll do the right thing—especially now that they're under the FDA's microscope."

Harry's voice was fading. She was falling back into the deep nothingness. But this time the darkness was only a resting place where she could be warm and safe, and sleep for a while.

Chapter 51

Gina and Harry sped down the twisting Geiger Grade, headed for the Reno airport. They had barely enough time to make their flight back to San Francisco. The Jeep wasn't all that great on curves, but Harry had it under control. When she looked down from the mountain, she was glad he was ignoring his usual urge to do the pedal-to-the-metal thing. After all they'd been through, to end up at the bottom of a ravine would be too much—even for them.

"Wish we had the Fiat," Gina said. "I really miss it. And it would be great fun taking these curves in my little baby."

"Yeah," Harry said, laughing. "If it didn't decide to have a tantrum and not start at all, or maybe sputter out in the middle of a hairpin turn."

"You hate my car," Gina said giving him an evil look.

"Nah, I don't hate it ... when it's running. Then it's a cute little bugger."

"Gotta take the bad with the good."

They rode in silence for a while before Harry said, "It's really too bad about Zelint."

Gina gave him her are-you-crazy look. "Too bad?"

"Well, we need drug companies to continue to invest in finding cures for all kinds of diseases. And Zelint? Their company is facing a multitude of criminal charges, not that they don't deserve them. But the headline is: They won't be developing AZ-1166 or looking for any other new meds. That's *not* a good thing."

"I guess," Gina said. "But rigging drug trials and committing murder ... well, you wouldn't call *that* a good thing."

"No, that was despicable."

"The whole business gives me the chills," Gina said, touching her throat. "Can you imagine, Delores claimed she never really saw anything, so she won't even have to testify against Ethan?"

"She and the other temps knew something was going on, but they never did anything about it, even claimed they hadn't actually seen anything wrong."

"Bullshitsky!" Gina said. "They couldn't figure out that patients were suddenly *gone*? They must have known something wasn't kosher."

"Kosher, huh," Harry said laughing. "Is that your latest Italian homily?"

"Homily, shmomily. That's New York talk, man. Get with it!"

Gina tilted back into the headrest. She still felt very weak, even after doing nothing but sopping up IVs and sleeping in a hospital bed for two whole days.

A chill rode her spine as she flashed on the pit where she and Tuva had been trapped.

Rotten garbage. That's all they were.

"Harry, those patients were murdered by Ethan so he could study their brains. Ugh! The man's not human."

He reached across for her arm, squeezed it hard. "That was only one of the reasons. Remember, that pit held participants from all over the country … sent specifically to Comstock so Zelint could manipulate the side effect stats of AZ-1166.

Gina's eyes clouded with tears. She could still see Tuva in her hospital bed, her neck swathed in bandages, her arms covered with purple islands the size of Australia.

It must have hurt like hell when she gave me that tight hug goodbye.

"What did you think of Carl?" Harry said.

"I liked Annie better."

"Oh, come on, babe. The man may have been reluctant to jump in at the beginning, but without him, Ethan would have gotten away. Carl did his job."

"I suppose."

"Man, what I wouldn't have given to be there when they grabbed our mad scientist," Harry said. "Carl really pounced on the evidence in the tablet and that little flash drive we stashed. Said that for now it was the only solid evidence they had to hold Ethan. They nabbed him just as he was stepping onto the airplane. Guess he thought he was really getting away with it."

"And all because you stuffed everything into that crawl space under the building, right next to where we parked the Jeep." Gina said. "Did it ever cross your mind that Rocky and Pete would find it there and trash it?"

"Are you kidding?" Harry said, laughing so hard he had trouble holding onto the steering wheel. "Those lazy parasites wouldn't have known what a crawl space was if it was staring them in the face."

Gina looked out the window. "Harry, stop the car! Pull over!"

"What's the matter?"

"Look!"

"Jeez! It's the hairy tarantulas again. First on the Carson Grade, and now on Geiger Grade. We've been had … coming and going."

"They're big and ugly," Gina said, smiling. "But they're pretty amazing, aren't they?"

"You kidding me?"

"Hey, I'm not going to pet them or anything, but they're beautiful in their own way ... real survivors."

"We're going to have to squash some of those beauties if we're going to catch our flight."

"Oh, hell, Harry. We can get the next flight. I don't want to kill them; not any of them. Everything has a right to live."

"Great idea. We'll spend the night in Reno."

"Harry?"

"Yes, doll?"

"I want us to get a cat. A rescue one."

"Really? Are you sure?"

"I'm sure."

He gave her a big smile, turned off the engine. They held hands and watched the huge spiders migrate across the road.

"Harry?"

He turned from watching the moving carpet of tarantulas and sat back into his seat. "What is it, babe?"

"You know, all my fretting and worrying, thinking and rethinking every single thing—"

"Yeah, that does sound like you," he said with a huge smile.

She took his hand and squeezed it as tight as she could. "It's almost too simple. But when you get right down to it … all that really matters are the ones you love, and the ones who love you."

Harry looked deep into her eyes before he pulled her into his arms, held her so tight she could feel his heart pounding.

The End

About the Authors

BETTE GOLDEN LAMB, a registered nurse, has developed parallel careers as a painter, sculptor, and ceramist. Her award-winning art works can be found in a number of galleries and private collections. J. J. LAMB is a career writer – journalism, short stories, and novels.

In addition to *Bone Pit*, the LAMBS have co-authored eight novels together, six of them as part of the RN Gina Mazzio medical thriller series. *Sisters in Silence, Heir Today...,* and *The Killing Vote* are stand-alone thrillers.

BETTE's *The Organ Harvesters* was named Grand Prize Winner in the 2014 Stellar Sci-Fi Contest, and was followed by *The Organ Harvesters-Book II.* J. J.'s *No Pat Hands* was a 2014 Shamus nominee from Private Eye Writers of America.

The LAMBS live in Northern California and are members of International Thriller Writers, Mystery Writers of America, and Sisters in Crime.

# # #

www.ingramcontent.com/pod-product-compliance
Lightning Source LLC
Chambersburg PA
CBHW071307200626
46813CB00015B/438